KU-449-186

Praise for *The Other Side of Night*

'A gripping and moving tale of loss and astounding sacrifice told so beautifully with a unique twist that was utterly satisfying'
— Imran Mahmood

'A fantastic read. Mind-bending, gut-wrenchingly tense and one of the most original stories I've read in years. It was an absolute treat'
— John Marrs

'Emotional, heart-warming and thought-provoking, one of those rare books that you'll still be thinking about long after the last page'
— Jenny Blackhurst

'Hold on to your sanity. This psychological thriller will keep you wondering which strange details are real and which emerge from the minds of the characters. The lonely boy, the disgraced police officer, the bizarre scientist – each has a dark secret, and a dark problem to solve. Imaginative and thought-provoking, fiction at its best'
— Mike and Kathleen Gear

'A mesmerizing tale of love, loss and the human condition, certain to transport readers while simultaneously transforming their imaginations. It will captivate and challenge perceptions while raising the question, what is reality vs grand illusion? It's guaranteed to be amongst the classics you'll read time and time again'
— Eric Bishop

'What can I say about *The Other Side of Night* that won't be a spoiler? Ingenious, constantly surprising and deeply moving. Put yourself in the hands of a master storyteller, and strap in for a mind-bending ride'
— Joseph Finder

By Adam Hamdy

Pendulum Trilogy
Pendulum
Freefall
Aftershock

The Scott Pearce Series
Black 13
Red Wolves

Y057016

**The item should be returned or renewed
by the last date stamped below.**

Dylid dychwelyd neu adnewyddu'r eitem erbyn
y dyddiad olaf sydd wedi'i stampio isod.

PILLGWENLLY

To renew visit / Adnewyddwch ar
www.newport.gov.uk/libraries

ADAM HAMDY

The Other Side of Night

MACMILLAN

First published 2022 by Macmillan
an imprint of Pan Macmillan
The Smithson, 6 Briset Street, London EC1M 5NR
EU representative: Macmillan Publishers Ireland Ltd, 1st Floor,
The Liffey Trust Centre, 117–126 Sheriff Street Upper,
Dublin 1, D01 YC43
Associated companies throughout the world
www.panmacmillan.com

ISBN 978-1-5290-8813-7

Copyright © Adam Hamdy 2022

The right of Adam Hamdy to be identified as the
author of this work has been asserted by him in accordance
with the Copyright, Designs and Patents Act 1988.

All rights reserved. No part of this publication may be reproduced,
stored in a retrieval system, or transmitted, in any form, or by any means
(electronic, mechanical, photocopying, recording or otherwise)
without the prior written permission of the publisher.

Pan Macmillan does not have any control over, or any responsibility for,
any author or third-party websites referred to in or on this book.

9 8 7 6 5 4 3 2 1

A CIP catalogue record for this book is available from the British Library.

Typeset in Scala by Jouve (UK), Milton Keynes
Printed and bound by CPI Group (UK) Ltd, Croydon, CR0 4YY

This book is sold subject to the condition that it shall not, by way of
trade or otherwise, be lent, hired out, or otherwise circulated without
the publisher's prior consent in any form of binding or cover other than
that in which it is published and without a similar condition including
this condition being imposed on the subsequent purchaser.

Visit **www.panmacmillan.com** to read more about all our books
and to buy them. You will also find features, author interviews and
news of any author events, and you can sign up for e-newsletters
so that you're always first to hear about our new releases.

For Elliot, who inspired this book with a simple question

Preface

What would you sacrifice for love?

As I look back on my life, I'm haunted by the question. Perhaps what troubles me most is that I never got to choose. The pain I suffer, the loss I feel, the regret that clouds every single day – I never chose my sacrifice. Someone made the choice for me.

Would I have taken a different path?

I don't know, but the opportunity would have been nice. Instead, like a character in a story, my fate was decided by someone else.

My son.

I think about Elliot every day. Sometimes in anger, often with remorse, mostly in pity, but always with love. You can draw your own conclusions about the morality of his actions. To this day, my own mind is not at peace with what happened.

Is regret real?

We feel it, but it doesn't exist anywhere. I can't point to it, any more than I can relive the events that caused it. But does that mean it isn't real? I devoted many of my years to science, and after decades spent pondering the intersection between perception and reality, I've come to the conclusion that regret and all the other emotions we feel so deeply are just as real as the clothes we wear or the air we breathe. I've dissected my life, studied the great thinkers of every age, and considered all the theories of reality I could find, and I've come to accept one inescapable truth:

Life is memory.

Everything we experience of the world exists only in our minds or the minds of those around us. The past is generally accepted as memory, so must we accept the present and future as fictions of our mind. Moments we perceive as 'now' have already passed, and the future is the imagined memory of things to come. We commonly think of time moving forward, but there are some who believe we're travelling backwards, that the past lies ahead of us and the future behind. In many ways, this view of the cosmos makes sense. We can see the past, but are blind to the future. Are moments gone any more real than those yet to be had? We are equipped to experience the now, to take in sights and sounds, tastes, smells, to touch and be touched, to feel pain, heartbreak, anguish, and yet as we move from one moment to the next, each instant fades and the new now becomes more real than anything we remember, but it too is memory the instant we experience it.

What was, what is, and what will be – I now understand these things exist only in our minds, but that doesn't make them any less real, any less inevitable. We are bound by the chains of causation that allow time to hold back chaos, and each link is essential to ensure we never escape our destiny. Every moment of suffering, every stab of pain, every shed tear is simply the price of order. We each long to be exempt from such tight bonds, to have one link unfastened to undo a moment, to alter the chain that constrains us, but such dreams are futile. We are stuck, bound to stories that have already been written. We just haven't lived them yet, and when we have, it's too late for them to be changed.

The story that follows has been decades in the making. I've pieced together court reports, electronic records, newspaper articles, video recordings, letters – everything I could to make my account as close to the truth as possible. I've relied greatly on the words of the woman who destroyed my son's life and then redeemed it: Harriet Kealty.

Harri strikes me as a lonely figure. Perhaps that's what law enforcement does to a person. Maybe daily exposure to the violent, dishonest, and downright murderous makes trust a luxury? Perhaps that's why police officers travel in packs, and end up socializing together.

She was thirty-one or thirty-two when she first met my son. She'd been born and raised in London, and spent her child-hood living in a four-bedroom terraced house near Battersea Park. Harri was twenty when her mum died, and her father retired to Melbourne shortly after she joined the police force. He died a few years later. There were a couple of cousins, one on the Isle of Wight, the other in Toronto, and a brace of school friends who met her once a year for drinks, but beyond that, Harri was a loner. She didn't keep a conventional diary, but every few days she would send herself a chatty email chronicling recent events. She kept the emails in a folder called 'journal' and as far as I can tell she never shared them with anyone. The emails read like round robins, and the fact she felt too isolated to share her news with anyone but her-self fills me with sadness. I consider myself a voyeur trawling through her private recollections, but given her role in Elliot's life this book wouldn't have been possible without the intru-sion. If I've wronged her, I hope she will forgive me.

I've been in two minds about sharing the trove that has enabled me to tell this story. They always say a magician should never reveal their secrets and I think the same is true of authors. If I hadn't revealed my access to Harri's emails, court records, and other histories, you might have thought me more imaginative, or a better storyteller, but I feel it is important you know I'm honest. I've traded mystery for accuracy. However much this diminishes your perception of me as a storyteller, you know that all I'm doing is colouring between the lines of reality.

Of all the books I've written, this is the most difficult. Not a page passes that I don't think of my son, alone, described by the social workers who came to assess him as 'troubled', 'withdrawn' and 'suspicious'. I long to reach out to my boy and hug him. I want to hold Elliot and make the pain go away. I want to tell him how sorry I am for abandoning him, to tell him how much I love him.

But I can't.

And that eats at me.

I'm hollow.

I miss him so much.

But he's gone.

Or rather, it's me.

I've gone.

I left him.

I left him alone in that house.

I didn't know what I was doing. I still don't. I can't come to terms with what I've done. That's part of the reason I'm writing this book: to try to make sense of it all. I've spent years telling stories, but this was the only one that really mattered, and I've never had the courage to tell it publicly because it's too raw. It still causes great pain, and all my failings as a father are laid bare. I want to hug my boy. I want to make him feel better, but I can't. And that's on me.

Me, and no one else.

I return to the house every year. I make the trip in summer when the Peak District is at its most beautiful. I travel the familiar track to the cottage we once called home, and wander through the untouched memorial to a happy life. I don't think anyone lived here after Elliot left, and the place is damp and imbued with a stillness of abandonment that crushes me every time I cross the threshold. The doors are bowed and flaking, the windows long broken, the frames woodwormed and splintered.

The roof has been pockmarked by the relentless march of time, and here and there the cracked slate floor is contoured by the residue of water puddles. I'm not sure how much longer the old place will withstand the elements, but where others might see a ruin, memory takes me beyond the decay and fills my eyes with glistening images of a husband and wife, happy together. Their joy at a child. The bubbling sounds of family life.

Years ago, I found an aluminium box concealed in the cubby behind the loose brick beside the fireplace in the sitting room. A trove left by Elliot, who was always obsessed with secrets. I remember showing him the cubby in happier times, before our lives were blighted by misery. I still recall how his eyes lit up when I said it would be a good place to hide pirate treasure or the clandestine messages of a spy. He always had such a wonderful imagination.

I can't remember what prompted me to look behind the loose brick all those years later. A desire to make physical contact with that moment, perhaps? To be linked to my son, no matter how tenuously? To relive a memory? My reward was a connection more real and haunting than I could have ever imagined.

I found letters Elliot had written to me.

I remember standing in the ruined room, hearing no sound, sensing nothing, as though time itself had stopped. I devoured them, pausing only to compose myself when some handwritten phrase broke me. Some of the letters are so raw I have only been able to read them once. Others I revisit often. This is one of my favourites, for reasons I hope will become clear.

Dear Dad,

Do you remember when you showed me this little pirate's hollow? You told me Jack Sparrow might hide treasure there. Or Alex Rider some top-secret plans. I remember that day. I hope you do too. I pray you find these. I like to think of you standing by the fireplace reading my words. These scrawled symbols on the page link our minds. It doesn't matter how many years have passed; the moment of your reading will be tied to the moment of my writing and through these words we can be together again. They tell part of my story, but you'll have to dig deeper if you want the whole truth.

You didn't deserve what happened. None of us did. But fate conspired against us and I was forced to make a choice. Although I sometimes wonder whether I ever really chose. When I look back on what happened, it always seems my path was chosen for me. Perhaps you'll be able to find sense where I have not?

I have two regrets. The first is that we can't be together. It causes me pain every single day, but without that pain, well, you know the alternative. You lived it. For a few agonizing weeks, you saw what life would have been like. My other regret is Sabih Khan. His face haunts my dreams and helps me accept my punishment.

I hope you don't miss me as much as I miss you. There's no need for sadness. We were blessed to have had more years together than we were due. It was an honour to call you father, but you know you were more than that to me – you were also a friend. The best I ever had. If you find yourself mourning me, take comfort in the knowledge that one day I will find happiness. Please don't be sad for me. I have as much as anyone could hope for, even if it's not everything.

    With all my love,

    Elliot

Those of you familiar with my work might be surprised by this tale, but before I became an author, I had another life. Writing is a metaphor for my journey. I came to it unwittingly, unwillingly and am captive to it.

Don't pity me. Like my son, I've suffered more than most and been trapped in ways few could understand, but I have almost everything I've ever wanted. There is just one thing missing, and it's the thing I miss the most.

I've tried to tell this story once or twice before, but even my closest friends don't believe it. Their sidelong glances of scepticism grind away at me and I've always lost heart before reaching the end. So I'm publishing it as a book, perhaps my last, and my readers can make of it what they will.

This is my son's story. I have no doubt it will be sold as fiction, but rest assured every word that follows is true.

David Asha

Part One

The Child

Extract from the court report of *R* v. *Elmys*

ROGER SUMPTION QC *for the Crown Prosecution Service*
Ms Hardcastle, you run Sunshine Start, is that correct?

ELAINE HARDCASTLE
Yes.

ROGER SUMPTION QC
Could you describe what you do?

ELAINE HARDCASTLE
We provide temporary care for children until they can be placed with a foster family or adopted.

ROGER SUMPTION QC
Can you explain how you first encountered the defendant?

ELAINE HARDCASTLE
Mr Elmys was going to adopt Elliot Asha. Well, he did, but when I first met him, he was still going through the legal formalities.

ROGER SUMPTION QC
I believe you told the police there was something odd about Mr Elmys's behaviour on the day he came to collect Elliot.

ELAINE HARDCASTLE
Yes.

ROGER SUMPTION QC
Can you elaborate? Tell us about it for the benefit of the jury.

ELAINE HARDCASTLE
It was last August. I remember because we were planning our annual sunshine holiday. It's a little treat we give the children at the end of every summer, sort of to make up for them not going away like they might if they were with family. I was sad Elliot was leaving us and missing it, but pleased he had a new home. Well, an old home.

ROGER SUMPTION QC
Can you explain?

ELAINE HARDCASTLE
David and Elizabeth Asha had made Mr Elmys trustee of their estate and Elliot's guardian. Elliot was going back to the family home to live with Mr Elmys.

ROGER SUMPTION QC
And how did he seem to you that day?

ELAINE HARDCASTLE
Elliot? He was sad. At least to begin with.

ROGER SUMPTION QC
And Mr Elmys?

ELAINE HARDCASTLE
I, well, we met in my office. I like to give new guardians the opportunity to ask questions while I'm doing final checks.

ROGER SUMPTION QC
Did Mr Elmys ask any questions?

ELAINE HARDCASTLE
No. He just watched me going over the paperwork. He seemed distracted.

GRACE OYEWOLE QC *for the defendant*
My Lord, as someone might be if they were suddenly responsible for a child.

HIS HONOUR JUDGE THOMAS
Indeed.

ELAINE HARDCASTLE
That's true. A lot of people who adopt struggle with the responsibility. But this was different. Am I, I mean, I hope it's not untoward or anything, but Mr Elmys seemed troubled.

GRACE OYEWOLE QC *for the defendant*
My Lord.

JUDGE THOMAS

Please keep to your recollection of events, Mrs Hardcastle. You're not qualified to give opinions on Mr Elmys's frame of mind.

ROGER SUMPTION QC

What happened then?

ELAINE HARDCASTLE

I asked Mr Elmys to stay in the welcome room. It's a play space we use to acclimatize children to their new families. I left him there and went to fetch Elliot, who was with Stephanie Cliffe, one of our counsellors. She was observing him interact with other children. Or rather, not interact. His parents' deaths had hit him hard. Is it OK to say that? I mean it's my opinion, but it's based on decades of working with children.

He was sitting apart, like he did every day, staring out of the window at the old oak tree that grows just beside the residential wing. Whenever I'd ask him what he was doing, why he was daydreaming rather than playing, he'd say he was counting souls. Each leaf was a person. One day they'd start to fall, and by winter they'd all be gone. I thought it was a very strange way for a ten-year-old child to look at the world.

Anyway, I found him by the window, and Steph and I took him to the welcome room. It was very distressing.

ROGER SUMPTION QC

Why?

ELAINE HARDCASTLE

He was crying. Fighting with us both. We don't use physical restraint at Sunshine, but this was as close as I'd ever come to having to do so.

ROGER SUMPTION QC

Would you say he was afraid of Mr Elmys?

GRACE OYEWOLE QC

I hesitate to rise, but my learned friend knows the rules. Can I ask that he sticks to them so that I do not have to address My Lord further?

ROGER SUMPTION QC

Then I will ask a different question. Did you get Elliot to the welcome room?

ELAINE HARDCASTLE

Yes.

ROGER SUMPTION QC

What happened then?

ELAINE HARDCASTLE

He ran away from us and went into the corner. He was very upset. He sat with his back to us, but I think he was crying. I asked him to come and say hello to Mr Elmys, but he ignored me. I reminded him Mr Elmys was one of his parents' oldest friends. 'They wouldn't have left you in his care if they didn't think he was a good man,' I told him, but he stayed put.

ROGER SUMPTION QC
What did Mr Elmys do?

ELAINE HARDCASTLE
When I looked at him, I thought he was crying, but he
caught my eye and turned away, so I can't be sure. These
are emotional experiences. Big rocks.

ROGER SUMPTION QC
Excuse me?

ELAINE HARDCASTLE
It's what I tell the children. When you go to the beach,
it's mostly pebbles, but occasionally there will be one
or two big rocks you have to climb over. Just like life.
Most days are pebbles, but every so often you'll hit a big
rock. Adoption is a big rock. A murder trial is another
big rock.

ROGER SUMPTION QC
Quite. Going back to that day, Mrs Hardcastle, what
happened next?

ELAINE HARDCASTLE
Elliot was shuddering and shaking. He was very upset.
I told Mr Elmys we would have to try another day if we
couldn't calm him down. I was about to go to the boy, when
Mr Elmys asked if he could try. I wasn't sure it was a good
idea, but Mr Elmys was already on his way. He crouched
beside Elliot and spoke to him.

ROGER SUMPTION QC
Could you hear what he was saying?

ELAINE HARDCASTLE
No. He wasn't whispering exactly, just speaking softly. After
a short while, Mr Elmys stood. I thought he'd failed, and was
about to go over, but Elliot got up and turned around. He
wiped his tears and then took Mr Elmys's hand. Steph and
I were blown away. I'd never seen anything like it. The boy
was transformed. He seemed calm, happy almost.
  'How did you do that? What did you say?' I asked Mr Elmys.
I've worked with hundreds of children and I was stunned.

ROGER SUMPTION QC
And what was the defendant's reply?

ELAINE HARDCASTLE
'We made a deal, didn't we, Elliot?' And he looked down at
the boy, who nodded. The two of them smiled.

ROGER SUMPTION QC
Did you ever learn the nature of this deal?

ELAINE HARDCASTLE
No.

ROGER SUMPTION QC
So, it was secret?

ELAINE HARDCASTLE
Yes. It was secret.

Chapter 1

Harriet Kealty had spent almost an hour sitting alone outside the Nantwich Bookshop, and was now nursing her third espresso. She watched the other customers and listened to their conversations as Steve and Denise, the friendly owners of the bookshop, and their staff shuttled in and out, ferrying orders of coffee and cakes. It was a Saturday, so the town centre was busy and the square opposite the crooked Tudor building was packed with shoppers buzzing from one market stall to another.

Harri checked her watch: 11.58. Two minutes off an hour. More than any reasonable person could be expected to wait. But she wasn't a reasonable person. She was desperate to reclaim a life she'd lost a few painful weeks ago. She'd been lured here by hope, and to leave would be admitting it had been extinguished.

But in the end, after another twenty minutes of sitting there with a gnawing sense of inevitability, Harri finally accepted defeat. John Marlowe, the man who'd emailed her, promising she would get her job back if she came to this meeting, had been yet another troll, a liar who felt entitled to waste her time and humiliate her because she'd been so successfully cast as the villain by the local papers.

Another dead end.

She asked Denise for the bill, paid in change, and drifted into the shop. There were tables and chairs arranged between bookshelves, and the hubbub of conversation filled the room. Friends and family bound together by shared experience. She had nothing to keep her company. Ever since that awful night, her life had been one misstep after another. She desperately wanted what all these people had: an ordinary life. She wanted to feel good. Overwhelmed by loneliness, her mind reached, as it had so many times, for Ben. He'd made her feel good for a while, and she was afraid she'd never meet anyone like him again. Self-pity brought tears to her eyes.

Great, she thought. A private humiliation and a public embarrassment. She hurried towards a flight of stairs and a sign that read 'Toilets'.

Her footsteps echoed around the narrow, crooked stairwell, and the sounds of the cafe faded as she emerged into an almost deserted second-hand books section. Cracked spines sliced long runs of other less damaged but clearly used books. Beyond the high shelves, almost directly opposite the top of the stairs, was a corridor that led to the toilets, where she might find a mirror in which she could check her make-up, and the privacy to compose herself. There was only one problem. The old man who stood between her and the corridor. He looked startled, as though her rushed arrival had caught him in some mischief.

'I'm sorry,' she said, fighting for composure.

'Please don't apologize,' he replied, obviously trying to recover his own.

'I didn't mean to startle you.'

He smiled indulgently and his face creased like an unmade bed. 'You didn't. I was just thinking.'

His eyes fell and for a moment Harri forgot her own worries. The man's sadness hit her like a wave. His craggy face was downcast and his eyes were heavy and shining with the prospect of a storm. His mop of grey hair was neatly combed, and he looked as though he was dressed for a date. His tweed jacket, black trousers, and white shirt were well pressed, and his red woven silk tie was bright and clean. If he was on a date, then like her, he had been stood up, because there was no one else around. He was tall, and might once have been handsome, but whatever gifts youth had conferred were long gone. Only a brightness in his eyes hinted at the charisma that might have drawn people to him and the energy he might have had long ago. His slight frame was angled against a supportive ebony walking stick. Harri took a generous guess he was the right side of ninety. She wanted to get past him, but felt awkward as it seemed as though he was expecting a conversation.

'My wife and I fell in love the instant we met. She's gone now, but she's always with me, you know, in all the moments we shared,' he said, and Harri feared he might cry. He took a couple of breaths, and she prayed he would hold it together, because she didn't think she'd be able to stop herself if she saw someone else weeping. 'She loved to read,' he added at last.

He managed a false smile. The world was full of people like him, their best days gone, their glories forgotten. All they loved, everything they'd done, nothing more than memories fading like writing in sand, washed away by the tide of time.

'I'm sorry. It's not long since I lost her and . . .' he trailed off, and they stood in awkward silence for a moment.

'It's all so overwhelming,' he added sadly. 'You take a journey together, and you know everything that starts will have an end, but you can never quite bring yourself to believe it.

Somewhere there's a secret tribe of quiet immortals, right? Some race of souls who never perish. You come to believe you'll find a way to join them, and you push the end from your mind.'

He took a step forward, and for a moment Harri thought he'd reach out and touch her, but he stopped a pace away and settled on his cane.

'It was sudden. Heart attack. We never had the chance to say goodbye,' his voice was cracked with age, but as he spoke of his loss, emotion fractured it further. 'I couldn't save her. It was one of those things. I'm so sorry . . .'

His words drifted to nothing, but his eyes stayed on Harri, before shifting away.

'She was very beautiful, you know? Like you.'

Harri didn't feel at all beautiful. She'd gained six pounds since her dismissal, and even though she wasn't overweight, she felt the extra baggage on her normally slight five-foot six-inch frame. She hadn't been to the salon for months and had her light-brown hair tied in a tail to conceal the tangles and split ends. Her usual wardrobe of suits had been replaced by scruffy trainers, jeans, and T-shirts, and whereas she'd once taken time over her make-up, she could barely muster the enthusiasm for lipstick. She might be many things, but right now beautiful wasn't one of them.

She thought he was just being polite, so she didn't thank him for his dishonesty, and grew increasingly uncomfortable in the beat that followed. She could hear the hubbub rising up the stairs, and longed to be part of the crowd. Fate had thrown her in the path of this broken old man, but she didn't have what it took to fix him. She was just as damaged. Her discomfort must have shown, because his demeanour changed.

'Listen to me.' His voice brightened, but his eyes told her the levity was forced. 'I'm a blathering old fool.'

'Not at all,' Harri said automatically. Her mother had raised her to be polite. 'Death is difficult.'

'If you could know the moment of your end, would you want to?' the old man mused.

She thought about all the bad things that had ever happened to her. Would it have helped to know about them in advance?

'No. No, I don't think I would,' she replied. 'It would hang over me like a cloud.'

'True.' He nodded. 'I promised myself I wouldn't get carried away, that I'd be strong, but it's so hard. I'm so alone, you see. Almost everyone I've ever known is gone. She was my love. She still is. Just being here is so difficult.'

'It's OK. That's normal. In the police we call it survivor's guilt.'

The man bit his lip and cast around the room, as though something in the old books might support him in his grief. He found strength from somewhere.

'You're good and kind. You have a big heart,' he said, and Harri almost broke down in tears. He was a soul in torment and he was trying to be nice to her. 'We all face the same end. Whatever our road, we finish the journey pleading with the void. Begging for just one more moment. But there's never enough time. The relentless turn of the seconds. The ticking clock. That is our enemy. I loved her so much.'

His eyes met Harri's and they shimmered.

'What would you give for just one more moment with someone who meant everything?'

Harri found herself wanting to take the old widower's hand and soothe the pain, but he moved back a half-step and eyed her with the sudden alertness of someone waking from a dream.

'Listen to me casting a shadow over your day. That's not who I am. I'm a bringer of smiles. You know what my wife used to say? "You are my star. You light up the darkest day." Don't you think that's beautiful?'

'Very,' Harri replied.

'That's what I should be doing; lighting up days, not darkening them. I'm sorry I've upset you.'

'Not at all,' she assured him.

'I've wasted your time at the very least. It's most selfish of me. Clinging to moments. Hoarding memories. I'm old. My day is done. Yours is ahead of you and I have no right to waste another second. It's been my absolute pleasure. Thank you for your kindness. Goodbye.'

Harri couldn't suppress a surprised smile when the old man abruptly pivoted around his walking stick and hurried past her. Within moments, he was clanking down the stairs.

She was about to head to the toilet when she noticed a book on the floor. It had been concealed by the man, and lay cover wide, spine broken, like a dead bird. Had he been looking at it when she'd startled him?

Happiness: A New Way of Life.

A woman smiled up from the cover. She looked annoyingly contented. Harri preferred thrillers and would never normally have been interested in such a book, but she was desperate, and if the smiling author, Isabella Tosetti, had just one useful nugget of advice, she'd take it. Harri picked up the book and checked the inner leaf. Fifty pence for a whole new way of life.

Bargain, she thought, and she took the book with her.

Chapter 2

There was a knock at the door, and she put down the book and crossed the small bedroom of the little flat she'd bought when she first moved to Stoke-on-Trent. It was on the sixth floor of a modern building on a quiet back street, not far from the old pot banks that stood to the south of Hanley. Harri's one-bedroom home might have been small, but the big windows in the living room gave her a panoramic view of the city and the emerald countryside beyond. It used to inspire her, but she didn't even glance at it now.

'Who is it?' she asked, pressing her eye to the spyhole.

'Me,' Sabih Khan said.

He was in a tailored suit which clung to his wiry frame, and his hair was as immaculately coiffed as ever, the black waves shining with product.

Harri opened the door for her old partner.

'All right?' he said, lingering on the threshold. 'I thought I'd stop by to see how you're doing.'

'Did Powell send you?' Harri asked, sensing Sabih's reticence.

'No,' he replied indignantly. 'I'm here because—'

She cut him off. 'Because you care?'

'You know, people ask if I miss you, but right now I can't say that I do.'

'Well, you know the way out.'

'I will come in, thank you,' he said, pushing his way past Harri.

She shut the door and followed him through the open-plan kitchen diner to the living room, and she flushed as she suddenly saw her home through a newcomer's eyes. It was a battlefield of misery and the casualties of her war with depression were scattered everywhere: clothes, magazines, unopened post, half-consumed cups of coffee, crumb-covered plates – some relatively recent, others relics from weeks ago. She hadn't felt this low since her relationship with Ben had ended. Harri registered the look on Sabih's face.

'I know what it looks like,' she said. 'But these aren't telltale signs. I've just been busy.'

'Empty bottles, discarded food, unkempt appearance,' Sabih responded, and Harri's hand rose instinctively to straighten her hair. 'None of these are signs of depression. Is that what you're telling me?'

He held her gaze, and they stood in silence as she eyed him defiantly.

'I was just passing,' he said at last. 'I'm not here to intrude on your business. If you say you're fine . . .' he trailed off. 'But if you need help—'

'Listen,' she interrupted. 'You can tell Powell, or anyone else who wants to know, that I'm doing brilliantly and winning at life.'

'I'm sorry, Harri,' Sabih said. 'I let you down. I never thought Powell would go for you like that. I don't know what to say. I wish I could take it back. Do better. Be stronger.'

And just like that he took the angry wind of indignation out of her sails. Harri couldn't cope with kindness. Not today.

She nodded, not trusting herself to reply. She'd thought about that night so many times, and wondered what she could have done differently. Her partner, her friend, was being beaten to death. If she hadn't stepped in to save him, well, he wouldn't be here. In her self-righteous self-pity she'd forgotten his suffering.

'How are you?' she asked. 'The ribs?'

'OK. Still hurts to breathe, and I don't think I'll be setting any track and field records for a while. The body heals. It's the mind that's harder, right? Do I still have what it takes? Will I be the first in next time, or a step behind everyone else?'

She could only imagine how his confidence had been knocked. Her own was shot.

'You'll be the classic fool rushing in,' she remarked.

He didn't look reassured. 'What about you?' he asked. 'How are you doing? Really?'

'I've been better. Some guy wasted an hour of my life today. Emailed me claiming he knew something about the footage of that night. Said I'd get it if I came to meet him in Nantwich. Never showed. I emailed him, giving a few choice thoughts on him wasting my time, but it's probably some troll with a fake account.'

'*Harami*,' Sabih said. 'Powell should have done more to keep your name out of the papers.'

Harri nodded. She'd devoted her life to the police, but none of that had mattered and her boss had hung her out for the vultures.

Sabih's phone rang and he pulled it from his pocket.

'Sorry, it's the guv'nor,' he said. He answered the call. 'Go ahead, guv.' There was a brief pause and Harri imagined Powell rattling off an instruction. 'I'm on my way.'

He hung up and gave Harri an apologetic puppy-dog shrug. 'Sorry. Duty calls.'

Harri felt a pang of envy. A few weeks ago, she would have been going with him.

'Ah, that was insensitive of me. Great body, sharp mind, not so hot on all these complicated human things,' he said, his index finger shuttling back and forth through the air between them.

Harri suddenly felt sorry for him. He'd been beaten and battered physically and psychologically, and he was grieving too. He'd lost a partner.

'Complicated human things?' Harri replied. 'What are you, a robot? Just say, "Let's grab a beer sometime", and leave with a smile on your face.'

'Let's grab a beer sometime,' Sabih said as he backed towards the door. 'You're the best, Harri. A top girl.'

She couldn't resist a smile at his awkwardness.

After he was gone, Harri stood in the little flat for a moment, listening to the distant sounds of the city, where thousands of lives far more productive than hers were being played out. She glanced around the messy room and thought about tidying up, but the brief surge of energy that had risen in Sabih's presence soon dissipated. The mess could wait. She left everything as it was, and returned to her book.

Extract from *Happiness: A New Way of Life*
By Isabella Tosetti
Printed with permission of Vitalife Press

Happiness as Love
Romeo and Juliet. Star-crossed lovers, ill-fated to suffer. A

picture of love that's endured to this day. One of pain and sacrifice. Love as tragedy. Alongside this runs a steady stream of novels, television, film and song that tell us love is the most powerful source of happiness.

Death cannot stop true love.

You had me at hello.

You complete me.

And so on.

The world's libraries could be filled with nothing but books on love, and still the poets would think more needed to be said.

Dr Martha McClintock demonstrated what we perceive as falling in love is actually a sense of attraction manufactured by our brain because it has used a combination of visual and olfactory stimuli to gauge that union with the man or woman in question would produce offspring with optimized immune systems. Less star-crossed love, more evolutionary biology. This is true even of same-sex relationships, because the matching of immune systems is blind to prejudice and untroubled by concepts of gender.

We've all heard friends say, 'I don't know what she sees in him,' or, 'He loses his mind when he's around her.'

The obsessive, infatuated lover is a staple of romantic poetry. In addition to manufacturing a powerful sense of attraction to help with evolutionary optimization, our brains increase the chances of mating by shutting down the regions of our brain associated with critical reasoning. Semir Zeki and his colleague John Paul Romaya found that people deeply in love experience temporary and specific loss of brain function whenever they think about their lover. Using brain-imaging techniques, Zeki and Romaya measured a significant deactivation of the frontal cortex. If we could see a person's faults, we'd be less likely to mate with them, so our brains quite literally blind us with love.

Eventually the hormone rush wears off and the brain stops its tricks. Some people wake up one day and wonder what they ever saw in the person lying next to them. Others stay together, and blind love, that evolutionary trap, turns into something else, something profoundly real.

Love can make you blind. It can give you fleeting brain damage, it can cause pain, anguish, and suffering. But when all that is gone, you're left with someone whose life you share. You hope you make each other better. You share experiences. You sacrifice, but each sacrifice must be repaid, or else there is imbalance and exploitation. The most powerful relationship (and always remember why I use the word powerful) is the one that is harmonious. A healthy relationship strikes a note of truth and brings equilibrium to the lives of the lovers. It is through that truth and balance that we find happiness, because without being true to ourselves and those around us, we manufacture an illusory self, and a gap is created between who we really are and who we're pretending to be. If there is no harmony in the relationship, that gap is likely to grow, and it is this gap between the true self and the projection we manifest into the world that is the source of so much unhappiness.

Love should create no gap. It should not force you to manifest any illusion about who you really are. Love that is worthy of the word will be real and true. It will provide fuel for your generator. In ordinary times, love should heal you. It should bring you happiness. If you find yourself in extraordinary circumstances and your world requires sacrifice, make sure it brings you harmony, and through whatever it is you do for the one you love, you must ultimately find balance and that all-important power. A love that helps you be true to who you really are is the most powerful love of all.

Happiness as Novelty

Misery is comfortable. It becomes familiar and if we grow accustomed to it, we seek it out. How many times in life have you thought, *Not again*? How many times have you felt yourself making the same mistake? The same bad lover, the same awful job, the same terrible friendship.

We're creatures of habit, and once we establish a pattern for ourselves, it's difficult to break. Whether it's nature or nurture, we're malleable creatures, programmable, designed to adapt to our surroundings, and if we come to have certain expectations in life, we will subconsciously ensure they are met. The bad lover will become an archetype we seek out. When the relationship inevitably deteriorates and finally breaks down, it will reinforce whatever feelings of self-loathing led us into his or her arms and reduce our self-esteem to make us even more likely to accept another inferior scoundrel.

The same goes for jobs and friendships, and pretty much every aspect of our lives.

So what can we do?

If you find yourself falling into an unhealthy pattern, don't wallow in the comfort of the familiar. Challenge yourself to break it. Do something different. Reflect on what is leading you into a cycle of repetition, of recurrence, trapping you into making the same mistake. The same play rehearsed over and over again with slightly different lines and an altered cast of actors.

If depression puts you in bed, ignore its heavy grip and force yourself to go for a walk. I have talked about the nourishing qualities of trees and the power of forest bathing and have no doubt you'll benefit from the phytoncides mentioned on page 286, but a walk will also broaden your world rather than shrink it. Change and optimism are hardest to deliver when we're low, but that's precisely when we need to be able to realize them. Don't wallow. Get up. Get up and get out. You want a different result? Get out there and do something different to get it.

The Gap

Why aren't you happy? Because you don't have the woman you want? Or the man? The job? The house? The car? Have you lost someone you love?

It is far easier for us to pinpoint the sources of unhappiness than it is to explain why we're happy. Does happiness even exist? Can you laugh during the bleakest moments? Of course. But would you describe yourself as happy? And when you are at your most contented, would you describe yourself as happy in the common meaning of the word? Or are you simply at peace? Free of desire, untroubled by longing.

We often mistake happiness for elation, and are encouraged to nurture the gaps in our lives by companies that will profit from desire. They lead us to believe transitory, endorphin-based elation is the happiness we need, but the quest for elation only creates an addiction that can never be satisfied.

Contentment is elusive and can be hard to realize. It's much easier to believe a new car will make us happy. Or a new house. Or a new relationship.

Happiness comes from within. You've heard that one, right? But it doesn't come from within. It *is* the within. If you let go of desire and regret (for what is regret but the desire to undo the past?), you will realize you have everything you need. There is no gap in your life. Once you accept that reality, you can find peace, contentment and a happiness more profound and lasting than anything you've ever experienced. End the quest for transient elation. Unlock the happiness within.

I want.

The words were scrawled in the margin in red ink. Harri noticed a couple of scribbles above them where it looked as though someone had tried to get a pen to work. She was a little annoyed to be reminded it was a used book and that someone else had read it before her. She'd been lost in Isabella Tosetti's words, and the knowledge another reader had got them first seemed to somehow diminish their significance. They'd been striking a chord with her, particularly the section about being love-struck. That's certainly how she'd felt the first time she'd met Ben. She absently turned the page and felt a sudden chill when she registered the handwritten words in the margin overleaf.

I want to live
Help
He's trying to kill me

Chapter 3

Harri hadn't been able to concentrate after finding the message. She hadn't been able to sleep much either. The words could have been a cruel prank, but something about them touched her finely honed instincts as a detective. There were the scribbles of someone trying to get a pen to work, and the message itself was simple and to the point. There were no dramatic flourishes, just a clear plea for help. She kept picking up the book to examine it. She hadn't found any more writing, but there had been a 'Leek Library Released for Sale' stamp on the endpaper. Finally, as the first grey light of dawn edged the curtains, Harri drifted into a fitful sleep and dreamed of the last life she'd failed to save.

Alan Munro.

The man who had cost her almost everything.

She was tormented by the desire to undo those last few moments. To reach out to him, to call to him. But just as in real life, she was too slow, and it felt as though she was pinned to the rocks beneath her knees. The light of impending doom blazed in her dream, so brightly it woke her with a start.

She sighed, wondering if the dreams would ever stop. Would the guilt?

She rubbed her eyes, got dressed and drove her old Volkswagen Golf into Leek.

She hadn't been to the library for years. Her mum used to take her every week as a youngster, and she'd grown to love reading. She remembered on her very first visit she'd explored the shelves tentatively, like a burglar prowling through a stranger's house.

How can all these books be free? she'd thought, but she'd quickly become acclimatized and treated the cornucopia of stories as her second home.

She'd never understood why the place wasn't always packed with people, but she now realized how easy it was to neglect even the most valuable treasures. Libraries, like the one back home in Battersea that had taken her on so many magical journeys, were constantly under threat of closure. Every few months, a campaign would be organized to resist the next round of cuts, and some appendage – early years' groups, mobile lending, adult classes – would have to be sacrificed to appease the gods of efficiency and progress. Except it wasn't progress to take knowledge and experiences from the poorest, and even though she was no longer a regular, Harri reached into her pocket whenever she saw a library fundraiser. She wanted future generations to have the same chances she'd had.

Narrowing and removing opportunity didn't seem sensible, but there was much about early twenty-first-century life that didn't feel right to Harri. She stood at the top of a set of stone steps, leaned against the handrail and watched a few early morning shoppers shuffle along the street towards the town centre. They moved against a backdrop of empty shops, boarded up and advertised for rent. The Internet was chewing the heart out of communities all over the world, but few people seemed to mind much.

'Eager,' a voice said, and Harri turned to see a tattooed woman in her early thirties. She had bright pink hair, piercings, a vintage AC/DC top and torn jeans. Her mouth was curled in a half-smile as though turned by perpetual thoughts of mischief. 'Someone needs their word fix.'

Harri smiled, and the woman produced a set of keys and unlocked the front door.

'We don't officially open for another fifteen, but you don't look like a book snatcher to me. You can wait inside,' the woman said. 'My name's Edie. Come on in.'

Harri followed Edie into the building and was immediately catapulted back to childhood by the dry scent of old books, still air, and the sight of shelf after shelf packed with knowledge and adventure. Leek library was a grand listed structure with lead-lined windows, a hall, and an imposing tower. It was a bridge to a different time, when Victorians had measured success by the social hubs they created: libraries, schools, and parks. Harri hovered near the door and took it all in, while Edie stepped behind a large counter.

'Don't be shy,' Edie said. 'You don't have to wait. I won't tell anyone you were browsing before opening time.'

Harri smiled again. 'I'm not here for a book. I was hoping you could tell me about the last person to borrow this one.'

She swung her backpack off her shoulder and reached inside for the book. Harri surmised that whoever wrote the message would have been the last person to have borrowed it before it had been released for sale. Anyone else who'd taken the book after the message had been written would have spotted it and alerted someone.

'*Happiness: A New Way of Life*, by Isabella Tosetti,' Edie

said, studying the cover. She took the book and opened the back. 'It's one of ours, but I'm not supposed to give out personal details.'

'I found something valuable inside,' Harri lied.

Edie looked at her expectantly.

'I'd rather not say what it is, that way I can confirm its rightful owner.'

Edie pursed her lips. She didn't look completely satisfied, but it was excuse enough. She turned to the computer terminal and typed in some characters.

'This was our only copy and it was last borrowed by . . .' she trailed off. 'Oh, I don't have to protect the borrower's details. She died a few months ago. Elizabeth Asha. It was so sad. She had cancer. We held a vigil for her. It was beautiful. Hundreds of people with candles out by their house. I went. Cried buckets. Donated money. They raised tons, but it didn't do any good. Her husband died not long after. They say it was suicide. He left their son . . .' she paused and shook her head. 'It was a tragedy.'

'That sounds awful,' Harri remarked. 'Poor family. Poor kid. How do you get over something like that?'

'I'm not sure you ever do,' Edie said, and the two of them reflected on a family's suffering for a moment.

'Do you mind if I use a computer?' Harri asked.

'Go ahead,' Edie replied, gesturing at a line of terminals near a big window.

LOCAL VIGIL DRAWS HUNDREDS
14 February

Hundreds of Leek residents joined the friends and family of Dr Elizabeth Asha for a vigil outside her home in Upper Hulme. Dr Asha, a physicist at Keele University, was diagnosed with a rare form of cancer eighteen months ago. She has been undergoing treatment, and the local community has come together to raise funds to pay for novel therapies.

Cynthia Hughes, a friend of the family, said, 'Beth is such a wonderful person. She deserves every chance. This is a celebration of her, but it's also a celebration of hope.'

Through a family spokesperson, Elizabeth Asha's husband, David, thanked all those who attended the vigil, saying he and the family had been touched by the kindness and support.

Katie Harper, *Leek Advertiser*

MISADVENTURE VERDICT
6 September

A verdict of death by misadventure was returned in respect of Dr David Asha of Upper Hulme, Staffordshire, who disappeared on 14 June. Dr Asha had been recently bereaved after the death of his wife, Elizabeth, who passed away in April, after succumbing to her long battle with cancer. Friends say Dr Asha had been distraught at his wife's death and had become increasingly isolated. He was seen near

Arthog in Wales on the day of his death, walking near the clifftops. He is survived by his son, Elliot.

Katie Harper, *Leek Advertiser*

Two lives and boundless tragedy summed up in a brace of short newspaper articles. The misadventure verdict had been delivered a week ago. These people weren't long gone. Harri looked away from the library monitor and wondered why a scientist would write a message in a book, suggesting 'he' (her husband?) was trying to kill her. She was intrigued by David Asha's death. The coroner might have ruled misadventure, but a depressed man hanging around clifftops probably wasn't there for the view. Could it have been suicide as Edie had suggested? Had he struggled with grief? Or was it guilt? What had happened to the child? Had he been taken into care? Was he safe?

Harri wasn't police any more, but she still had the heart and soul of a detective, and they could never take that away from her. She got to her feet, gave a nod of thanks to Edie, and left the library.

Chapter 4

Harri could see faces in the high cliffs. The judgemental brow of an old aristocrat. The patrician nose of a Roman senator. The gritstone cracks and crags sparked her imagination as she steered her Volkswagen Golf along the lane that led from Upper Hulme to Ash Ridge.

To her left, a grand reservoir shone cobalt beneath a cloudless sky, and beyond it were rising green fields stocked with grazing cows and sheep. The cliffs loomed to her right, half a mile beyond boulder-strewn stretches of gorse. Harri had walked these inland cliffs many times and had always been moved by the rugged landscape. It was a place where the imagination could run wild. It wasn't just the striking beauty; she loved the grandeur. It gave her a sense of perspective, camouflaging her. The vast wilderness dwindled her significance, and she liked the idea of being hidden from the universe so it could neither notice nor judge her. She particularly relished the prospect of insignificance now, but she wasn't here for a walk. She was on a private mission, following a thread that started with what she assumed was Elizabeth Asha's message in the book.

Harri turned right and followed a narrow lane that circled around the cliffs. She had to slow a couple of times to allow sheep to move out of the road, and stopped and left the car to deal with gated cattle grids on three occasions. Finally, a mile further on, Harri saw what she was looking for: Longhaven, the Asha family home.

Harri parked on a patch of grass beside the driveway and got out. The two-storey detached cottage was the only building in sight. It stood behind a drystone wall in a large garden that looked as though it hadn't been tended for months. Weeds mingled with flowers, and shrubs and creepers spread beyond their beds. A gate blocked the short drive that connected the lane with a parking area in front of the house. Behind the property, a gentle hill met the cliffs, and Harri could see a footpath leading from the stone wall at the very end of the garden up to the high ridge.

She drew back the bolt, and the gate squeaked treacherously as she walked through. The cottage had six small square windows on each floor, evenly distributed either side of the front door. The window frames were painted black, a distinctive contrast against the grey walls and storm-cloud slate roof.

A shiver traced a cold finger down her neck, and Harri looked up to see a young boy with brown hair and sad, striking blue eyes staring at her from the upper window to the right of the front door. He stepped out of sight when he realized he'd been spotted.

A wrought-iron owl had a heavy hoop in its beak, and Harri took hold of the knocker and rapped it against the door. She heard muffled words and footsteps, and after a few moments, the door opened, and she was shocked to see a face she recognized.

She'd met Ben Elmys a little over a year ago, soon after she'd first transferred to Staffordshire, and for a brief time she'd loved him. She still did. He represented a life that might have been. A different life. A good one. But he hadn't wanted it.

'Hello,' he said awkwardly.

He'd changed since their last date at the Hand and Trumpet, a fine pub on the Cheshire border. He'd lost weight, leaving his six-foot-one frame teetering on the edge of gaunt. His shoulders were hunched and his face, which she recalled being so bright and alive, exuded a hangdog sadness. His eyes still made her think of polished amber. His brown hair was tousled and in many ways he reminded Harri of the child she'd seen in the window. Was he the boy's father? Is that why he hadn't called her? Did he have a secret life?

'Ben?' She couldn't help betraying her surprise. 'What are you doing here?'

'I live here,' he replied.

'I was . . . I mean . . .' She was flustered now. He was the last person she'd expected to meet.

'I'm in the middle of something.' He wiped his hands on his black T-shirt. The words 'I'm Fine' were stitched in red across his chest. He slipped his fingertips into the pockets of his jeans in an effort to appear casual, but Harri sensed a little too much effort. Was that it? Was that all he was going to say? Wasn't he going to even acknowledge the fact they'd once been in love?

'I was hoping to ask some questions about David and Elizabeth Asha,' Harri said, keeping her tone friendly and light.

Ben's face fell. 'They're dead.'

'Is that their son?' Harri probed, nodding towards the upstairs window.

He didn't even bother glancing up. 'Yes.'

'Elliot, isn't it?'

'Yes.'

It was like drawing teeth.

'If that's all,' Ben suggested, moving to shut the door.

'Why didn't you call me?' Harri asked hurriedly.

He said nothing.

'You broke up with me, Ben. You didn't respond to any of my messages or calls.'

'I know,' he replied. 'I . . . things changed.'

Harri didn't know what to make of his response. It was so vague it was meaningless.

'I read about the vigil people held.' She tried to connect with him. 'It sounded very touching.'

'It was,' Ben replied. 'The Ashas were good people.'

'Is that why you didn't call? Was it because of what happened?'

Why hadn't he told her about the Ashas and what they were going through? If they were the reason he'd broken things off, an explanation would have helped her understand. He'd said a friend had been ill, but that didn't even begin to convey the tragedy of what had happened to Elizabeth and David Asha.

He looked as though the question had stirred painful memories. 'I can't explain. It was just bad timing. I'm sorry if I hurt you. Why are you here? You're not with the police any more, are you?'

Harri's hackles rose. He obviously knew about her dismissal from the force. He'd been keeping tabs on her, but still hadn't called. 'No. I'm not. Why do you ask?'

'Isn't that normally who knocks on doors, raking through people's lives?' Ben replied.

If it was meant to be a scathing remark, it fell wide of its target because he delivered it with an innocent tone and an uncomprehending smile. Was he mentally unwell? He was still handsome, but the air of trauma was impossible to ignore. What had happened to the confident man she'd fallen for? This was a damaged soul in need of repair.

Much like you, Harri caught herself thinking. *Maybe you could find solace with each other?*

It was a testament to her strength of feeling that she was still drawn to him after how he'd treated her. This man had rejected her in the coldest possible way. He'd ended their relationship, dropped her calls, and ignored all her messages. Was it a connection she wanted? Or absolution for failure? Before she'd died, Harri's mother had called her a collector of broken toys. She was drawn to damaged people and always tried to make things better for them. She was a helper, a saviour. That's why she'd joined the police force. She'd wanted to save people, help the innocent, punish the guilty. Maybe the attraction she felt wasn't an expression of her vulnerability, but instead a manifestation of her habit of trying to heal others. Did she like Ben even more now she knew he was broken?

'Maybe if we'd met under different circumstances, we could have made each other happy,' Ben said. 'But the timing was wrong. And now this.'

'What do you mean "this"?' she asked.

'You're digging into the deaths of my friends. I don't think it's going to give us much of a future.'

'Why?' Harri asked. Was he admitting there was something for her to investigate?

'I wish we'd met in different circumstances.'

'Different how?'

Did he still feel something for her?

'If none of this had happened,' he replied. 'If we'd met in another world, I think we might have been good together, don't you?'

Ben looked at her earnestly. Why had he said that? Was he trying to mess with her emotions? Throw her off balance? Or did he still have feelings for her?

She was in uncharted territory. She'd never had to interview someone she knew personally, but she took her lead from Ben's strange and chilly reception, and used a cool no-nonsense tone she'd perfected on hundreds of other suspects.

Is that what he is now? Is he a suspect?

'I didn't come here to talk about us. I want to ask you about Elizabeth Asha,' Harri said.

'No one called her Elizabeth. She was Beth.'

'I'd like to know about Beth,' Harri tried.

'Did you ever meet her?' Ben asked.

He didn't seem all there. Was he on drugs?

'No. I'd like to ask you some questions about how Beth and David Asha died.'

Ben's eyes glazed over and his gaze drifted past her to the garden and valley beyond. 'But when the high gems shimmer and the shutters fall, I still feel those worlds tenderly traced.'

He doesn't seem well, Harri thought, but she immediately checked herself. *Don't get confused. You don't owe this man your compassion.*

They'd bonded over a shared love of poetry, but that was then. The lines sounded out of place, detached from the world, perhaps reflecting his current state of mind.

'Were you listening?' he asked suddenly, as though a slipped cog had suddenly re-engaged with reality. 'It's from a poem I wrote for someone dear to me.'

'Beth?'

Ben didn't answer and his attention drifted again. This did not seem like a person who should be in charge of a child.

'Is there anyone else here?' she asked.

'No. Just Elliot. And we're busy,' he said. 'We don't have time for questions.'

His words were hard, but his expression was almost pitying as he shut the door on her.

As she walked away from one of the strangest encounters of her life, Harri looked back and saw the boy, Elliot, watching her from the upstairs window.

Maybe it was her imagination, but he seemed to be judging her.

Chapter 5

Harri had first met Ben Elmys a little over a year ago, shortly after she'd moved to Staffordshire.

Everything had seemed so much lighter. She'd left the stress and danger of London for a slower pace of life and had been pleasantly surprised to be partnered with someone as sparky as Sabih Khan. They'd hit it off immediately, like a younger brother and older sister reunited after years apart. They'd never met before, but that's how it had felt – easy and familiar. They'd slipped into a natural rhythm of banter and honesty, and when Sabih had found out she'd registered for eHarmony, he'd mocked her relentlessly, but she didn't care. She was determined to make the most of the move to the country, and at thirty-one, she was resolved to find someone to share her life with. Once he realized how much it meant to her, Sabih stopped teasing about finding love in the algorithm.

'So, today's the big day,' he said as she pulled up outside his house at the end of their shift.

The algorithm had given her one man she was interested in. A guy called Benjamin Elmys, and she'd made the mistake of giving Sabih a running commentary of their email exchanges.

'All ribbing aside, I hope it goes well for you,' Sabih said as he climbed out of the car. He'd turned and leaned in through the open door. 'Just remember to take your baton in case he's a weirdo. I'm sure he won't be, but don't be afraid to club him if you're not sure.'

Harri scowled at him.

'He'll be normal though,' he went on. 'Everyone knows there aren't any weirdos on the Internet.'

He flashed a grin and shut the door.

Harri drove to Newcastle-under-Lyme, the market town on the outskirts of Stoke-on-Trent, and parked in the multi-storey near the cinema. She checked her make-up and fixed her hair. Butterflies filled her stomach and her heart thundered like a tiny drum as she thought about what might lie ahead.

The centre of Newcastle-under-Lyme is pedestrianized, with shops and cafes either side of a broad pavement. Harri's nerves grew as she walked the red bricks towards the Guildhall, a large Victorian building that marked the very heart of town. There was a cafe on the ground floor where she was due to meet Ben. She passed old couples, young lovers holding hands, and parents pushing prams, and felt her loneliness more keenly, suddenly aware she was surrounded by the consequences of love. Only today was different. Today brought hope she might have found someone.

She hurried to her date, not wanting to keep Ben waiting, but a small part of her longed to turn around, to run away. She was afraid she might not like him, nor he her, and she wasn't sure she could cope with another disappointment.

She forced herself on, and her stomach was churning by the time she entered the Clockhouse, the cafe that occupied the Guildhall's clock tower. There weren't many people inside, and Harri recognized Ben immediately. He looked even better than his profile picture. The interest she'd felt online became the electricity of attraction in the flesh, and fear gave way to excitement as she walked towards the table near the back of the cafe.

He smiled when he saw her, and his grin lit up her world. He stood, and she saw he was tall and muscular. Not heavily built, but athletic.

She'd never believed in love at first sight, maybe because it hadn't happened to her, but as she moved towards this man, profound knowing hit her, reverberating deep within her soul, and she felt an attraction that was impossible to resist. There was lust, the intrigue of exploration, of getting to know a new person, but there was something more, something deeper that came from her ancient, primal self. It was as though she'd found the part of her that was missing.

She hadn't read Shakespeare for years, but his words came to her, 'No sooner met but they looked, no sooner looked but they loved.'

She had always dismissed them as a shorthand for what had been, for her, the arduous and ultimately disappointing journey of falling in love. But she understood them now. They signified the instant attraction felt when a match was so perfect it seemed as though the gods themselves were smiling down on the couple. Judging by the grin on Ben's face and the bright shimmer in his amber eyes, he felt something similar.

He tried to pull out a chair, but the legs caught the edge of an uneven floor tile and sent it toppling over. They both lunged for it before it hit the floor, and their hands touched as they caught the chair back. Her skin tingled at his touch.

'Sorry,' he said quickly.

He moved his hands so they were no longer on hers, and

she was surprised to feel disappointed. He righted the chair, and she took a seat.

'This is odd,' he said as he sat. 'Knowing someone you've never met in person.'

'The perils of Internet dating,' Harri replied.

She knew he worked at a university, that they had a common love of poetry, movie soundtracks and country walks.

He nodded and smiled. 'Have you met many people through the site?'

'You're my first,' Harri replied. 'You?'

'The same.'

She was glad. She already couldn't bear to think of him with someone else.

A waiter approached. 'What can I get you?'

'Black coffee,' Harri said.

'Me too,' Ben added, and the waiter withdrew.

Harri smiled, and Ben responded in kind, and for a moment they sat at the table like a couple of blissed-out fools.

'When you come to me, unbidden, beckoning me to long-ago rooms, where memories lie,' Ben said, and Harri's eyes widened. 'Maya Angelou,' he added.

'I know. That's one of my favourite poems,' she replied.

'Mine too. It's beautiful. So evocative.'

It might have felt strange to hear poetry from someone she'd just met, but somehow it was perfectly natural with Ben.

'Can we pretend we've known each other for ever? That we trust one another? That there's nothing we could say or do that would offend? No truth that would deter? Can we be ourselves even if we act a part with others?'

Harri was bemused, but intrigued. She wasn't sure she was ever completely herself with anyone.

'I want to be honest with you,' Ben went on, 'but I know that's not how these things work, is it?'

'It takes time,' Harri replied. 'We're vulnerable creatures. We carry our hurt with us, and each wound forms new scar tissue that makes it harder to see the person beneath. It takes time to open up to someone new.'

'And we are new to each other, aren't we?'

Harri felt as though the world had gone dim and he was the only person in it.

'Yes,' she agreed. 'We are new to each other, but at the same time I feel like I've known you for ever.'

It was a brave thing to say, but no more so than his quoting Maya Angelou, or his suggestion they be completely honest with each other.

'I feel it too,' he admitted, and Harri breathed a little easier. 'I feel as though I've been waiting for you.'

Her stomach churned. This was getting intense.

'Two black coffees,' the waiter said, breaking the spell and bringing the real world rushing back as he deposited two steaming mugs on the table.

'Thanks,' Ben said.

'Thank you,' Harri added as the waiter left them.

They spent the afternoon in that cafe, talking, letting their drinks go cold. Ben was gentle, kind, calm, charming and funny, everything she could have hoped for in a man, but more than that, she tried her very best to live by his suggestion and felt she could be herself around him, because he was so real and honest. For the first time in years, she'd met someone who made her feel safe. Not physically, because years patrolling the streets of London meant she knew how to handle herself. He made her feel secure in being who she really was, that it was

OK for her to be honest. She could share her thoughts and feelings, her opinions, insecurities and longings and he wouldn't judge her or turn them against her.

His movements were as gentle as his sense of humour, and his voice was soft. He seemed genuinely interested in everything she had to say.

They shared similar taste in films, books and food, and talked a great deal about their common love of poetry. Coffee turned into lunch and lunch into dinner. They spent the whole day together relishing each other's company, laughing and grinning, neither willing to break their new-found bond.

The cafe could have been the grand dining room at the Savoy for all the joy and excitement Harri felt. Every mouthful of the simple sandwiches they'd ordered tasted glorious, simply because she was with him. And she could see he felt the same way. His eyes shone with happiness and desire, and even though they'd only met that morning, she'd started to dare to dream she'd finally found someone she could spend her life with. They talked and listened to each other, but looking back, Harri could hardly recall exactly what they'd said.

Finally, a different waiter came over and told them the cafe was closing, and Harri glanced around and realized the place was deserted. She checked her phone and saw it was a few minutes before eleven.

'Wow. I'm sorry,' Ben said. 'I lost track of time.'

'Me too,' Harri replied, and they both chuckled.

Ben settled the bill in spite of Harri protesting they should split it, and they walked outside. The summer nights were waning into autumn and there was a slight chill.

Harri wished Ben would put his arms around her, that he'd invite her back to his place, but he didn't.

'I had a wonderful time,' she said.

'Me too.'

The town centre was empty, and when the waiter shut the cafe door, it seemed as though they were the only people in the world.

'Would you like to do this again?' Ben asked. 'Not this, but something else,' he added awkwardly. 'Maybe a walk. I know a great place out near Maer.'

'That sounds nice,' Harri replied casually, trying not to betray her elation.

Ask me home, she thought. *Just ask me home.*

'I'll call you to arrange a time,' Ben said.

There was an awkward moment of silence.

'Would you like me to walk you to your car?' he said at last.

'If it's not out of your way.'

'Of course not.'

So they walked side by side through the deserted town, past the silent shops and still cafes, and the stillness and silence created a weight of expectation that stifled language. They didn't say a word until they reached the car park, and under the ugly glare of the yellow strip lights, they loitered by her car.

Ask me home, Harri shouted inwardly.

'Do you need a lift?' she tried.

He shook his head. 'I walk from here.'

'Well . . .'

'Well, goodnight,' he said, stepping forward to give her an awkward kiss on the cheek before hurrying away.

Harri watched him go, disappointed their date had ended, but thrilled she'd met him, and she got in her car and drove home with the radio on loud, excited, dreaming of a life together.

It was the happiest she'd been in a long time.

Chapter 6

She would never forget how she'd felt that day and even the memory of what had followed couldn't entirely tarnish the joy of their first encounter. She hoped she'd feel that way again, but right now there was no sign of romance on the horizon, and she wasn't sure she wanted it after running into Ben. Seeing him had reminded her just how much she'd been hurt and she wasn't sure she was strong enough to endure such pain again. Not now, with the rest of her life in tatters. She focused instead on her investigation into the death of Elizabeth Asha.

It was 8 p.m. on a Tuesday and people were already wasted. Harri swerved to avoid a couple who staggered along the pavement. The glassy-eyed woman had wild red hair that came to her waist and she was grinning as a puckish man slurred bawdy propositions at her. His arm was coiled around her shoulder and he clasped her possessively. Harri longed for love, though she knew it wouldn't come from a meaningless encounter with someone she didn't care about. But at least she'd have companionship, and maybe that was the next best thing? Even companionship, however fleeting, seemed unattainable. Men used to approach her, but they didn't any more. Maybe they could sense the cop in her? Maybe they could tell she was looking for something deeper than a night of casual lust? Or perhaps they could tell she was damaged?

She didn't think herself beautiful, but she knew she wasn't unattractive. Her light-brown hair looked good when she brushed it, her skin was clear and her features were small and refined. Only her eyes were big, and they had been described as 'endless' by a pathetically hopeless romantic she'd dated for a while back in London, and 'like Betty Boo's' by an unimaginative dolt during a particularly hostile break-up. She wasn't sure whether she had it, but she definitely didn't flaunt it if she did, and years of police work had taught her the importance of sensible clothes for chasing down a suspect or winning a street fight. She was used to being anonymous, and over time anonymity had become an addiction. She wasn't sure she had the confidence for attention any more. Another reason she'd liked Ben so much. He'd seemed to value her as a person and hadn't just been after her body. As it turned out, though, he hadn't been after her at all.

She drew a couple of glances when she entered the Moon on the Hill, a busy, modern pub on the outskirts of Hanley. Most of the people who'd looked at her returned to their conversations immediately, but three sets of eyes stayed on her as she pushed her way through the crowd. They belonged to Neil Watson, Ian Romney and Ishan Juneja, her former colleagues. Watson and Romney nudged their neighbours, and soon all eight men, police detectives from Hanley, were eyeing her. Sabih Khan was the last to notice her arrival, and she thought there was a flash of embarrassment as he hurried towards her.

She nodded at the group, but only Juneja and Watson

replied in kind. The responses from the others ranged from impassive to cold.

'So, this is what it feels like to be a civilian,' Harri said as she and Sabih met and made a gap in the crowd. 'Frosty.'

'Don't be silly, H,' Sabih replied. 'It's just a little odd, that's all. Why don't you join us?'

'I don't think that would be a good idea. I'm the awkward silence, the knowing look, the bad smell no one wants lingering.'

'You're so dramatic.'

'Tell me I'm wrong.'

Sabih hesitated, and Harri scoffed.

'I just came to ask a favour,' she said. 'See what you can find out about these three.'

She handed Sabih a piece of paper, which he examined.

'Benjamin Elmys, David Asha and Elizabeth Asha,' he observed. 'Ben Elmys? Isn't that the name of the guy you dated?'

'I need you to do this,' Harri replied, ignoring the question.

'It had better not get me into trouble,' Sabih remarked.

'It won't.'

'I'll call you.'

'Thanks,' Harri replied. 'Tell the lads I said hi. I know it will mean a lot to them.'

Sabih smiled, and she flashed one of her own before she left the pub.

Sadness nagged at her as she started down the street. She missed the camaraderie, the laughs, the feeling she was part of something more than herself. She hadn't had much of a social life, and her colleagues and job had filled the gap. Or maybe the immersive life she'd lived as a police officer had left no space for anything else? Either way, she felt the loss keenly. She'd once considered those men her friends, and even though none of them had openly shunned her just now, they hadn't embraced her either. Only Sabih had remained truly loyal, but maybe he felt he had to, given what she'd sacrificed for him. No matter what happened, things could never be as they were. She was an outsider now.

Her car was parked on Etruscan Street, but as she approached the corner, she heard a noise coming from a service alleyway that ran parallel with the side road. She glanced down the alley and saw Puck and Red, the drunk couple she'd passed. They were having sex against a graffiti-covered industrial bin. The man had his back to her, but Red caught sight of Harri watching. Her eyes flashed in the darkness, as though she delighted in being seen. Did she think Harri was jealous?

Harri blushed and ran on, wondering if on some level she was.

Chapter 7

The trees rose like the crooked fingers of a god, making patterns in the sunlight. A week after their first date, Harri met Ben for their second, a walk in the forest that covered Maer Hills. They parked nose to nose in a lay-by in a country lane off the A51. He drove an old black Land Rover Defender with privacy windows, and she was in her Golf, which seemed so out of place in the rugged countryside. He was beaming when he got out of his car, and her cheeks ached with her own grin.

'It's good to see you again,' he said.

She wished he'd take her in his arms, but he greeted her with another little awkward kiss on the cheek. She hid her disappointment.

'You too,' she replied.

'Have you been here before?'

She shook her head.

'It's really beautiful.'

He led her to a stile at the end of the lay-by and held her hand as she climbed over. She didn't want him to ever let go. But he did, and they started along a narrow footpath that was almost lost to the surrounding vegetation. Nature was trying to reclaim the scars man had scored across the hillside, but there was enough of a cut remaining for them to push their way through.

'It gets better,' Ben assured her.

He was right. After thirty paces, the blackberry bushes and thick shrubs fell away to reveal a broad track. They walked side by side in the warm sunshine. There was an edge on the breeze that made it feel as though these were the last days of summer, and Harri wondered whether she'd have a companion for the long winter nights, someone to keep her warm, to hold her against the frost's sharp bite.

She looked at him, his face almost burned out by the sun which flared behind his head.

'It's beautiful,' she said, glancing at the avenues of trees that stood either side of them.

'Wait until you see the view from the top.'

'Are you from here?' Harri asked.

Ben shook his head. 'You?'

'No. I'm from London. Battersea originally. Then all over.'

'What brought you up here?' He was looking at her now, and she felt those butterflies again. His words didn't matter. His eyes told her everything she needed to know. They gazed into hers as though nothing else existed and she was his world.

She flushed and looked away.

'The job. London was getting me down and I had to make a choice; career fast-track or a better, slower way of life. I chose a better life.'

'I'm glad you did.' He grinned.

'So am I,' she replied. 'What about you?'

'I came here for work.'

'You said when we were emailing that you're a scientist.'

He nodded. 'I work at Keele University, in the physics department.'

'I was never any good at physics. Too much maths.' Harri immediately regretted her reply. She didn't want him to think her stupid.

'It's like that for a while,' he responded. 'But there comes a time when you realize God wasn't a mathematician. She was an artist. The best physicists are poets. They're the only ones who can bridge the gap between the artist and her work.'

'You believe in God?' Harri asked.

'Not really, but I do believe in fate. Some things are just meant to be.'

She felt a thrill of excitement as he took her hand. They smiled at each other and walked on without saying another word. The breeze set the trees swaying and the rustle of leaves and creak of branches was their accompaniment. A chorus of singing birds rose above the rustle and creak, and as she and Ben climbed the hill, Harri wished they could stay in this moment for ever. It was full of promise, unspoiled by complication or disappointment. Everything could be perfect. It should be perfect, and it should last for ever. But it wouldn't, and so, even as they continued along the track, perfection was tinged with sadness, the imperfection of what was to come.

When they finally reached the top of the hill, Ben led her to a gate at the edge of the summit. A steep slope dropped into the field before levelling off some sixty feet below them, and they had an unobstructed view of west Staffordshire and beyond it the Cheshire Plain. Trees sprouted like tiny heads of broccoli in the distance and small hedges cut the landscape into a crooked chessboard.

'Beautiful,' Harri remarked.

'I've always come here alone,' Ben said. 'Do you have any family?'

She shook her head. 'My parents are dead.'

'I'm sorry. Mine too,' he replied with a longing so powerful it seemed to close the gap between them. 'I have friends who have adopted me into their family, but it's not the same. One day I'd like one of my own. Even if it's just someone to grow old with.'

There was such sadness about him Harri felt a chill, as though a cloud had passed in front of the sun, but it was still shining brightly, lighting up the magnificent landscape.

Poets often write about love as perfection, but what if it was their flaws that made them such a good fit? Maybe their imperfections made them perfect for each other? Maybe they'd struggled to find love with anyone else because they were only ever meant to find it here in this moment? They were pieces for this puzzle and no other.

'You're not alone any more,' she said. He'd told her they should be honest with each other, and she would never have made herself so vulnerable with anyone else, but their connection felt so real she couldn't help herself. 'Neither of us are.'

He nodded, but something in his eyes told her he didn't believe what she'd said. She wanted to ease his pain, but she didn't know what else to say, so she pulled him close and they kissed. It was long and passionate, the embodiment of the connection they shared, and she knew he was the man she was meant to be with. They held each other at the top of that hill.

She was right; he was what had been missing from her life.

They were no longer alone. They had each other.

Chapter 8

She remembered that day in the woods and wished she could go back there to a time when everything had seemed so perfect and her life had been full of promise. She'd felt such love for Ben. She still did, but now it was tinged with the pain of rejection. He'd come back into her life in the most unexpected way, and she had entered his world on a quest for answers. They didn't have a future together, that much was clear, but in solving the mystery of what happened to David and Elizabeth Asha, Harri might learn why the man she'd fallen in love with had spurned her so coldly.

She felt as though she had stepped into a science fiction film. She was standing in an observation area just off a corridor that bisected one of the buildings in Keele University Science Park. Angelika, a willowy PhD student, was beside her, and they watched what was happening on the other side of a long window that took up most of one wall. Beyond it, an Arabic man in his late twenties was waving his hand through the air as though he was doing t'ai chi, but his movements were about more than spiritual form and martial discipline. He wore a thick black glove covered in what looked like tiny solar panels. The glove was linked to a sophisticated projector, and allowed him to wirelessly manipulate a realistic hologram of an intricate machine about the size of a small car.

'It's a particle accelerator,' Angelika explained as the man moved the vibrant, insubstantial machine to examine its innards.

Harri noticed circuits, tiny generators, and myriad parts she couldn't even pretend to recognize.

'It's a machine that helps researchers understand the building blocks of the universe. This team are working on making design improvements to the next generation of accelerators,' Angelika said, before she stepped forward and pressed a button on an intercom panel. 'Dr Abiola, there's someone here to see you.'

A tall, slim, regal woman glanced over. Her voice came through the speaker. 'Just give me a moment, Ang.'

Angelika left the intercom on, and Harri heard the gloved man muttering to himself as he examined the ethereal components. There were two others in the room with him and Dr Abiola – a Chinese man who looked to be in his mid-twenties and who seemed to be inwardly chuckling at a joke, and an intense-looking South Asian woman in her early thirties.

'I think it's good to go,' the gloved man said.

Harri caught Dr Abiola flash a look that suggested she thought otherwise.

'Reassemble,' the gloved man said, and the holographic machine came together.

A low hum filled the observation area as the hologram simulated the operation of the particle accelerator. Harri sensed something was wrong immediately. A housing near the top of the machine began vibrating, and the hum turned to an ugly grind.

'End simulation,' the gloved man said, and the machine froze instantly. 'I don't understand it.' He craned forward to examine the projection, his frustration evident. 'I can't get the tolerances right.'

'May I?' Dr Abiola asked, gesturing for the glove.

He handed it over, and Dr Abiola slid it on. She manipulated the hologram, disassembling the machine in a way that Harri found hypnotic. Shimmering sections floated through the air, gliding around Dr Abiola like strange ghosts. The others looked on in awe, and even though she couldn't understand what was happening, Harri got the impression she was watching a genius at work.

'You were close, Tarek,' Dr Abiola said, replacing one of the parts with another she brought up from a menu directory. 'I'd suggest swapping the generator with a series six device.'

She removed the glove and handed it to Tarek, who somehow managed to look both exasperated and grateful.

'I should have thought of that,' he said. 'The tolerances . . .'

'It's OK,' Dr Abiola assured him. 'That's why we have simulators, rather than a billion-pound prototype,' she gestured at the hologram. 'If you'll excuse me.'

She stepped away from the group and glided towards the door, eyeing Harri all the way.

'Can I help you?' she asked as she entered the observation area.

'Dr Abiola, I'm Harriet Kealty. Thanks for agreeing to see me. I'd like to ask you some questions about David and Elizabeth Asha, and Ben Elmys.'

Her smile fell and her face clouded over. 'I see. Thank you, Angelika,' she said, and the young PhD student nodded and withdrew. Dr Abiola waited until she was gone. 'Why don't we go for a walk?'

Chapter 9

They went into gardens that lay between a cluster of four contemporary buildings in the north-west corner of the science park. The landscaping reminded Harri of a doodle she might have absently drawn as a bored teenager. Gravel swirled in endless loops, and winding stone paths cut through beautifully manicured asymmetric lawns. A dozen benches were scattered around the space, most beneath well-trimmed trees. Only a couple were occupied, one by a man on his phone and the other by a young woman who was reading a book.

'You want to know about Beth and David?' Dr Abiola asked. Her tone was smooth, her accent sufficiently upper-class that Harri found herself making a conscious effort to soften her harder London edges. 'What would you like to know in particular?'

They walked the widest path, which encircled the whole garden.

'They both worked for you?' Harri asked.

'Yes. Beth was one of my first PhD students. A long time ago, when I was young and fresh,' Dr Abiola replied.

Harri studied her closely. She could have passed for mid-thirties, but delicate wrinkles around her eyes and mouth hinted she was much older.

'Beth was brilliant at particle dynamics. She helped build that holographic simulator you saw in there. David joined us from Cambridge eleven years ago. He was a brilliant physicist. I can't believe what happened to them both. It's so sad.'

'They met here?'

'Yes, and fell in love. They married ten years ago.'

'What about Ben Elmys?'

Harri noticed Dr Abiola's eyes narrow slightly.

'Ah, Ben. A brilliant man, but not quite of this world.'

'How so?'

'Have you ever read *The Lord of the Rings*, Ms Kealty?'

'I saw the films,' Harri confessed.

'Ben is like one of the Rivendell folk, the Eledhrim – the elves. A projection into this world from somewhere else. Part of this reality, but disconnected by a mind that sees beyond it.'

'I'm not a huge fan of magic,' Harri said. She thought she was a good judge of character, and that certainly hadn't been her impression of him after two and a half dates, but their more recent encounter suggested he might have a looser connection to reality than she'd previously thought.

'Neither am I. I'm a scientist, but it's the best way I can describe him. Brilliant, but he's different. I'm sorry he's no longer here.'

'He left?'

'Shortly after David died. He said he needed to devote himself to Elliot,' Dr Abiola replied.

'When did Mr Elmys start here?' Harri asked.

'Six months after David.'

'What was their relationship like?'

'It's funny – for a while I thought Ben and Beth might have had a thing,' Dr Abiola said.

'Why?'

'He was always hanging around her. Even when she and David got together. And . . .'

Harri waited expectantly. The more Dr Abiola spoke, the more she made Ben Elmys sound like a weirdo. It certainly fit with what Harri had experienced when she met Ben at Longhaven, but it was so different from the man who'd inspired dreams of love a year ago. She knew she still had feelings for him because she was instantly jealous of the thought of him with Elizabeth Asha. She chided herself inwardly for feeling envious of the poor woman.

'And what?' Harri pressed.

'I don't want to disrespect their memories,' Dr Abiola said at last.

'The truth is never disrespectful.'

'But rumour and scandal are,' Dr Abiola replied thoughtfully. 'I recognize you from the newspaper, you know.'

Harri flushed, suddenly acutely aware of her disgrace.

'It's OK,' Dr Abiola said. 'For what it's worth, I thought you were innocent.'

'I was, but others didn't feel the same way as you, so I work privately now,' Harri replied, breathing a little easier.

'Who for? Is it Mrs Hughes, their housekeeper?'

Harri recalled the name from the article about the vigil.

'She loves Elliot. If anyone is checking on him, it has to be her.'

Harri ignored the question. 'Why are you changing the subject? What were you about to tell me, Dr Abiola?'

The graceful woman came to a halt and took a deep breath.

'People often used to comment on Elliot's resemblance to Ben, and, well . . .'

It took a moment for Harri to understand what the academic was getting at.

'You think Ben Elmys is Elliot Asha's father?' Harri had registered some resemblance, and had even flirted with the same conclusion. 'You think David Asha would have been friends with his wife's lover?'

Harri's mind came alive. A love triangle. The oldest motive for murder. But who killed who? And exactly who was this man? Maybe it was a good thing he'd broken up with her.

'As I said,' Dr Abiola continued, 'rumour and scandal. I think Ben is a lost soul. Personally, I don't believe he's interested in love. Not as we might understand it. I think he lives for something else. Excellence. Achievement. I really don't know what, and even if I did, I probably wouldn't understand it. I think Beth and David took pity on him. He was a stray, and they gave him a home.'

Like most gossips, Dr Abiola was backtracking now that she'd planted the seed in Harri's mind. She was talking about his honourable motives and decency, but if she truly believed that, why share the scandal? Why colour the air with tawdry suspicion? Harri went off the confident academic, but knew better than to give any sign of her feelings. This woman was a useful source.

'What kind of work do you do here?' Harri asked.

'We study the tiny particles that make up the universe. A mix of theoretical modelling and practical work in the lab.'

Harri felt the germ of an idea form. She wondered what kinds of materials David Asha and Ben Elmys might have had access to.

'I have to ask you a difficult question, Dr Abiola. The cancer that killed Beth Asha –' Harri paused for a moment as she thought about how best to phrase such a delicate idea – 'do you use any dangerous substances in your work? Is it possible Beth's death could have been caused by exposure to a toxin?'

The question chilled the air between the two women, and Dr Abiola's demeanour changed instantly. She looked at Harri with ice in her eyes.

'We have strict safeguards here,' she replied. 'We would never allow our employees to be exposed to—'

'I didn't mean—'

'Who are you really working for, Ms Kealty?' Dr Abiola asked, stepping back. 'I don't think I can talk to you any more. Not without a lawyer present.'

She turned and walked away briskly.

Harri called after her, but the academic didn't respond, and went inside the nearest building.

Another fail, Harri thought, before she headed for the car park.

She replayed their conversation and tried to understand why Dr Abiola would have reacted so strongly to the suggestion Beth Asha might have been exposed to a toxin. Was she worried about the university's reputation? Or was she covering up something?

When she reached her car, Harri saw something fluttering on the windscreen. She grabbed it and was going to toss it away without reading it, but none of the other cars had flyers and the moment she touched the scrap of paper she felt as though she was being watched. She glanced round and saw Ben Elmys standing in the trees at the edge of the car park.

'Hey!' she yelled. 'What are you doing?'

He froze for a moment, but found his legs when she started running towards him. By the time she reached the treeline, he was gone, swallowed by the thick woodland that surrounded the campus. Harri checked some of the paths through the trees, but there was no sign of him.

As she headed back to her car, she realized she was still holding the flyer. She smoothed out the scrunched-up piece of paper and read the typescript.

An edge
Shaving moments
To curl and wither
Doomed to decay
In flawed minds
What is
What was
And what will be
All lost
The misremembered lyrics
Of a once cherished song

Harri glanced back at the woods, conflicted. The poetry was beautiful, and it reminded her of their first date when he'd quoted Maya Angelou and they'd shared their love of the form, but the circumstances of this piece made it unsettling. Had he always been otherworldly? That was the polite way Dr Abiola had put it, but she hadn't been spurned by him. Harri wondered whether she'd been blinded by the love hormones Isabella Tosetti's book had talked about. Or had something happened to Ben to change him?

'Just talk to me!' she shouted at the trees. 'Don't leave me notes.'

There was no reply. Simply leaves fluttering in the wind.

Harri shivered as she got into her car.

This wasn't the first time he'd messed with her mind.

Chapter 10

Twelve months earlier, Harri steered her Golf into the car park at the Hand and Trumpet for her third date with Ben. She felt the faintest breath of autumn as she stepped outside, but the September sun kept the chill at bay.

Children scampered around a large pond in the centre of a freshly trimmed lawn, and the scent of cut grass mingled with the fragrance from flowers hung in baskets bursting with bright colour. A terrace outside the pub buzzed with chatter, and every table was occupied.

It had been four days since their second date and Harri hadn't been able to stop thinking about him. They'd stood at the top of the hill for ages, holding each other, kissing, and she'd wanted him to make love to her. He'd wanted it too. She'd sensed his passion building, but neither of them had given in to desire, and after the sun had touched the horizon, they'd walked back to their cars, kissed, and parted with an agreement to meet again.

She'd counted the seconds, and Sabih had teased her for acting like a love-struck teen, but she didn't care. This was what she'd been searching for. A soul to complete her. Someone whose very existence made her feel more alive. If he didn't ask her back to his place, she would invite him to hers. Kisses would not be enough this time. Today, she planned to find out whether their physical connection was as powerful as their emotional bond.

Harri saw Ben when she reached the top of the wooden staircase that connected the beer garden with the terrace. He was sitting at a table for two, tucked in the corner, behind the door to the pub. She smiled broadly, and her empty stomach lurched with excitement. He hadn't seen her, so she could afford to grin like a fool, and she had good reason to. Meeting someone wasn't easy. Her police work meant long, unsociable hours, and she was often grouchy or despairing as a result of the things she witnessed on the job. It was hard to stay cheerful in the aftermath of a serious road traffic accident, or following an interview with a hospitalized victim of domestic abuse. She'd had a patchy love life in London, a string of meandering relationships that took winding routes to dead ends, so she was overjoyed to have found someone who was so perfect.

Ben caught sight of her as she reached the top of the stairs, and instead of trying to play it cool, her smile broadened. She felt sufficiently safe with him to be herself, her silly, lovestruck self. If this date went well, she had no doubt they'd be together, and the thought of what might be at stake filled her belly with more butterflies than she'd experienced as an excitable seven-year-old on a snowy Christmas Eve.

Ben smiled in reply, but there was something feeble and insincere about it, and Harri felt more sadness than joy. She was gripped by a sudden panic and talons of anxiety wrapped themselves around her spine and weakened her legs as she crossed the deck. She'd been so sure he felt the same way about her, but what if he just wasn't that keen? Had he met someone else? Was he secretly married? These and other painful thoughts clawed at her as she approached the table like a condemned prisoner.

'You know what's coming, don't you?' he remarked.

He didn't even bother standing. The kind, attentive, warm man had been replaced by a sullen, distant figure. He was right. Everything about him – his withdrawn demeanour, false smile and coolness – told her what to expect, and her eyes brimmed as she sat down.

'Why?' she asked, feeling utterly bewildered. Had she imagined their connection? They were so right for each other.

'I can't explain,' he replied flatly. 'You wouldn't believe me, and you wouldn't understand even if you did.'

'Try me,' she said, wiping her eyes. She felt exposed and foolish in the short tea dress she'd worn to showcase her legs. She tucked them further under the table.

'I can't,' he replied, and she was gratified to see a flicker of pain cross his face. This wasn't as easy for him as he was trying to pretend. 'I wish I could, but I can't.'

Harri couldn't wipe the tears fast enough. She had her back to the other customers and was glad to be spared the embarrassment of strangers seeing her break down. Her pain reached him and his demeanour softened.

'A friend is ill,' Ben explained. 'I have to be there for her.'

Her? Who was this 'her' that was taking him away?

'I'll wait,' Harri suggested. 'Please don't do this. Don't throw this away. I know you feel the same way as me. I just know it.'

For a moment it looked as though he might cry, and then the cold shutters came down and he composed himself.

'I love you, Harri.'

This wasn't supposed to be how it went. Had he really just

told her he loved her as he was breaking up with her? She should have been elated, but instead felt a cold knife in her heart, twisting and turning, hollowing her out.

'I love you too,' she said pathetically. 'I don't understand. Please don't do this.'

She was sobbing now.

'I'm sorry, but I can't be with you. Not now. One day you might understand.'

He stood and leaned down to kiss her forehead. She held his arm pathetically.

'I'm sorry. I really am.'

He pulled his arm away and then was gone.

She sat at that table alone in the middle of a crowd, crying, trying to make sense of what had just happened, but there was no explanation to be found. Eventually her thoughts turned in on herself.

What's wrong with me?
Why didn't he want me?
Why don't I deserve love?

Extract from the court report of *R* v. *Elmys*

GRACE OYEWOLE QC *for the defendant*
So, Mr Elmys broke off your relationship a year before you started investigating him?

HARRIET KEALTY
Yes.

GRACE OYEWOLE QC
And yet you felt it appropriate to proceed with an investigation for which you had no official authority? Not even a private commission.

ROGER SUMPTION QC *for the Crown Prosecution Service*
It is my turn to rise and remind my learned friend of the rules.

HIS HONOUR JUDGE THOMAS
I see no reason for you to be on your feet. The question is pertinent to the matter at hand.

GRACE OYEWOLE QC
Thank you, my Lord.

HARRIET KEALTY

I was worried about the child. If Mr Elmys had a role in what happened to the boy's parents . . .

GRACE OYEWOLE QC

Events that were investigated to the satisfaction of not one but two police forces in England and Wales. Are you sure you didn't have a personal motive for pursuing the investigation?

HARRIET KEALTY

My motive was the truth. It's always been the truth.

GRACE OYEWOLE QC

Commendable, I'm sure. So, you don't feel your personal relationship with my client tainted your feelings towards him?

HARRIET KEALTY

No.

GRACE OYEWOLE QC

And what about your feelings towards Detective Sergeant Sabih Khan?

HARRIET KEALTY

Sabih? What do you mean?

GRACE OYEWOLE QC

Did you blame him for the events that led to your dismissal from Staffordshire Police?

ROGER SUMPTION QC
My Lord, I rise with great reticence . . .

GRACE OYEWOLE QC
We will have to come to these matters at some point, but
if my learned friend feels now is not the time, I will oblige
him by moving on.

JUDGE THOMAS
Please do, for the sake of harmony. But you are right to say
we must return to these matters.

GRACE OYEWOLE QC
So, ignoring what some might have considered a conflict of
interest, you continued your investigation. Where did you go
next?

HARRIET KEALTY
I went to see Cynthia Hughes, the housekeeper. I thought
she might be able to tell me more about the family and that
she might share my concerns about the child's welfare.

Chapter 11

There are places where time seems to get lost. It meanders down crooked lanes, seeps into ancient stone, and haunts shadowed alleyways, never passing, always lingering, holding a small part of the world in stasis. Ipstones was such a place. A small village hidden in the Staffordshire hills, found by few who weren't looking for it. Harri went there soon after her meeting with Dr Abiola, when she'd discovered the poem on her windscreen. She drove the meandering journey to a place that hadn't changed much in two hundred years.

St Leonard Church, an imposing red stone building, looked as though it had weathered a thousand storms. It stood to the north of the village, and Church Lane flowed south from it, like the curved root of a tuber. Harri drove through the village, passing quiet residential cul-de-sacs that branched off the main road. She parked in a lay-by beside St Leonard and indulged in her habit of reading the headstones in the churchyard as she walked along the lane. She was often moved by how much love and celebration of a person's life could be imparted by a short inscription, and this churchyard did not disappoint. She caught sight of an old headstone that was covered in text. It was just the other side of the grey wall, so she drew closer and leaned on the capstones to see better.

IN MEMORY OF ANNA CECILIA, SHE DEPARTED
THIS LIFE JUNE 17TH 1812 AGED 31. SHE WAS
DISTINGUISHED BY A MOST ADMIRABLE DISPOSITION
OF THE HEART, THE DELIGHT OF HER PARENTS, AND
THE ADMIRATION OF ALL WHO KNEW HER. AT 16,
SMALLPOX STRIPPED THE BLOOM OF BEAUTY, BUT
HER AFFECTION AND TENDERNESS FOR ALL WERE
UNDIMINISHED. SHE WAS FINALLY RELEASED FROM
MORTAL SUFFERING AND RECEIVED INTO A WORLD
WITHOUT PAIN, WHERE GOD HIMSELF WIPES THE
REMNANTS OF LIFE'S TEARS FROM EVERY EYE.

Harri choked up a little, thinking of poor Anna Cecilia disfigured by disease. Who knew what cruelties she had to endure in life and what strength it had taken to persevere and earn the admiration of all who knew her? Such kind words in death, the legacy of a life well lived. Harri wanted people to think well of her, both now and when she was gone. Could the ghost of this poor young woman be her guide? Could she find a better perspective? Harri's own misfortunes seemed pale in comparison, and she walked on wishing she could be more like Anna Cecilia.

There was no one around and no traffic. Just the song of birds and the slightest wind in the trees. Maybe when she was old and grown up she'd move to a place like this and live a peaceful life with a family. She might be on the wrong side of thirty, but she liked to kid herself she still wasn't a grownup. That way all the missteps she'd taken didn't matter. If she was still a child she could pretend she wasn't supposed to know what seemed obvious to others: how to make a success of life.

Anna Cecilia lived and died in the time you've wasted trying to find your way, Harri thought darkly.

She tried to shake the sense of failure, and checked an address on her phone. She walked to the second of a row of three terraced cottages, number 46 Church Lane – a narrow grey stone home which exuded warmth and comfort in every aspect of its tiny character. A vine grew up a trellis and over the apex of a porch roof, and bunches of late harvest white grapes clustered here and there. Window boxes full of chrysanthemums hung beneath the upstairs and downstairs windows and flowers fought bees and butterflies to see who could make the most vibrant contribution to the house's colour palette. Beneath a wooden awning, a small bookcase stood against the wall beside the front door, and a sign told people to '*Love and Lend, these books are free to borrow, provided they are returned.*' The shelves were lined with an eclectic mix of fiction and non-fiction, and if she'd been local, Harri would have been tempted by offerings from Mari Hannah and Anthony Horowitz.

She noticed the granite threshold slab had been worn to a shallow U and wondered how old the little home was, and how many footsteps it must have taken to weather stone.

She knocked on the front door, and a short while later was greeted by a rosy-cheeked woman in her early sixties. She had short brown hair with the occasional wisp of grey, and wore black leggings and a loose floral top.

'Hello,' she beamed.

'Mrs Hughes?' Harri asked.

'Yes.'

'My name is Harriet Kealty. I'm investigating the death of Beth Asha.'

Dr Abiola had mentioned Cynthia Hughes had been the Ashas' housekeeper, and thought her sufficiently interested in Elliot Asha to have hired a private investigator. She seemed a potentially rich source of information. Harri was going to have to work hard to get it, though. Cynthia Hughes's mood curdled.

'I know who you are and what you're doing.'

'How?' Harri asked.

'Mr Elmys told me. He said you'd come prying.' There was a bitter chill in Cynthia's words.

'You're still in contact with him?'

'I look after young Elliot every now and again. I've got nothing to say to you.'

'Not even if it protects Elliot?' Harri was gratified to see a crack in the ice, but it quickly frosted over.

'Protects him from what?' Cynthia asked. 'People were always talking scandal and nonsense about Ben and David and Beth. You always look to the worst, don't you? Why can't you ever think the best?'

'I just want to find the truth,' Harri replied.

'Who do you think you are?' Cynthia countered. 'Mr Elmys says you're not even a police officer any more.'

Why had Ben been talking about her to the Ashas' housekeeper?

'I'm a private investigator,' Harri lied. In truth, she wasn't really sure what she was.

'Then I don't have to talk to you.'

Harri knew from experience that most people were too polite to shut the door in someone's face, and if anyone had offered her odds on Cynthia Hughes being too well man-nered to leave her on the doorstep, Harri would have gambled her meagre police pension. And she would have lost it. Cynthia fixed her with an unflinching stare and closed the door on her.

Harri rapped her knuckles against it. 'Mrs Hughes?'

'Go away.'

Harri hesitated. Mrs Hughes was right; she didn't have the authority to question anyone any more. Feeling impotent, Harri went back to her car. This time she kept her eyes firmly away from the headstones. She didn't want inspiration and forgot her dreams of becoming a better person, shunning Anna Cecilia's tale of suffering. She'd never measure up to the saintly woman, so there was no point.

Harri's self-pity deepened when she neared her car and saw a piece of paper fluttering on the windscreen. Was it another message from Ben? Why was he doing this to her? She lifted the wiper blade and unfolded a note in the same typescript.

I long to return to that so real place
Where you took your hand in mine
Your fingers traced along my arm
Drawing maps of worlds to come

We walked the wisps of emerald green
By our forever elsewhere house
A new-laid path stretched on ahead
Diamond stars shone with high promise

I long to return to that so real place
Where you took your hand in mine
But your hand is gone, rolled over, rolled on
The stars are ill aligned

Our elsewhere house lies empty and still
What was is now no more
But when the high gems shimmer and the shutters fall
I still feel those worlds tenderly traced

The style was coarse, but it was heartfelt. Whatever its redeeming emotional qualities, it was wrong. Why was he leaving her notes? Why didn't he just talk to her? How had he known she was here? And how had he managed to get the poem onto her car without her noticing, when she was standing no more than fifty metres away? She looked around, but the village was as deserted as when she'd arrived, just the sound of birds and the gentle brush of leaves. Was Ben asking for her forgiveness? Was he trying to woo her? Did he still love her? It had taken Harri months to get over him, and fate had brought them back together at a time when she was vulnerable. She wasn't sure she was strong enough for these games.

Wondering what she'd got herself into, Harri shivered in the warm sunshine and pocketed the note. She got in her car and drove away from the village as quickly as she could.

Chapter 12

Darkness always seems deeper when you're scared, the wind bites harder when you're alone, and shadows take on nightmarish shapes when you are at your most vulnerable. Harri experienced all these accentuations when she returned home. The long dusk had turned to night and the wind had picked up and swept a broil of clouds over Staffordshire. She parked around the corner from her building and hurried along the otherwise deserted street with her front door key protruding between her index and middle fingers like a talon. The sounds of the city seemed so distant, and she felt as though she was in an isolated pocket of the world where anything might happen.

Hanley had once been an engine of the industrial world, but was now a patchwork of retail parks, offices, and apartment blocks that were separated by veiny terraces of Victorian houses. They had managed to cling to the world, remnants of a prosperous time now long gone. With the demise of industry, the town had become a place in search of identity, and, robbed of the qualities that had once made it special, it had floundered and transformed into another sprawl of chain stores, fast food mastheads, and branded pubs. It was the sort of place where a woman's body could be found in an industrial bin and no one would be able to recall quite where she'd been discovered, but they'd all remember she'd been wearing a pair of Marks & Spencer boots with the heels cut off. Harri knew because she'd once attended a crime scene exactly like that. She realized she was in M & S boots and for a dark moment she pictured Ben Elmys standing over her body engaged in the bizarre ritual of cutting off her heels. She smiled at the absurdity of the image she'd conjured. He might be behaving strangely, but he wasn't dangerous.

She thought she heard a noise and glanced round, but the street behind her was empty. She hurried along the pavement, and gripped the key even tighter.

You're being paranoid, she told herself as she unlocked her front door. *Am I?*

She tried not to think about the information she'd been privy to as a police officer: that most murder victims know their killer, that women were more likely to be slain by someone they were romantically involved with than a stranger, that countless incidents of stalking or acts of violence trace their roots to online relationships.

She pushed the door closed behind her and checked it was locked, and her anxiety faded as she crossed the lobby to the mailboxes. She opened hers to find a sad collection of junk mail and leaflets. She didn't bother taking them.

As she turned away, she became aware of something in the stairwell next to the lift. The fire door was ajar and there was a figure seated on the steps. He stood, and pushed open the door, and Harri tensed and took a lungful of air, ready to scream. The man stepped from shadow to light and she recognized Sabih Khan.

'Sorry,' he said. 'I didn't mean to freak you out. One of your neighbours let me in.'

'Sab, you . . .' Harri trailed off and took a couple of deep breaths to settle her heart.

'What's got you so jumpy?'

'This case,' she said, walking to the lift.

'So it's a case now?' Sabih pressed the call button.

'Yes. The deaths of David and Elizabeth Asha.'

'I knew you were up to something,' Sabih replied. 'I'm guessing your former beau, Benjamin Elmys, is the suspect.'

'It's too early to say whether he's a suspect, or even if there's been a crime. I could be chasing nothing,' Harri replied. 'But it feels like there's something there.'

She didn't even experience the slightest glimmer of betrayal when she took the most recent poem from her pocket and handed it to Sabih. Her old partner started reading as the lift opened. He followed her absently into the car, and the doors slid shut behind him.

' "I long to return to that so real place, where you took your hand in mine," ' he read, leaning against the doors. 'How is that even possible? "You took your hand in mine".'

Harri flushed, suddenly feeling exposed by having shared something that had clearly been intended to be private. She understood what it meant.

'I think it's about not having a choice,' she replied. 'But having a choice at the same time.'

'OK. Whatever,' Sabih scoffed. ' "Your fingers traced along my arm, drawing maps of worlds to come".'

Sabih looked from Harri to the note and back again, like a West End tourist who'd been handed a flyer for a religious cult, and for a moment his mouth opened and closed wordlessly. Harri hated him in that instant. Ben Elmys might be strange, but she'd felt a depth to his words that drained away when Sabih spoke them. They sounded meaningless and tacky. She regretted giving him the poem because he was robbing her of something special and diminishing the man she loved. *Used to love,* she corrected herself, but she wasn't sure that was true. She wasn't over Ben. He had seemed possessed of a soul unlike anyone else she'd ever met. He might not be perfect, but she had thought he was perfect for her. Now, in this tiny lift, Sabih made him sound like a moody teenage poet who'd listened to too much Bon Iver.

The clunk and rumble of the elevator mechanism announced they had arrived, and the doors opened.

'I think I should arrest him for crimes against poetry,' Sabih said as they stepped out.

Harri was about to protest, but caught herself. *You're developing some sort of weird Stockholm syndrome,* she told herself. *He rejected you. You owe him nothing. Any love you might have felt for him has to be in the past, or you'll never move on.*

'I think it's good,' she replied, taking the poem. She couldn't help herself. She felt she needed to defend Ben.

Sabih followed her along the corridor to her flat.

'He's been dreaming about you,' Sabih said.

She'd surmised as much, but having someone else articulate it made the prospect sound unsavoury.

'His old boss said he was away with the fairies,' Harri replied as she unlocked her front door. 'But I don't think he is. I think there's something else going on.'

'Guilt?' Sabih asked.

'I don't think so,' Harri replied, wondering whether her feelings for Ben were clouding her judgement.

They stepped inside her little flat and she switched on the

lights. She ignored his raised eyebrows when he registered the place was still a mess.

'Whatever the cause, I'm not surprised his brain's on the fritz. He was in a car crash when he was twenty. Three of his friends were killed.'

Harri realized why Sabih was here. He had the background she'd asked for, but her former colleague's diligence took second place to an immediate sense of pity for Ben. No one could experience something like that and remain unchanged.

'Benjamin Elmys was the only survivor,' Sabih continued. 'In a coma for three months. Went off to study in Australia. Came back to the UK a little over ten years ago. Maybe the accident tripped a fuse.'

Sabih grinned and tapped his temple, but his smile fell when he realized Harri wasn't in the mood for cheap cracks. He reached into his pocket and produced a USB drive, which he placed on the kitchen counter, between a dirty plate and a grimy glass.

'It's all here, along with everything I could find on Elizabeth and David Asha. Elizabeth died of cancer. David died a few weeks later. Fell from – or jumped off – the cliffs outside Barmouth, near a village called Arthog. I spoke to one of the uniforms involved in the investigation. PC Simon Lake. Good lad. A witness, Margery Allen, was walking her dog, saw Asha pacing around on the cliff edge. The body was carried out to sea – never recovered.'

'He just left his kid?' Harri asked in disbelief. What could make a father so desperate he'd be willing to inflict such trauma on a child?

Sabih shrugged. 'Well, we don't know that he did, deliberately. The witness didn't see him go over the edge, no firm evidence of suicide, so it's death by misadventure, remember? Either way, the boy ended up in the custody of your weirdo.'

Harri winced at the word. 'Don't call him that.'

'Sorry, I thought you two were over.'

'We are, but still . . . don't call him that.'

'Well, whatever he is, he holds everything in trust for the boy.'

'And if anything happens to Elliot?' Harri asked.

Sabih shrugged. 'Why are you so interested in these people?'

Harri grabbed the copy of *Happiness: A New Way of Life* from the sofa, and opened it at the page with Beth Asha's message. She handed it to Sabih.

' "He's trying to kill me"?'

'I bought this in Nantwich. It's an old library book,' Harri explained. 'The last person to borrow it was Beth Asha.'

Sabih whistled and shook his head. 'Have you lost your mind? This is why you're digging into these poor people's lives? You bought an old book and now you think you're solving a murder? Come on, Kealty. This isn't normal. You can't build a case off a few scribbles.'

Smouldering embers of resentment caught on the wind of Harri's anger. His words hurt all the more because they were coloured by truth. The message in the book was a tenuous reason to pursue an investigation. Would she have taken it quite this far if Ben Elmys hadn't answered the door? Would she be treating it like a case if the man who'd spurned her hadn't been involved? Was she looking for answers? Some reason to explain why he'd rejected her? Or did she want revenge?

'Normal? What's normal? I've lost everything, Sab. My

career, my so-called friends on the force, my life. What am I supposed to do? What exactly is normal for someone like me?'

Sabih closed the book and tossed it on the sofa. He took her shoulders and squeezed gently.

'I'm sorry, Harri. It's all my fault, but this isn't what you need,' he said. 'You can't go poking into people's lives. You're not police. Not any more.'

His words couldn't have caused greater hurt, and Harri trembled as she fought back tears of shame. Had she been suppressing her feelings? Was that what the Elmys investigation was? A chance to play pretend? To stall the reality that the job that had defined her for so many years was no longer hers? She still harboured the hope she could get it back. If only she could find the man who'd filmed her that night.

Was she clutching at straws? The poster girl for lost causes? Is that why she was investigating Elizabeth Asha's death? Did she secretly hope she and Ben might have a future together? Or were her true motives darker? It was a rare twist of fate that put a man who'd spurned her in such a position. Did she just want to see if she could make him suffer for the pain he'd caused her?

'I'm sorry,' Sabih said. 'That was harsh.'

'I'm lost, Sab,' she replied, finally breaking down. 'I'm really lost.'

As her tears fell, Sabih pulled her close, and she cried into his shoulder.

'I'll help you. Whatever you need. I owe you that, at least. It's going to be OK,' he said, but she really didn't believe him.

Chapter 13

Harri could taste salt in the air. The west wind picked it up from the swells and spray, and carried it over the trees to the lay-by where she waited next to her car. There was an old red-and-yellow brick cottage opposite, with brine-corroded drainpipes, dirty windows and grime-grey net curtains obscuring its innards. The house exuded a stillness that suggested it hadn't been inhabited for a long time, and Harri pictured herself living there on the outskirts of Arthog, a tiny Welsh village whose main advantage was the magnificent mountains of Snowdonia stretching out to the north. The densely packed forest obscured her view of them from where she stood, but she'd been in awe driving the last few miles of the journey. More than the rugged cliffs of the Peak District, these mountains touched her soul. They reminded her of the grandeur of the world into which she'd been born, and in which she could lose herself.

Something moved high in a tree to her left and she peered through the dancing leaves to see a buzzard. The bird looked directly at her, and for a moment she felt as though it might be questioning her. What did it want of her? What answer would she give? She held her breath and took a gentle step forward to get a better look, and the bird stayed fixed on her. It was a majestic creature, and she wondered what it was thinking.

Did it see beauty? Or was the world divided into threat and prey? It opened its wings suddenly and with a single burst of energy took to the sky, as a police car pulled into the lay-by.

'That was a big one,' a grinning police officer said as he stepped out. His North Wales Police uniform indicated the rank of constable. Some might have found him attractive, with his buzz cut, tall muscular frame and cheerful smile, but it was the eyes that put Harri off. They reminded her of a beagle: sad, eager to please, but not a whole lot there. 'Constable Lake. You can call me Simon.'

'Harriet Kealty. Harri,' she replied. 'Thanks for sparing the time.'

'DS Khan said you're conducting a private investigation,' he said. 'I'm glad to hear it. I always felt there was more to this case. Never could get my guv'nor to back a deeper dive.'

Maybe she'd misjudged him. His instincts seemed pretty sharp.

'It was such a sad one,' he remarked.

They stood in silence for a moment, and Harri thought about the mass of tragedy that was crammed into that short sentence. *It was such a sad one.* Two dead, and an orphaned child. So much trauma, it was almost enough to take her breath away, and as Ben had said, she was just an intruder, raking through other people's lives. She could hardly begin to understand the emotional toll on those directly touched by events.

'This is where I found Mr Asha's car,' Lake gestured at the lay-by.

'Anything unusual about it?'

He shook his head.

'And the place where he . . .' Harri trailed off.

'It's a five-minute walk from here,' Lake replied.

He signalled a narrow footpath that snaked into the woods.

They saw no one as they neared the crashing waves. The wind only troubled the treetops, but Harri and Lake were in the calm shelter of the thick trunks and they engaged in chewing-gum chatter, sharing nothing of any real value, but keeping their mouths working and awkward silences at bay.

After a few minutes, Harri felt a breeze on her face and saw blue sky and emerald-green grass through the trees. They emerged from the forest onto a rolling clifftop. Judging by the sheep droppings, the wispy short grass was naturally cropped, but there were no living creatures in sight. There was big sky above them and an ominous line ahead, an uneven slash that cut the horizon, the ragged edge of the clifftop which separated earth from sky. Harri saw distant swells and her legs went funny when she realized how high up they were. Even grass wouldn't grow near the edge. It was the preserve of brave scree and foolish rocks.

As they left the forest behind them, Harri looked to her right where the mountains of Snowdonia rose grey and purple beneath the blue sky. Across an estuary that separated the mountains from the spit of land on which they stood, nestled in the embrace of the foothills, was a small beachfront town.

'Barmouth,' Lake remarked. 'And Elsewhere.'

'Excuse me?' Harri said, surprised at the name.

Lake was a couple of paces ahead of her, so she skipped to catch up.

'Elsewhere,' Lake repeated, gesturing to their north. 'Its proper name is the Elsewhere House, but locals just call it Elsewhere.'

As she drew level with him she saw beyond a curve in

the treeline. Standing in a semi-circular clearing was a grey stone house with a jet-black slate roof. The tiles were held in place by metal clips that shone like silver knuckle bones. The house itself was a large square box with two small windows on the ground floor, either side of the front door, and two much larger double bay windows on the first floor. Harri understood the building's name. A structure so grand in such a striking location almost didn't seem of this world.

What she didn't understand was whether the reference in Ben Elmys's poem, about 'our forever elsewhere house', was connected to this place. Or was it coincidence? But there were too many coincidences. What were the chances of her finding a cry for help written by a woman who knew a man she'd once dated? That he'd happen to mention an elsewhere house? Coincidence was the enemy of every good detective, and Harri was irritated by the thought she was missing a huge piece of this puzzle.

'Beautiful spot, eh?' Lake remarked.

Harri nodded absently. It was truly stunning, but her mind wasn't on the aesthetic qualities of the place. She was trying to recall the rest of Ben's poem, and puzzled over its significance.

'It's vacant,' Lake went on as they continued towards the cliff edge. 'Used to belong to an old couple who were as lovely as anyone you could hope to meet and totally devoted to each other, but, well, she died and he moved away and it was sold as a holiday home. Now spends most of its time empty. Seems a shame.'

The house had no garden or fence. It was as though it had grown from the clifftop, like an appendage that was as much a part of the landscape as the rocks and trees, which only added to its magical quality. Her instinct felt right; this must be the place Ben had mentioned in his poem.

'This is where it happened,' Lake said, and Harri's stomach curled like week-old ham when she realized how close they were to the edge of the cliff. 'It's OK,' he assured her. 'There's an outcrop below us. You really have to *want* to fall.'

Harri smiled uncertainly and took tiny steps forward. The wind whipped, making her feel even more exposed. As she inched towards the precipice, she saw more of the water below. The waves turned choppy and swirled around rocks at the foot of the high cliff. Her knees went weak and her toes bunched like fists, as though some ancient part of her was trying to find purchase. She craned over and saw the small outcrop Lake mentioned. It was home to a nesting seagull, and about a hundred feet beneath it, the roiling sea crashed angrily.

She stepped back and immediately breathed more easily.

'Quite something,' Lake said.

Harri wondered how low someone had to be to take that final step. She shuddered and turned away. Was this why Ben had referenced the house in the poem? Was it because it was where his friend had died?

'There was a witness?' she asked.

Lake nodded. 'Margery Allen. She was walking her dog, heading south when she first saw him. She passed him again when she was going home. Both times she said he was pacing around, muttering to himself. She walked about a quarter of a mile that way, towards Barmouth, before she glanced back, and when she did, he was gone. She didn't think anything of it, until we started canvassing after he'd been reported missing and we found the car.'

'And David Asha was reported missing by Ben Elmys?'

Lake nodded.

'Any chance I could talk to the witness?'

'She lives in Barmouth,' Lake replied. 'She's listed in the phone book, but be careful, she can be a bit scratchy.'

Harri shivered as she looked around. She'd dealt with suicide in the past, but for a father to take his own life in such circumstances and leave his child alone . . .

'Will you let me know if you find out what happened to this family?' Lake asked. 'Like I said, the guv'nor wouldn't let me scratch my itch, but that doesn't mean it's gone away. Something doesn't sit right.'

Harri nodded. 'Of course.'

'You want my theory?' Lake offered. 'I think he was done in by the death of his wife, but when the hospital lost her body, that was too much—'

'The hospital lost her body?' Harri asked. David's body never being found was a common enough set of circumstances, but Beth's body going missing in a hospital could have much darker implications.

'Yeah,' Lake replied. 'Mr Asha was thinking about suing. At least that's what his lawyer said. Talk about a mess.'

Harri shook her head absently. 'Maybe. Or maybe it was good planning. A missing body means no autopsy. No toxicology tests. No way to be sure what happened to her.'

Chapter 14

Harri thanked Lake for his help, and the two of them parted ways. Lake took the forest trail back to his car, and she walked north along the clifftop path. The wind whipped her hair and she reached into her pocket for a band and tied a loose tail. A shiver kissed her neck and ran down her spine. She looked around, but saw no one apart from Lake, who was almost at the treeline.

Her eyes settled on the strange, solitary house for a moment. She saw a black slate plaque by the front door, which bore the words 'The Elsewhere House'. She was disconcerted by the name, and the proximity of the building to the place where she believed David Asha had taken his own life, and managed to convince herself someone was watching her, even though there was no one in the windows. She was only being paranoid.

Harri turned away from the unsettling building and watched the waves roll in. She didn't stray off the path, but she could hear them crash against the rocks far below. There was something soothing about the erratic rhythm and, just as the mountains made Harri feel like a tiny, insignificant part of something vast, the beat of the ocean connected her to a world beyond the horizon. As she walked along the strip of worn, faded grass, she entertained the notion of moving here. There was nothing left for her in Stoke. She could sell her flat and buy a home on the coast. Maybe not somewhere as grand as the Elsewhere House, but a little cottage inland, perhaps? A new start, far away from the places and people that ruined her career. She smiled to herself and wondered why she hadn't considered it before. Maybe depression had clouded her mind?

She walked on, hatching plans, picturing herself at home among the mountains and forests, living a slow-lane existence, working only as much as was needed to pay her bills, and spending the rest of the time enjoying the world and its beauty.

She followed the path down a steep slope to the estuary. Romance gripped her as she took in the ancient mountains that stretched into the distant north. She could live here wild and free, and maybe meet someone who would love her. Would she ever love them as much as she'd loved Ben? Maybe. Hopefully.

Brimming with dreams, she crossed the slatted wooden railway bridge that stretched between the two shores, and checked her phone for Margery Allen's address. It turned out she lived in one of the blocks of flats on the seafront, not far from the bridge.

As she neared the Barmouth side, Harri encountered walkers, families, and tourists. The bridge offered a marvellous view of the estuary, which shimmered between the mountains and cliffs like a quicksilver ribbon. Harri went through a turnstile that had been warped and marred by time, and up some stone steps to the shorefront road. People strolled around with ice creams and cones of chips, basking in the lazy, warm, late-summer weather, and Harri fell in love with the idea of living among pleasure seekers. This was a place of leisure where people came to find calm and relaxation or have fun, and some of that must rub off on the locals. Could she become a calm pleasure seeker?

She crossed the road, hurried towards a row of grand Victorian apartment blocks, and approached a sky-blue building that had huge bay windows on every floor. When she reached the porch, she scanned the column of buttons for flat number five.

The front door opened, and a slim woman with a heavily lined face and a potent scowl emerged. An English springer spaniel followed her, sniffing around enthusiastically. The woman's tweed walking suit made her look as though she might have been Winston Churchill's governess.

'What do you want?' she asked as her dog pressed its nose against Harri's legs.

Harri was taken aback by the curt tone.

'Well? You're about to push my button,' the woman added, nodding towards Harri's finger, which hovered above number five.

'Oh, I'm sorry,' she replied. 'Are you Margery Allen?'

'Of course I am,' Margery snapped. 'The real question is who are you?'

'My name's Harriet Kealty. I'm investigating the death of David Asha.'

Margery glanced down at her dog, and Harri sensed a shift in her mood. 'I'm afraid I don't have time. I've got to walk Fred.'

'I can come with you. This won't take long. I promise.'

Margery snorted, shut the front door, and brushed past her. Harri wasn't sure whether that was a refusal, so she chanced her luck and fell in beside the brusque woman and her dog as they started down the path.

Chapter 15

'I told the police everything,' Margery said as they waited for a car to pass.

'It would really help if you could just go over exactly what you saw.'

Margery frowned, and Harri followed her across the road towards the bridge.

'I like it up there.' Margery nodded towards the cliffs on the other side of the estuary. 'Away from all the tourists and bother makers.' If there had been any doubt she was referring to Harri, she eradicated it with a pointed glance. 'My heart sank when I saw him. Unhinged. Degenerate. Talking to himself. I thought he was holding something.'

'What?' Harri asked.

Margery tutted. 'Are you going to constantly interrupt like that? It's very rude, you know. And you throw me off my rhythm. Where was I . . .'

'You thought he was holding something.'

Margery scowled. 'It was something small. A ball or a stone. He kept looking at it.'

Harri had to skip as Margery strode down the steps. She really did walk fast.

'Did you hear what he was saying?'

'I didn't get too close. Just the odd word. Something about courage, I think, but I couldn't swear to it.'

They wove through groups of slow-moving walkers and tourists.

'And you passed him on your way back?' Harri asked.

Margery nodded, but there was hesitation in the gesture. She had the expression of a child being forced to the dentist. The conversation was going somewhere unwelcome.

'And it was another quarter of a mile before you noticed he'd gone? What's that? About five or six minutes?'

They approached the old turnstile and Harri ferreted in her pocket for some change to put in the donation box to contribute to the upkeep of the bridge.

'More like three or four. I'm a fast walker.'

'I've noticed,' Harri said.

Margery snorted again. 'Is that all? I'd really like to get going now, and you're slowing me down.'

'I'm sorry,' Harri replied. 'I do have one last question.'

The sound of their footsteps thudding against the planks merged with the hubbub of the small crowd and the rattle of an approaching train.

'Why are you lying?' Harri asked. She was fishing, but something about the way Margery had reacted to being asked about the return journey suggested she wasn't being completely honest.

She saw a flicker of uncertainty cross Margery's face, and the older woman stopped walking.

'How dare you? I don't think I've ever—'

Harri was familiar with this particular brand of indignation. Billy Tompkins, her old patrol partner in London, used to say people squeal the loudest when you've got the tightest grip on their balls.

She cut Margery off. 'I've been around long enough to spot a liar. I just don't understand why you're not telling the truth. Unless you were involved?'

Margery's scowl fell away. 'Involved? You don't think . . . Why would I? I didn't even know the man.'

Harri was surprised to see tears form in Margery's eyes, and she gently led the older woman to the west side of the bridge, behind the tiny rail terminal. Fred, the springer spaniel, sniffed the struts that supported the handrail.

Margery wiped her eyes. 'I was a headmistress once. A good one. They made me take early retirement. Your views are outdated, they said. You're too cold. Too inhumane. Too distant.' The tears were gone, replaced by seething fury at past injustice. 'Too distant? Ridiculous. Do children need a friend, or do they need a teacher?' Margery's chin quivered and her eyes lost focus for a moment. 'I didn't do anything. I could see the man was in trouble, and I didn't help him.' She hesitated. 'Now I've got to live with that for the rest of my life. It's my punishment.'

'What punishment?' Harri asked. 'What did you do wrong?'

Margery took a deep breath and her vulnerable core was replaced by the hard shell Harri had encountered at the woman's front door. Margery's eyes burned with resentment, and Harri had no doubt she hated the idea of showing weakness, particularly to a stranger.

'You're right. I've been lying. I never looked back. I was too busy running away.'

'Why?'

Margery hesitated again. 'I saw him do it. I saw him jump. I was trying to pass as quickly as I could. The poor man needed someone to help him and I went on by.' Her eyes welled again, and she wiped them angrily, as though they were traitors. 'He was right beside me. He looked straight at me, smiled the kind of sad smile of someone who was grieving, and stepped off the cliff.'

She paused, wrestling with something. 'I saw him jump.'

'Did he say anything?' Harri asked.

Margery nodded. '"They're going to think I murdered her."'

'He said that?'

'Yes,' Margery replied. 'A man died because I walked on. Too cold. Too distant.'

She fixed her hair with a resentful stare, but Harri didn't care about the old woman any more. Her mind was turning over questions. Had guilt driven David Asha to suicide? Had he played a part in his wife's death?

'His statement, what he said, that might be important,' Harri suggested. 'Why didn't you tell the police?'

'You think I want that on a file somewhere? That I watched a man jump to his death?' Margery Allen asked.

'I'm sorry,' Harri said absently.

She reached to touch the woman's shoulder, but Margery stiffened and stepped back.

'That's quite enough of that,' the former headmistress said. She made a play of adjusting Fred's collar. 'Well, now you know. There's nothing more to discuss. If you'll excuse me, I don't think Fred is in the mood for a walk after all.'

Margery pushed past Harri. 'Come on, Fred.'

Harri watched the fearsome woman stride north, returning the way they'd come. The poor dog struggled to keep up. She took her phone from her pocket and made a call.

'Sab, it's me,' she said. 'I need your help with something.'

Chapter 16

Harri walked back to her car, and when she reached the Elsewhere House, she paused to admire the view, storing it up to take with her. She tried to picture herself living in Arthog, surrounded by the towering mountains and the endless sea, but her encounter with Margery Allen had tainted her dream, and every time she saw herself in a cosy cottage, there was no love, no family. She was alone. She didn't know whether Margery Allen was a spinster, but the old lady certainly did a good impression of one. Would that be the price of such beauty? Would Harri be doomed to spin out the rest of her years alone? It wasn't as though she was setting the men of Staffordshire on fire. The one man she'd felt anything for might well be involved in murder. She'd cancelled her eHarmony subscription after losing her job; a combination of financial prudence and 'I'm worthless' depression.

She wondered if she should reactivate the account, but she'd lost interest after her experience with Ben, and she wasn't sure she could face the liars, damaged shells, and creeps that would emerge from the website, their profile pictures and messages promising so much, and yielding nothing except disappointment.

Harri walked briskly through the forest back to her car and started the three-hour journey to Stoke. She kept puzzling over what Margery Allen had said. Why would David Asha smile at her? And why would he say, 'People will think I've killed her', unless he believed he knew there was something untoward about his wife's death? Harri couldn't answer the questions, and found herself drifting back to David Asha's relationship with his son. How could he abandon Elliot in such circumstances? How could he leave his child alone in the world? Tragedy had torn that family apart, and their suffering made her reflect on her own life. She could never imagine herself being so irresponsible, but pain twisted people in terrible ways.

She wound through mountains, which eventually gave way to hills, and as the sun touched the horizon, it threw long shadows ahead of her and painted the rolling landscape red. By the time the hills were smoothed into the Shropshire plain, the sun was gone. Lights dotted the flat landscape and stars sprinkled the sky. The magic of the mountains faded, and the romantic dream of living by the sea went with them. She owed it to herself to get her job back. She needed to right the wrong she'd suffered. Cracking an unsolved murder might help get her part of the way there. She had to find out what really happened to Elizabeth and David Asha, and whether Ben had a hand in their fate. By the time she reached the outskirts of Newcastle-under-Lyme, she knew she'd be staying put for a while. She couldn't give up on her old life, on herself, just yet.

Harri turned onto Mount Pleasant, a residential street on the edge of town. When she'd first moved to Stoke-on-Trent, the sprawl of little towns that formed the city had confused her. There were six that made up the federation of Stoke-on-Trent – Burslem, Fenton, Hanley, Longton, Stoke and Tunstall – each with their own planning policies, which meant the city often felt like an uncoordinated sprawl. And then there was Newcastle-under-Lyme, which was sometimes described as part of Stoke by ill-informed outsiders, simply because it had merged with the larger conurbation over the years. But Newcastle locals were proud of their distinct identity and most people tended to view the satellite town as a more upmarket place to live.

Harri drove halfway along the run of well-kept semis. Seven-seater family cars dominated the street, parked outside beautiful pre-war houses. Harri pictured families inside, gathered around the television, and immediately gave herself a telling-off for romanticizing what she didn't have. These imaginary families were just as likely to be in separate rooms, lost in their own digital worlds, spending time with distant strangers, rather than the people they lived with, who were now only tied to them by an accident of genetics and financial necessity.

God, that's bleak, she thought, as she stopped outside the address Sabih had given her. She texted him, and a short while later he emerged from the house and waved to a group of men who'd gathered in the hallway. He hurried to the car with a frown on his face, and jumped into the passenger seat.

Harri smelled the whiskey immediately.

'I hope you know what you've done,' he said, a slight slur shaving the edges from his words. 'I was winning.'

'Sorry,' Harri responded. 'I might need a warrant card.'

'I wasn't even supposed to have my phone on.' He settled into his seat. 'My cousin is very strict about poker night. He says I'll have to pay a fine.'

'Again: sorry.'

He fixed Harri with the intense, unpredictable stare only drunks can muster. She had no idea whether he was going to turn angry or happy.

'They should never have let you go. You were a bloody good cop.'

Matey. He was going to get matey.

'I know,' she replied.

'I know you know. But sometimes you need to know that others know what you know, so that you know. In here.' He patted his chest, and made a fist, which Harri thought was meant to symbolize a heart. 'You get me?'

'I get you,' she replied, reaching into the door pocket beside her. 'Have a couple of these.' She handed him a packet of gum.

'I'm hurt,' he said. 'My breath is as fresh as . . .' He blew on his palm and inhaled. 'Damn!' He opened the pack and popped a handful of pieces in his mouth. 'Thanks. So, where are we going?'

'To hospital,' Harri replied, putting the car in gear.

Chapter 17

It was a five-minute drive to the hospital, and Harri used the time to tell Sabih what she'd learned from Margery Allen.

'Must have been grim,' he said as they entered the hospital canteen. 'To see someone actually jump like that. And he said, "They're going to think I murdered her"?'

Harri nodded.

'What a thing to say,' Sabih remarked.

Harri scanned the large second-storey room. There was a long buffet of congealing food, fridges full of fizzy drinks, a few worried-looking couples talking quietly over cups of tea, a man with a young girl whose right arm was in a cast, and, over at a table by the run of windows, a lone doctor in blue scrubs. Harri had met Kelly Jackson once before, but Sabih knew her better, and she wanted her former partner's warrant card and easy charm in case Kelly had read the newspapers and wasn't inclined to talk to a disgraced former police officer.

Kelly saw them and waved. She was blonde and had a figure that used to torment Sabih. Harri had told him she wasn't interested in his horny musings about how hot Kelly was, and he hadn't broached the subject again, but she saw from his expression that his desire hadn't waned. He was eyeing Kelly like a lion slavering over a baby antelope. Harri shook her head, but if Kelly knew what was on Sabih's mind, she gave no hint of it.

'Detectives,' she said, standing to shake their hands. She had a broad Potteries accent and a folksy smile.

'I'm not—' Harri began.

'It's good to see you, Kel,' Sabih interrupted. Perhaps he wasn't all that drunk. Kelly wasn't aware Harri had left the force, and Sabih's knowing look suggested he saw little point in enlightening her. 'Thanks for squeezing us in.'

'My shift just ended,' she replied as they sat. 'Tea? Coffee?'

'No thanks,' Harri replied, and Sabih shook his head.

'What can I do for you?'

'We're investigating the death of Elizabeth Asha,' Harri said. 'Sab says you treated her.'

'Yes. Poor woman. I felt sorry for the whole family. It was so sad,' Kelly replied.

'And her body is missing?' Harri went on. She felt Sabih shift in his seat and glanced at him to see a momentary frown.

Kelly sighed. 'We just don't know what happened.'

'When did her body go missing?' Harri asked.

'The night she died.'

'Was her husband here?'

'Yes. He and Ben Elmys, their friend, were in the room when Beth died. I was with them. Her body disappeared after we left, before the orderlies came to remove it.'

'When was this?' Harri asked.

'Four or five months ago,' Kelly replied. 'I think she died in April.'

Some months after their last date. He'd said their break-up was linked to his friend's illness. Had Beth's condition deteriorated while Harri and Ben had been seeing each other?

Maybe that was why he'd broken things off? Perhaps he'd been knocked by her illness? But why didn't he tell Harri?

'You said the body disappeared after you, Ben, and David left. Were they with you the whole time?' Sabih asked.

'For a while, but then they went,' Kelly replied.

'Could they have taken the body?' Sabih suggested.

Kelly smiled uncertainly. 'You're kidding. Why? What for?'

'Could they?' Sabih pressed.

'I suppose,' she hesitated. 'But I've seen a lot of distraught, grieving families and these two men loved that woman. They'd never have done anything untoward. She meant a lot to both of them.'

Harri hoped Kelly was right. She couldn't believe the man she'd dated was capable of such a thing, but she had to be sure.

'Is there a camera system?' she asked, looking around the canteen. She caught sight of a couple of CCTV cameras hanging from the walls.

'Yes, but they say the one outside Beth's room malfunctioned the night she died.'

Harri and Sabih exchanged a glance, and she saw the gleam in her former partner's eye.

This was a case.

She'd started the investigation, but now she didn't want it to be a case. She didn't want to know Ben wasn't the man she thought he was. Even if he didn't love her, she still loved him and she didn't want to discover a love so pure had been birthed by a twisted man.

'We'd like to take a look,' Sabih said.

'I can put you in touch with hospital security,' Kelly replied.

Harri thought back to her conversation with Dr Abiola and

how she'd reacted to the suggestion Beth might have been exposed to a toxin.

'Can lymphoma be caused deliberately?' Harri asked.

'I suppose so,' Kelly replied. 'Certain substances are capable of triggering it. Are you suggesting . . . no . . . why would anyone want to do that?'

Harri looked at Sabih. They knew from bitter experience there were dozens of possible motives, but they left Kelly's question hanging.

Sabih bounced out of the hospital, his arms animated, his fingers clicking in time to an imagined beat. She hadn't seen him so lively since the night he'd been attacked near the railway tracks. The night her life had been ruined. The night his had been saved. She was happy for her old partner and pleased to have played a part in breathing life back into him.

'Why didn't you tell me her body went missing?' he asked.

'Dramatic effect,' Harri replied. She couldn't help but be uplifted by his mood. 'I wasn't sure lymphoma could be caused deliberately, so I didn't want to—'

'Yeah, yeah,' Sabih interrupted. 'Don't give me that. You could google that. You were just stringing me along, but now here we are. We've got a lot of missing pieces but it looks like there's cause for interest at least.'

'Right,' Harri said. 'Why else would someone steal a body?'

'Organ harvesting,' Sabih joked darkly. 'To conceal the cause of death, of course. I bet Ben Elmys had access to the kind of toxins Kelly mentioned. The husband probably did too.'

'True,' Harri acknowledged as they made their way back to her car, but she didn't like how this was shaping up. She'd had these thoughts in the abstract when she'd been convinced something or someone would come along and tell her she was unhinged and that her suspicions were unfounded because Ben Elmys was a good man.

'He kills her and then, overwhelmed by guilt, takes his own life,' Sabih said. 'Or the two of them conspired and the husband couldn't cope with what they'd done, and jumped.' He was getting excited. 'You fancy a drive out to Leek?'

'Now? What about your poker night?'

'How am I going to focus on cards, knowing there might be an unsolved murder with my name on it?'

Harri wasn't so upset she didn't want credit. This might be her way back onto the force. She shot him a disapproving glance.

'Our names,' he corrected himself. 'Our names on it.'

Chapter 18

It was easy to believe the world had ceased to exist. Beyond the twin pools of light there was nothing but black, and Harri convinced herself that if she veered off the narrow country lane, the car would tumble into a void. There were no stars in the sky, obscured by clouds perhaps? Or lost to the endless abyss? She was glad she wasn't alone. Not that Sabih was much company. He'd fallen asleep on the drive through Hanley, and his chest was rising and falling to the rhythm of a dream. At least she'd have someone's hand to hold if she drove them off the edge of the world.

But I don't want his hand, she thought, *I want Ben's.*

She was conflicted, travelling to investigate a man she still loved. How could she begin to be objective? What would she do if they discovered compelling evidence of his involvement in Elizabeth Asha's death? Police procedure was clear, but as a private citizen she didn't have to declare the conflict to Sabih, and that made her feel worse. Ashamed and a little guilty.

She followed the road round a bend and finally saw light up ahead. She relaxed almost instantly, and thought it was funny that a single bulb or candle against a vast backdrop of nothing could have that effect. Wasn't that the essence of hope? Optimism against overwhelming odds. A distant light touched something even more primal. It was a sign we weren't alone and that others were also determined to hold back the void. It was a symbol of shared hope.

She drove towards it, and a few minutes later, she pulled to a halt just before the driveway that led to Longhaven, the Asha family home.

Sabih stretched, yawned and smacked his lips as he woke up.

'Where the hell are we?' He looked around in mock dismay. 'This really is the middle of nowhere.'

Harri switched off the headlights and the world was lost to darkness. Only the single window in the furthest corner of Longhaven resisted the night.

'A kid lives here?' Sabih asked. 'What the heck is there to do? Count all the nothing?'

They got out and walked up the drive to the cottage. Harri knocked. A few moments later, Cynthia Hughes opened the door. Her face fell the instant she registered who was calling.

'Mr Elmys said you'd be back.'

'Did he?' Harri asked.

'He says you've got a thing for him,' Cynthia smiled. 'That you still fancy him. You've got to move on. This family's suffered enough. The boys don't need you coming here with ideas of revenge. I know it's hard, love, but you've got to accept he's not interested.'

Harri flushed. This was an excruciating humiliation. It was bad enough to have been rejected by the man, but to be chastised by the housekeeper in front of Sabih was too much.

'We're here investigating a suspicious death,' Sabih said, producing his warrant card, and saving her from further embarrassment. 'Detective Sergeant Sabih Khan.'

'I don't have anything to say,' Cynthia replied.

'Is Mr Elmys home?' Harri asked, regaining her composure.

'No.'

'Will he be back later?' Harri pressed.

'He's on a research trip.'

'I thought he'd left the university,' Harri remarked.

'It's his own research. For a personal project,' Cynthia replied.

'Does he take many of these trips?' Sabih asked.

Harri could see he was thinking along the same lines as her. A scientist without a job going on late-night research trips could be up to all sorts of mischief.

'Take your search for scandal somewhere else,' Cynthia replied. 'These lads have been through enough. These are good people. This is a good house.'

She started to shut the door, but Harri put her foot in the gap and stopped her. She couldn't bear the thought of coming away with nothing. She had to know the truth, but she wasn't sure which one was of more interest. The truth about what happened to David and Beth Asha? Or the truth about why Ben had ghosted her?

'Can I use your toilet?'

Cynthia eyed her with suspicion.

'We've been driving for ages, and it's a long way back to civilization.'

Cynthia didn't respond.

'Please,' Harri said. 'Don't make me go by the side of the road. Not in the dark.'

Cynthia looked at Sabih. 'You stay here.'

Harri glanced at him, and he shrugged.

Cynthia opened the door and allowed Harri inside. The hallway had a black slate floor and was lined with full-length bookcases. The shelves were packed, mostly with non-fiction science books, which stood behind photographs of David and Beth Asha and their son, Elliot. They looked a kindly, happy couple and the love they had for Elliot was clear in every picture.

'Must be difficult for the boy to grow up surrounded by memories of his parents,' Harri observed.

'Where else would he go? This is his home,' Cynthia replied. 'Here it is.'

She stopped outside a dark wooden door. The brass handle gleamed like a honey sun, and reflected a miniature figure. Harri glanced to her right and saw Elliot sitting on the floor of a large room, surrounded by papers and A3 pages covered in scribblings.

'Mind your business,' Cynthia said crossly, and as she reached for the door, Elliot turned and caught Harri's eye. He kept his gaze fixed on her, and his eyes burned like a couple of coals blazing in a hearth.

Does he hate me? Harri wondered as the door clicked shut.

'Well, go on then,' Cynthia urged.

Harri stepped into the small room and found an old-fashioned brass-lever light switch. She flipped it on, before closing the door and sliding the lock into place.

The tiny room was lined with family photographs, and Harri studied them carefully. The biggest was on the wall beside the mirror, and it was the only one that featured the three Ashas with Ben Elmys. He was as handsome as ever, and the photograph captured some of the charms that had attracted Harri the first time they'd met, but the warmth and kindness that had struck her was absent. The others were smiling, but he seemed angry, and she got the sense he was looking out of the image and accusing her. She caught sight of her reflection and told herself not to be such a sensationalist. It was just one bad photo.

Then she saw it, hanging on the other side of the mirror, by the door. A picture frame, but this one wasn't home to a photograph. Instead, there was a piece of paper with words printed in a font Harri recognized. She stepped closer to read it.

> *At the edge you stand*
> *Searching for truth*
> *From Elsewhere*
> *I watch and wait*
> *Back turned*
> *Soul distant*
> *But I keep faith*
> *Now and forever*
> *We will be together*
> *When this life is done*

Chapter 19

Harri cried out, startled by a loud knock.

'Everything all right?' Cynthia asked through the door.

'Yes,' Harri lied and she heard Cynthia mutter disapprovingly, before moving along the corridor.

Harri was trembling. Had he followed her to Arthog? Had he been watching her on the cliff? Why? What had happened to the man she'd fallen in love with?

She flushed the toilet and washed her hands. She couldn't bring herself to look at the poem as she dried them, and she inhaled deeply to settle her nerves before opening the door. She pinned a smile to her face and stepped out.

Cynthia Hughes was nowhere to be seen, but the door opposite was partly open again, and Harri caught sight of Elliot through the gap. He had his head down and seemed to be concentrating, so she edged closer in an attempt to see what he was looking at. The house was strangely still. No radio or television, not even the sound of a computer fan. Just the tick of a distant clock, which did little to mask the sound of Harri's breathing. It seemed loud to her, so she held her breath and crept forward until she was at the threshold and could peer through the gap in the doorway. She leaned against the frame and watched him.

Elliot was reading handwritten notes scrawled in what

looked like indecipherable code. What was it? Why was he reading it? She scanned the page, looking for something, anything she might understand, but the letters and symbols were beyond her.

'Do you believe in ghosts?' Elliot asked, and Harri tried to conceal the fact he'd made her jump.

He'd turned to face her, and she found his sad eyes unsettling. He wasn't angry, just broken. Children weren't supposed to know such complete grief.

'My mum said she'd always be with me, but she never answers when I talk to her,' he revealed, and Harri's heart broke for him. 'Why would she tell me something that isn't true?'

'It is true,' Harri replied.

'Then why doesn't she answer?' he asked. 'Or my dad. Have I done something wrong?'

The weight of his grief was almost too much for Harri to bear. She had no idea how he carried it on such small shoulders.

'Some people think our loved ones talk to us all the time. We just don't know how to listen,' Harri suggested.

She recalled how the deaths of her own parents had affected her, and how she'd longed to have just one more conversation with them. She'd been grown when they'd passed, and could only imagine the confusion and frustration she would have felt as a child.

'I'm listening very carefully,' Elliot said. 'I'm doing everything I can.'

He fell silent and the only sound was the ticking clock.

'I miss them so much,' he confessed at last. 'Mum was

sick, but Dad . . . well, he just left. Why would he do that? I thought he loved me. Why would he go?'

'I don't know.'

'I still love them so much. Ben says my heart doesn't know they're gone and my brain won't let me forget them. When I felt bad like this before, I could talk to them or hug them, smile together, but now they're not here to make me feel better. I don't know what I'm supposed to do. Where do I put all the love I have for them?' His voice trembled, and Harri found herself on the verge of tears.

'I'm so sorry, Elliot.'

She wished she could take his pain away, but she didn't know how, so she did the next best thing and changed the subject in an attempt to take his mind off his loss.

'Can you tell me about that poem in there?' she asked, gesturing to the loo. 'Is it new?'

'He said you'd come asking questions,' Elliot replied sadly, as though Harri had somehow let him down.

'What are you doing?' Cynthia Hughes asked, appearing behind Harri.

Harri became flustered. 'I . . . we were just talking.'

'Come on,' Cynthia added. 'You've done your business. It's time to go. Move along.'

She chivvied Harri to the front door with a combination of *come ons*, tuts, and irritated sighs. Harri kept her eyes on Elliot, who moved to the doorway to watch her.

'I just want to—'

'Not interested,' Cynthia cut her off. 'Out with you.'

She gave a final nudge, and Harri backed over the threshold where she was rewarded with the front door swinging shut in her face.

'Went well, then?' Sabih remarked. He was leaning against the house, a few yards from the porch. 'Friendly bunch.'

'I—' Harri began, uncertain how to explain what she had just seen. 'There was something weird in that house.'

'Don't be so hard on yourself. I'd describe you as strange rather than weird.' Sabih started down the drive. 'Come on.'

Harri followed. 'Very funny. I'm being serious. There was a poem in the loo. It was written for me. He confessed to watching me from Elsewhere.'

'Elsewhere?' Sabih asked, hurrying towards the car.

'It's a house near the spot where David Asha jumped.'

'And this poem was a confession that he spied on you?' Sabih got in the passenger seat.

Harri opened the driver's door. 'Not as such,' she replied, climbing in.

'Did you get a photo?' Sabih asked, holding up his phone.

Harri rolled her eyes in irritation, and slammed the door. How could she not have taken a photo?

'Take it easy,' Sabih urged. 'This Elsewhere is famous, right?'

She started the engine. 'I wouldn't say famous, but the locals use the name. Its proper name is the Elsewhere House.'

'So lots of people know what it's called. Maybe the poem was about someone else and you're just reading yourself into it? Maybe it was about David Asha?'

Harri nodded, but she wasn't so sure. It was possible, because that was where David Asha had taken his own life, but she couldn't shake the feeling the poem was about her and that she'd been meant to find it, but that was impossible, wasn't it? She put the Volkswagen in gear and drove away from the strange cottage. A shiver ran down her spine. A release of tension? Or a premonition of things to come?

'I'm not interested in poems, though,' Sabih said, and Harri knew what was coming. 'How many people know you and he dated?'

Harri kept her eyes on the road. 'I don't know who he told.'

'Well he told the housekeeper at least,' Sabih remarked. 'We need to think about how to handle this. It won't look good if we need to make a case. You'll seem compromised.'

'I'm not,' Harri protested, perhaps a little too strongly. Her stomach churned at the thought of making a case. This was all getting too real. Could she really cast Ben as a villain?

'I know that, but a jury won't. You know how these things go. It's not about truth, it's about appearances. Got to give people the comforting illusion life's fair.'

Harri didn't reply. She focused on the beams of light making road from darkness. Was he warning her she'd have to withdraw from the investigation? There was something else on his mind. She could sense it in his prolonged pause.

'Let me ask you something,' he said at last. 'Did you really find that message in the book?'

Harri's mouth opened and closed in disbelief. He'd seen it. Was he accusing her of forgery?

'Of course I did,' she replied. 'Do you think—'

He cut her off. 'Don't you think it's strange you found a random message that ties you to a man you once dated?'

The coincidence bothered her too, but she hadn't yet found the missing piece that would make sense of it.

'You know what I think about coincidences,' Sabih went on. 'They don't exist. There's always a reason.'

'What reason?'

'To throw shade on you?' Sabih suggested. 'You were still on the force when you met him, right?'

'You think he dated me to compromise some investigation months down the line? That's crazy.' But even as she railed against the idea, part of her couldn't dismiss it entirely.

'Or maybe he planned to use you as a source?' Sabih said. 'Find out if the police were investigating the death of his friends, feed some information that would keep us off the right trail.'

'So why did he dump me?' Harri asked.

'Who knows? The only thing I do know is that I don't believe in coincidences. Either you're working an angle . . .'

Harri took a breath and was about to respond to the accusation when Sabih raised a calming hand.

'Which I don't think is what's going on. Or he's working an angle, and he's been planning this since the very first day you met.'

Chapter 20

The fear was something few men would ever understand. The short walk home from the train station. The hurried march from car to front door. The dash down a gloomy footpath. Isolation and darkness stoked women's fears of encountering the wrong man. The creep with the angry glint in his eye who could be triggered by the wrong word. The charmer who just wanted to be friends, but who would turn hostile at the politest refusal. Harri thought of them all now, as she walked from her car to her apartment building. She was never usually this anxious, but Sabih's suggestion that Ben Elmys was playing her was unsettling.

She'd dropped Sabih off at his place and driven home, but it wasn't until she stepped into her pin-drop quiet street that she realized how vulnerable and exposed she felt. Harri was a former police officer and could handle herself, but tonight she wished she had someone beside her.

She hurried up the path and poked her key in the lock. She opened the front door, and there was a slight delay before the motion-activated lights came on and illuminated the deserted lobby. She shut the door behind her, didn't bother checking her mailbox, and went straight for the lift. She was halfway across the open space when she heard a noise coming from the stairwell. The door was ajar, but she couldn't see anything in the thin monolith of darkness. Her stomach lurched when she heard another sound, a low shift, movement across concrete. She slid her key between her index and middle fingers and jammed her thumb behind it.

She pressed the call button, and shuddered when she heard another noise.

Please let it be Jenny's cat, she thought, and prayed she'd see her neighbour's grey-and-black tabby emerge from the doorway. But nothing came, and the nagging inner voice that told her the poem was meant for her also warned her that whatever lay beyond that door was not as harmless as a cat.

Harri jumped when the lift doors slid open. She hurried inside and pressed the button for the sixth floor. She slumped against the side wall beside the console as the doors eased shut.

A hand reached into the gap.

Her heart skipped a beat and started racing at a thunderous pace. The safety sensor activated and the doors bounced open to reveal Ben Elmys. Harri lost the power of speech when he stepped into the lift. She wanted to scream, but fear choked her. He was dressed like an assassin, in a black pullover and black jeans, and he looked at her with an intensity that burned her soul. She tried to scream again, but could only manage a strained choking sound.

'It's OK,' Ben said, stroking her arm.

His touch was like a cattle prod, and she jumped away from him, which she realized, with sinking dismay, took her away from the doors. They closed, and the lift started to rise.

'I'm not going to hurt you,' Ben said.

'I'm not afraid of you,' Harri managed at last.

'No? You look afraid. Terrified even. But you shouldn't be.

We're connected. I know you feel it. You felt it the very first time we met.'

The words were delivered with such sadness, Harri almost felt sorry for him.

That's the kind of thinking that gets women killed, Harri corrected herself instantly. *Never make excuses. He shouldn't be here, not like this.*

'We need each other,' Ben said. 'You might not see that now, but I hope one day you will.'

'You shouldn't be here,' Harri said. 'This is my home.'

'When you came to my home, I wasn't scared.'

'What do you want?' she asked. Her voice had a sting. She started to resent the presumption of this man. He'd invaded her space.

'To see you,' he replied. 'And to tell you that whatever happens, I forgive you. It's important you know that.'

'What do you want with me?'

Ben's eyes narrowed and his face fell. He looked frustrated. 'We're meant to be together. I really believe that,' he replied. 'I know you feel it. You do feel it, don't you?'

Harri didn't respond.

'The time wasn't right,' he said, closing on her. He reached out and touched her chin. 'But it will be. One day it will be, and I hope when you're finally given the choice, you'll think about how good we could be together.'

Harri held his gaze, and for a moment she saw the warmth that had drawn her to him. He'd looked at her with the same intensity when they kissed by the gate in Maer Hills all those months ago. The memory of the kisses they'd shared stirred in her chest, they were so passionate, so all consuming, so right. She felt herself waver.

Then she came to her senses, and stepped away.

This man isn't what he seems, she told herself.

The lift stopped and the doors slid open.

'Don't ever come near me again,' Harri said as she pushed past him.

She was worried he'd try to stop her, but he just stood aside and watched her go.

She took out her phone and dialled Sabih. She glanced over her shoulder and saw the lift doors close. Sabih didn't answer, but she didn't need him. A moment later, she was inside her flat, her locks secure, her bolts drawn, a chair wedged against the front door.

She went to the fridge and grabbed a bottle of beer. As she sat on the arm of the sofa, watching her front door, she wondered how long it would be before she stopped shaking and felt sufficiently calm to sleep.

Extract from the court report of *R* v. *Elmys*

ROGER SUMPTION QC *for the Crown Prosecution Service*
And you went to see Detective Sergeant Khan the day after
Mr Elmys came to your home. Is that correct?

HARRIET KEALTY
Yes.

ROGER SUMPTION QC
Please tell us what happened.

HARRIET KEALTY
He, Sabih, DS Khan, didn't answer my call and I wanted
to tell him about Mr Elmys coming to my home. I wish I'd
never gone now. I had no idea what would happen.

ROGER SUMPTION QC
I understand, but you did go, and you spoke to DS Khan,
didn't you?

HARRIET KEALTY
Yes, I went to Hanley Police Station. I don't have many
friends left on the force, but there are still a couple of people
who will do me a favour. One of them let me through

security and I met DS Khan coming out of a meeting. I told
him about Mr Elmys's unwelcome visit and asked him to log
an official complaint in case anything else happened.

ROGER SUMPTION QC
And that complaint is exhibit 3J?

HARRIET KEALTY
Yes. After we'd done the paperwork, DS Khan told me the
hospital footage had come in and asked if I wanted to see it.

ROGER SUMPTION QC
This is the footage from the closed-circuit television camera
outside Elizabeth Asha's hospital room the night she died?
Exhibit 4D?

HARRIET KEALTY
Yes.

ROGER SUMPTION QC
And what did it show?

HARRIET KEALTY
It showed David Asha and Ben Elmys standing in the
corridor outside Mrs Asha's room. Mr Asha looked
anguished. Mr Elmys seemed distracted. They were
whispering to each other. Mr Elmys looked directly at
the camera, and just after that the video ended. The
hospital says the camera malfunctioned at that point, but
when I asked DS Khan to rewind the footage, we noticed
something in Ben Elmys's hand.

ROGER SUMPTION QC

The court will recall I drew attention to this when presenting the footage. What do you think the object might have been?

GRACE OYEWOLE QC *for the defendant*

My Lord, it is with great reluctance that I find myself on my feet again. There's no way the witness could know what, if anything, my client was holding.

ROGER SUMPTION QC

The witness's background as a police officer, and her work on this investigation, make her opinion relevant.

JUDGE THOMAS

I tend to agree. Please answer the question, Ms Kealty.

HARRIET KEALTY

DS Khan and I worked on the assumption the device was some kind of jammer, something that could disable the camera. Twenty-two minutes after the camera went out, Ben Elmys and David Asha were picked up by another camera at the main entrance. I checked the distances and timing. They had long enough to have hidden Elizabeth Asha's body somewhere in the hospital grounds.

GRACE OYEWOLE QC

Another speculative leap, my Lord. Hospital management still cannot say what happened to Elizabeth Asha's body.

JUDGE THOMAS

But it is missing, is it not? And therefore it is appropriate to note who might have had the time to move it without detection.

HARRIET KEALTY

I believe they had time. I believe they could have moved Elizabeth Asha's body.

Chapter 21

'What's she doing here?'

Harri was startled by the tone of her former boss. She looked up from the screen on Sabih's desk as Detective Chief Inspector Lee Powell strode towards them. He was a strutting cockerel at the best of times, and never missed an opportunity to highlight another's failings or broadcast his own successes. Harri was convinced the reason he'd pushed so hard for her dismissal was because he viewed a London high-flier as a threat to his job. He looked older than Harri remembered, like an aging soap star whose best days were behind him. His pressed white shirt shone, his black shoes gleamed, his creases were pin sharp, and his tie was held in perfect position by a silver clip. His shirtsleeves were rolled up, but Harri suspected this was for 'man of the people' effect, rather than comfort.

Harri flushed with shame when she saw him, and angry words bubbled in her throat. This was the man who'd abandoned her, betrayed her, failed her when she'd needed him most. She knew expressing her anger would be counterproductive, so she said, 'I'm here to report an assault.'

Powell gestured at the monitor, which showed Ben Elmys and David Asha leaving Royal Stoke Hospital on the night of Elizabeth Asha's death. 'Is that the Asha investigation?'

Harri looked at Sabih. 'You told him?'

'I—' Sabih began defensively, but Powell spoke for him.

'Told me? Do you imagine any responsible police officer would let a potential murder investigation go unreported? Thank you for any help you've given, drawing this matter to police attention, but this is now an official investigation, and you will have nothing further to do with it.'

'This is my case,' Harri objected.

'Your case?' Powell replied. 'Even if you were still on the force, you wouldn't be anywhere near this investigation. Your prior involvement with the suspect excludes you.'

The way he said the word 'involvement' made it sound sordid, and Harri was wounded by the insinuation and Sabih's betrayal. Her former partner couldn't meet her gaze, which was probably just as well. She was furious with him.

'You're not welcome here any more, Kealty,' Powell said. 'You know the way out.'

Powell didn't wait for a reply. Maybe he was afraid of the response his humiliating tirade would provoke? Or perhaps he simply didn't care? He marched across the room, went into his private office and slammed the door.

Harri was left to face the pitying looks of Watson, Romney, Juneja and her other former colleagues. Some went beyond pitying and their thin smiles told her they positively enjoyed her humiliation. She was too stunned to react immediately. She hadn't considered Sabih was obliged to file an official report, and was annoyed at her own naivety.

' "You know the way out"?' She finally found her voice. 'This investigation wouldn't exist without me.'

'I'm sorry,' Sabih said.

'You should tattoo that on your forehead. Thanks for screwing up the only thing I had going for me.'

'Harri, I'm—'

'It's one thing to tell him about the investigation. But you didn't have to tell Powell I dated Elmys.'

Sabih was about to respond, but Harri didn't give him the chance. She got up and stormed out, ignoring the gleeful looks she got from some of her former colleagues.

Harri was shaking when she finally made it outside. Her mind raced with all the things she could have said to Powell. She hated him even more for the way he'd humiliated her in front of people who already held her in such low regard. Her cheeks burned and she longed for a way to vent her fury, but she would just have to swallow it and accept it as part of her, like so much of the negativity she'd experienced these past weeks.

Her phone rang, and when she pulled it from her pocket, she fumbled and dropped it. She prayed the screen hadn't shattered against the pavement, but when she picked it up she saw a spider's web of cracks splitting the glass.

Great. Just great.

Tears formed as she answered the call. 'Hello,' she said, almost choking on the word.

'Ms Kealty?' a woman's voice asked.

'Yes.'

'It's Sarah Abiola from Keele. Would you be able to come out here? We need to talk.'

Chapter 22

Harri had shed the worst of her tears on the drive over. She couldn't believe Sabih had betrayed her. She'd sacrificed everything for him. He wouldn't even be alive if it hadn't been for her, and he'd rewarded her by breaking promises he'd made to 'always have her back' and 'never forget what she'd done'. He'd laid her personal life bare and worst of all he'd exposed it to Powell, the man who'd done most to ruin her. The man who could have taken her side and backed her in disciplinary proceedings, but who instead seized the opportunity to drive the knife in.

She sobbed at the betrayal. She'd given so much of herself to the job, and everything for Sabih, and it still wasn't enough. They felt they could throw her out like rotting trash.

She pulled herself together as she reached the outskirts of Newcastle-under-Lyme and had managed to stem the tears by time she parked the Golf on campus.

She went in the lobby of the Endeavour Building, which stood at the heart of Keele Science Park. The smoked glass and brushed black steel structure was eight storeys high. The security measures were far stricter than anything she'd seen in the lab where she'd first met Dr Abiola. Harri introduced herself to the receptionist, and the bored man handed her a visitor's pass. She followed his instruction to wait in a seating area opposite the reception desk, where she took the opportunity to wipe her reddened eyes. She checked her make-up on her phone's selfie camera. She looked puffy and miserable, but there was nothing she could fix in the few minutes she had available. Dr Abiola would have to take what she got: a broken, humiliated failure.

'Ms Kealty?'

Harri looked up to see a movie star in a black suit. Well, he wasn't a movie star anyone would recognize, but he had the good looks of an idol.

Harri cleared her throat and straightened her top as she stood. 'Yes.'

'Thank you for coming. I'm Nick Sullivan. I run security for the science park. Dr Abiola is waiting for us.' He smiled to reveal rows of gleaming pearls. 'If you'll follow me.'

Harri nodded and followed him silently through the building, passing through long anonymous corridors. They reached a security door near the heart of the ground floor, and Nick tapped a code into a keypad to open it.

When they stepped into the small windowless antechamber on the other side, Harri saw Dr Abiola standing next to a security guard who was posted at a desk by a steel door that looked as though it belonged in a bank vault.

'Thank you for coming, Ms Kealty,' Dr Abiola said. 'I was bothered by an issue you raised when we last met. Nick, if you wouldn't mind?'

Nick pressed his palm against a scanner beside the steel door.

'I was suspicious of who you might be working for. I thought you were trying to gather evidence against the university to suggest we might have been negligent in exposing one of our employees to a toxin,' Dr Abiola said.

Behind her, the steel door slid back an inch from the frame, revealing a pressure seal which deflated.

'Once I'd had a chance to reflect on our conversation and look further into your background, I took a different view,' Dr Abiola added.

'My background?' Harri asked, suddenly ashamed. Would she ever escape her past?

'I told you the first time we met that I didn't believe the allegations surrounding your dismissal . . .'

Harri couldn't bear to hear it. 'My dismissal was not a reflection of guilt.'

The heavy door had completed its slow slide. Nick stood beside the open doorway, studying his shoes intently, pretending not to listen, and Harri shrank inside.

'I understand. And I believe you, but even if you are a killer, you are hardly likely to admit it to me,' Dr Abiola said.

'I'm not a killer,' Harri replied, flushing crimson.

'Good, but that's not my concern. What I am interested in is your track record prior to the event that led to your dismissal. You were a good detective, first in London, then up here, and, according to the people Nick knows in the Met, you had an excellent clearance rate.'

Dr Abiola walked through the open doorway. 'Come,' she urged gently. 'Through here.'

The security guard at the desk eyed Harri the way people always did when they discovered why she'd been kicked off the force. She wanted to explain herself, but she knew it would do no good. So she shone her warmest, most innocent smile at the man, and followed Dr Abiola through the doorway. Nick came in behind them.

They entered another small antechamber that was separated from a larger room by a reinforced glass window that spanned the eighteen feet of the far wall. Another security door had been cut into the window, and was also surrounded by a vacuum seal. Beyond the window were rows of shelves that stored radioactive and toxic substances. At least that's what the large, bright warning signs said.

'It seems your instincts are still good,' Dr Abiola said. 'The government imposes strict controls on organizations authorized to use certain materials. We have safeguards . . .' she trailed off. 'Well, you can see the level of precautions we take.'

Harri looked around. They were in a vault at the heart of the building, and the materials room that lay beyond the reinforced glass divider was a vault within a vault. She couldn't believe what she was hearing.

'An inside job?' she guessed.

A burglary would have been almost impossible, and the university would have noticed a break-in sooner.

'Our safeguards were circumvented,' Nick admitted. 'Someone has stolen a small quantity of Cobalt 60. We're conducting a full investigation, but it seems clear it was an insider.'

'Cobalt 60 is used as a tracer in chemical reactions and for radiography. It is radioactive, and can cause lymphoma,' Dr Abiola revealed.

'Why are you telling me?' Harri asked. 'Surely this is a police matter?'

'There is an official notification process,' Dr Abiola replied. 'But it will help the optics if we're seen to have taken our own steps to recover the material,' Nick added. 'You're a former police officer.'

'And you already have an interest in the matter,' Dr Abiola remarked. 'You said you work privately now. If there is no conflict, we'd like to engage you as a private investigator to help us track down the missing cobalt.'

Harri didn't know what to say. She'd never even considered becoming a private detective, but somehow she'd stumbled into her first case and secured her first client. She'd been obsessed with trying to prove her innocence and get her job back, but was she wasting her time? Was this her new life?

Chapter 23

She didn't feel like an imposter as she stood on the ridge and watched the cottage through a pair of binoculars. She wasn't just a busybody raking through people's lives or an ex trying to find out why she'd been jilted. She was a private detective with a client who wanted the answer to a question: what had happened to the missing Cobalt 60?

Her engagement meant more than that. Maybe it was a legacy of years of police work, but she'd always assumed people would believe there was no smoke without fire. Dr Abiola was trusting her, and had said she believed Harri was innocent. It gave her hope for the future, because she'd feared wherever she went people would tar her as a killer and assume she'd been responsible for the death of Alan Munro, but this quieted that worry. At least some people were prepared to give her the benefit of the doubt. It was a tiny beacon of hope after so many weeks of darkness, and she was determined not to betray the faith of someone who'd believed in her.

Harri had parked her car on a farm track on the other side of Hen Cloud, the rocky outcrop east of the Asha family home, and had hiked a mile to her vantage point. The rugged countryside was a mix of gritstone cliffs, stretches of colourful gorse, and fields of short grass, cropped by small herds of sheep and cattle. There were a few horses and ponies, but in the main this was functional farming land or wilderness, a disorganized patchwork patterned by crooked drystone walls that crisscrossed the landscape.

Harri was hunkered beside one such wall and rested her elbows on it to help support her binoculars. She'd been watching Longhaven for over an hour, and her patience was finally rewarded when Ben Elmys led Elliot Asha from the house. The two of them exchanged words that had become indistinct by the time they reached Harri. They climbed into Ben's black Land Rover Defender, and moments later, it was a speck on the winding lane that snaked east towards the main road.

Once the car was out of sight, Harri climbed over the wall and crossed a patch of gorse to the footpath that led to the cottage. The black grit trail was bordered by purple wildflowers, and bees and butterflies took flight as she passed. The cottage didn't look as inviting from the rear. There was a small patio and a garden of wild grass and flowers that stretched from the back of the house to the drystone wall that delineated the edge of the property. The back garden looked neglected and in danger of going to weeds.

Harri kept her eyes on the lane as she hurried down the slope. She reached the stone stile, climbed over the wall, crossed the overgrown garden and the moss-covered patio and went to the back door. She produced a set of picks and solved the Yale lock.

She pushed the door open slowly, and checked inside. A red tiled floor, white walls, old shelves, a boiler, washing machine and dryer were all still and silent. She stepped inside the utility room and shut the door behind her. An archway to her left led to a larder, shelves almost empty. She walked through a doorway into a large farmhouse kitchen.

An Aga squatted opposite, and pine units covered most of the walls. A large oak table and two long benches stood in the heart of the space, and a set of copper pans dangled from cast-iron hooks above a wood-topped butcher's block that was off to her right. Photographs of the Asha family lined a dresser to Harri's left.

This might have once been a warm, vibrant family kitchen, but it was now a mess. Used plates and pans filled the large butler's sink, books, files and papers covered the table and benches, and the remains of meals on plates were half concealed beneath scattered documents. This didn't look like a healthy environment for a child, and the mess made Harri reflect on the state of her own home. It was the sign of a damaged mind and she told herself she would do something about her own situation the moment she got back to her flat.

Harri removed a PCE-RAM radiation detector from a bag slung over her shoulder. The device looked like a simple mobile phone, with a small keypad and a large black-and-white screen. There was a circular sensor at the top that was designed to detect decaying particles. At least that's how Dr Abiola had explained it when she'd demonstrated how to use the device. Harri switched it on and examined the display to see the readings within normal range. Dr Abiola had told her what to look for: a sudden spike in levels would indicate the presence of an isotope. If she found the Cobalt 60, she was to phone an emergency number and the relevant authorities would be notified and a clean-up team dispatched to recover the radioactive material. Under no circumstances was she to touch it.

Harri ran the detector over the papers scattered on the table and saw nothing abnormal. The documents seemed to be a mess of mathematical formulae, and there was a line or two of strange poetry here and there. The formulae made no sense to Harri, and neither did the out-of-context poetry. She swept the rest of the room before moving into the hallway.

The detector registered normal as she walked on. She opened the cloakroom door and leaned in, reaching into her pocket for her phone. She'd get a picture of the Elsewhere House poem this time, but her plan was thwarted. The poem was gone and had been replaced with a photograph of the Elsewhere House itself. Unsettled, Harri backed out. Had he put the poem there for her visit? Or was the photograph another message? Why would Ben have a picture of Elsewhere in his house?

She reminded herself of Sabih's advice that she shouldn't be so paranoid, and tried to convince herself these changes had nothing to do with her, but deep down she knew they did. Ben had told her she was connected to him, but she couldn't see how, and that blind spot tormented her almost as much as the question of what had really happened to Elizabeth Asha.

Harri shut the door and moved to the room opposite, the one Elliot had been sitting in when he'd asked her if she believed in ghosts. It might once have been a dining room. There was a small fireplace set in the opposite wall, but there was no other furniture, just stacks of books and papers arranged on the floor. Harri ran the detector around the space, but it registered nothing.

She went down the hall to the living room, which was near the front door. There was a sofa, some shelves with photographs of the Ashas, and yet more papers scattered on a Persian rug. On top of a pile of papers was an iPod and a set of headphones. Harri heard the tinny sound of something playing through the earpieces, so she picked them up and put them on.

She recognized Ben Elmys's voice instantly.

'*Your challenge will be to live through the sacrifice. It is greater than you can possibly imagine. You will give all of yourself and more. People will call me evil for what I will do to you, but they don't know the truth, and you must trust that I have acted for the greater good. When you've lost faith, and all seems broken, the last beacon of hope will break the rock of despair.*'

Harri shook her head in dismay. What was Elliot Asha listening to? It sounded like gross religious raving, the brainwashing of a cult.

She prepared to listen to more, but her heart stalled and she shrieked when she felt a hand on her shoulder.

Chapter 24

Harri stumbled back and almost fell over a pile of papers. She turned to see Ben Elmys. He stood, blocking the door, looking hurt, offended even. Behind him, Elliot Asha wore an expression of puzzlement. Harri's heart raced and she fought for composure.

'What's she doing here?' Elliot asked.

'Good question,' Ben replied. 'What's the point of telling me to stay away from you, if you can't keep away from me? You told me not to invade your home, but here you are. I should really call the police, but they're already here, along with some other meddlers you've drawn into this.'

Harri backed towards the window and glanced over her shoulder to see Ben's Land Rover had been joined in the driveway by a blue BMW 3 Series. When she looked round, Ben was only inches away from her and he leaned in far too close for comfort.

'One day you'll realize you've been wrong about every-thing, and you'll wish you could take it back. But you can't. Your path is set. Just like mine. You don't understand. None of you understand.'

Harri held her breath and for a moment she wasn't sure whether he might hit her or kiss her, but his gaze softened and his mood shifted as though clouds of melancholy had swept over him.

'Forgive them, for they know not what they do,' Ben muttered. 'Isn't that what the book says? And that's what I'll do. I will always forgive you, because that's also part of my journey. I still love you, you know?'

There he was, playing with her mind again. Toying with her emotions and reopening the wound he'd scored into her heart. How could he be so cruel?

He stepped away, and Harri inhaled deeply, grateful for the sound of people moving in the hallway. Moments later, two women entered the living room and looked around with the critical eyes of a couple of tax inspectors. The older of the two wore a cheap sky-blue skirt and matching blazer and had short red hair. The younger woman was in jeans and a red blouse, and her blonde hair was pulled into a tight bun which made her look quite severe.

A familiar face appeared behind the two women.

'Harri? What are you doing here?' Sabih Khan asked. Harri knew him sufficiently well to recognize his sheepish expression. He clearly still felt guilty.

'She's poking around in things that don't concern her,' Ben replied. 'Much like you people.'

'Now, Mr Elmys, we're here to check on Elliot's welfare. My name is Amanda Booker, but you can call me Mandy. And this is Nessa Dooley,' the older woman said with one of the least sincere smiles Harri had ever seen. 'If we can have some privacy, we can get started.'

Everyone looked at Harri pointedly.

'Don't feel the need to go, Ms Kealty,' Ben said. 'Please finish whatever you were doing.'

Harri blushed and eased past him and Elliot. Mandy and Nessa stood aside and let her go by, and she joined Sabih in the hallway.

Nessa shut the door and there was indistinct conversation as Harri and Sabih moved away.

'What the hell are you doing here?' he asked. 'Don't tell me you broke in?'

'Who are they?' Harri countered as they walked towards the kitchen.

'Social workers. Powell insisted we call them to make sure the child isn't at risk.'

'Powell,' Harri scoffed.

'Easy, tiger. He's just doing his job.'

'Like you?' Harri asked bitterly.

Sabih ignored the dig, glanced around the kitchen, and took in the mess. Harri shut the door behind them.

'Reminds me of your place,' he said.

'You don't get to make jokes,' she responded.

'I'm sorry, H, you know I had to make it official. And I had to tell Powell about you and Elmys. The housekeeper knew, for god's sake. He would have found out anyway.'

Harri glowered at him.

'Don't be like that, H,' he pleaded. 'Come on. Please.'

'Keele hired me to do some background on him,' she replied. She didn't want to listen to more of his pleas for forgiveness.

She didn't trust him enough to share the whole truth, but giving him a nugget might prove useful. The concealment saddened her, because not so long ago there had been no secrets between them and he'd felt like family.

'I thought Ben and the kid would be gone long enough for me to search the place.'

'Social services wanted to do an unplanned visit to see the boy's normal conditions. We met Dr Strange and the boy on the lane a few miles from the main road,' he revealed. 'Lucky really, otherwise we would have just turned up and found you.'

'I shouldn't even be talking to you,' Harri remarked.

'Your fight is with Powell, not me.'

'So are you going to share notes? Like I've just done.'

Sabih was saved from answering. The door swung open and Ben entered, putting Harri on edge.

'Have you two been trading secrets?' he asked with a dark smile. 'I hope so. I'll be able to listen to the concealed recorders later.'

Harri shot Sabih a concerned look.

'Come on,' Ben said. 'Do you think I'd bug my own home? What makes you think I'd even need to? We're all nothing if not predictable.' He beamed a broad grin, as though the three of them were old friends. 'I'm going for a walk while the two busybodies do their mind probe on Elliot. Would you like to get some air, Ms Kealty?'

'Don't you need to stay?' Harri asked.

'They want to interview Elliot alone. I suppose they don't want me there giving him signals and threatening him and whatnot,' Ben replied. 'Would you like to come? The fresh air might do you good. You can bring the muscle if you don't feel safe being alone with me any more.'

'The muscle?' Sabih scoffed. 'My name is Detective Sergeant Khan.'

'I know who you are,' Ben responded. 'I never forget a name. Especially not yours.'

Sabih shook his head and shot Harri a quizzical look. She

felt exactly the same way. Who was this guy and what was he on?

Ben fixed her with his intense gaze. 'Well?'

'OK, Mr Elmys. If this is what you want,' Harri replied. 'And no, I don't need the muscle. I can handle myself just fine.'

Transcript of a video recorded by Ben Elmys Eleven Years Later

This video was discovered in Pilgrims Cave, near Lud's Church in the Peak District.

BEN ELMYS

Remember the day at Longhaven, Harri? When those two social workers came to check on Elliot? We walked up to the ridge. It was windy. I tried to find patterns in the gorse. Isn't that so much of life? The search for meaning in the meaningless? But do you know what I've realized after all these years? Life is just what happens. There is no divine plan, no script, no moral in the tale. Just a sequence of events that binds each of us to a story without purpose. The cosmic storyteller sets our path, but there is no point to it. We are the universe experiencing itself, reflecting on itself. We are existence. Still we look for meaning, determined to make sense of it all. I didn't find patterns in the gorse that day, but I did discover one in your eyes.

I remember them, so hostile and angry, as though I was responsible for all the wrong in your life. I know I hurt you, but I had no choice. You'll understand soon. You'll understand. Beyond the anger I saw that day, there was beauty and the promise of the kindness that might one day be mine. I wanted you to see it in me, but your zeal for what you perceived to be the truth had blinded you.

'Did you find what you were looking for?' I asked as we walked side by side.

You were so suspicious. Rightly so, perhaps. I can only imagine how your opinion of me had altered since we first met.

'You seem remarkably calm about all this,' you said.

'Because I've got nothing to hide, Harri.'

'Don't call me that.'

You were quite angry I'd used your name. Then you asked me an interesting question.

'What's the greater good?' you said. 'What do you have planned for the boy?'

I have a feeling you thought you'd trapped me.

'I heard the recording. The one you play to Elliot,' you added.

You wouldn't let it drop. You kept at it.

'What's the greater good?' you insisted. And when I didn't answer, 'OK. What sacrifice is Elliot going to make?'

I've had a lot of time to think about that day, to ask myself whether I should have told you everything then, held you close and kissed you. I still think about the time we spent together when we might have been lovers. I felt the promise of the world on your lips.

What would you have done if I'd taken you in my arms that day? I know you loved me when we first met. I could feel desire radiating from you. But by then, by the time you broke into my home, I wasn't so sure. Had the love gone? I saw fear and suspicion in your eyes.

I couldn't summon the courage. Remember that, Elliot. Remember how cowardly I was.

'Do you think there's one person out there for each of us?' I asked you.

Do you recall that question, Harri?

'Or do you think we can be happy with anyone who's a rough fit?' I went on. 'Are we fated to be unhappy unless we find perfection?'

'What's the point of us talking if you're not going to answer my questions?' was the reply you snapped back. You were testy. 'What are you going to forgive me for?' you asked. 'Whatever happens, I forgive you. That's what you said. Well, what do you think you'll have to forgive me for?'

You know now, of course.

Do you remember what I said?

I told you, 'We all have to do things we're not proud of. Things that will hurt others.'

'What are you not proud of?' you asked me.

'Is this where I confess and you crack the case?' I replied. I might have done if you'd pressed me, but you didn't, so I carried on with the veneer that has defined so much of my life. 'I've done nothing wrong. Things aren't always what they seem. You of all people should know that. Involuntary manslaughter, wasn't it?'

It was as though I'd touched you with a red-hot poker. Do you remember you stopped and grabbed me?

'I never hurt that suspect,' you were almost snarling.

'And yet here you are,' I replied. 'Kicked out of the police, working alone.'

'Whatever you think you know about me, I'm not the one being investigated for murder,' you said.

You took a half-step back. I think you realized you'd said too much.

'So that's what the police are doing?' I scoffed. I knew, of course. 'Good luck. You're all wasting your time.'

Do you understand now why I said that?

'You never answered the question. Do you think we could ever love each other? Under different circumstances?' I asked.

And do you remember what you said?

'There are no different circumstances. Things are how they are. The crazed genius act might work on other people, but it won't wash with me.'

I remember smiling, beaming like a fool. It was such a sparky answer.

'You hurt me, Ben,' you said. 'You hurt me more than you can ever know.'

'I know exactly how much I hurt you,' I replied. 'And how much I hurt myself too, but I had no choice.'

'Why do you keep saying that?' you asked.

'Because it's the truth,' I replied.

I took your hands at that point, didn't I? You were horrified, but I felt complete. I knew then that we were meant to be together, but you weren't sure whether you were being held by a murderer. Perhaps you were. I'm still not sure what I am. But for me, that was a moment I'll never forget.

In you, I'd found everything I'd ever need.

'Things aren't always what they seem, are they? You say you were innocent. Perhaps I am. Whatever happens, know that I only want happiness for you,' I said.

You pulled your hands free, and backed away.

'Don't ever touch me again.'

You almost spat the words. You were so angry. Do you remember? I think you were afraid. Maybe you did still love me?

And what did I say? I told you, 'I can't make that promise. I can't promise never to touch you again.'

And you hated me for saying that. I could see it in your eyes. They burned bright with indignation at what you thought was a threat, but which was simply a statement of truth. I couldn't imagine never touching you again.

'Get away from me,' you said.

'Mr Elmys,' Sabih Khan shouted.

DS Khan, I mean. Poor man. Poor, poor man. Know that not a moment passes when I don't regret what happened.

'They want you back,' DS Khan yelled up from the cottage.

Do you remember what I said to you before I left?

'I think we would. I think if we'd met somewhere else, in another time, another place, I think we would love each other.'

Your eyes told me that the first time we met, your lips told me that when we kissed, and you should know that I felt it too. I still do. It was as though I'd wounded you with those words. You deflated and for a moment all your indignation seemed to dissipate.

'So why did you end it?' you asked.

'It was one of the hardest things I've ever done,' I replied. 'But it had to be that way. There's no point dwelling on the past. I only hope one day you'll be able to forgive me.'

Chapter 25

Harri tried to make sense of the strange man who had so infuriated her. How dare he touch her? And why was he playing with her emotions? How could she ever forgive him for breaking her heart?

There were no answers to be found in the breeze that swept over the top of the ridge. She watched Ben walk down the slope to the cottage and waited until he had gone inside. Sabih glanced up with what might have been a sheepish look, but she was too far away to see him properly. When he went inside, Harri headed down the slope.

She stepped into the utility room and shut the back door behind her. There was no one in the kitchen, so she walked along the hallway, but the house felt empty. There were no conversations, just a rhythmic tapping that seemed to be coming from the living room.

Harri edged forward, afraid of what she might find. The taps sounded like a metronome.

Beating a countdown to your doom, she thought darkly.

She told herself not to be ridiculous, the house was brimming with social workers and a police officer. Nothing bad could happen to her.

But where are they? her fearful inner voice asked.

She ignored the question and inched closer to the door,

which was ajar. She peered round – *tap, tap, tap* – Elliot was lying on the rug, headphones on, hitting a pencil against a floorboard.

Harri felt foolish and walked inside with a sense of relief. Elliot turned and removed his headphones.

'They're not going to help,' he remarked.

'Excuse me?' Harri replied. She didn't have much experience around children, but she was pretty sure they weren't supposed to speak the way this one did.

'I know why you're here.'

'Why don't you tell me?' she asked.

'You want our secret,' Elliot said.

'So you know it too?' Harriet responded, trying to bluff the child into disclosing what it was. 'I bet you want to tell someone.'

Elliot looked thoughtful and for an instant Harri believed he might open up, but his face quickly bunched into a scowl.

'You're so wrong. About everything. And if people know the secret, it won't be special any more. The magic won't work.'

'What magic?' Harri asked, suddenly worried for the boy.

Elliot eyed Harri with suspicion and she could see him trying to figure out whether he could trust her.

'He talks about you every day,' the boy said.

There was a time when the revelation would have pleased Harri, but now it just made her uncomfortable.

'What's the secret, Elliot?' Harri asked.

He wavered, clearly sizing her up.

'You remember you asked me if I thought ghosts are real,' she said, trying to form a connection with the boy.

He nodded.

'I think they are real, but not in the way they show them on

TV or in the movies.' Harri tapped her chest. 'I think they live in here. That's where my mum and dad are. They're always with me, watching over everything I do.'

Elliot considered the idea.

'I think your mum and dad are with you, Elliot. I think they're watching you.'

'He says one day I'm going to have to go away,' Elliot whispered.

She was getting close now. Close to the secret. She felt as though she could almost reach out and touch it. She just needed the boy to trust her.

'He says I'm going to have to go away and never come back.'

Harri felt nauseous. Was this child suggesting Ben planned to kill him? She couldn't believe it of the man she'd fallen in love with a year ago, but she wasn't so sure about this more recent incarnation. She had to know. She had to be certain.

'What does he mean?' she asked. 'Where do you have to go?'

Elliot eyed her thoughtfully.

'He says you're special. He says we'll always be together.'

'I am special,' Harri agreed. 'That's why you can trust me. Please, Elliot, you can trust me. You can tell me if you're in danger.'

He looked as though he was about to speak.

And then Mandy walked in and ruined the moment.

'All done here. Thank you for your time, Elliot. We've just been talking to Ben outside, and you seem well cared for. We'll follow up in a month or so, but you're all good.'

Well cared for?

Harri wanted to shake the woman out of such blindness, but Sabih appeared at the door.

'Coming?'

'Elliot was just telling me something,' Harri tried. 'Something important.'

'No I wasn't,' Elliot said.

Mandy gave Harri a cynical look. 'We really should go. Our presence here is no longer in the child's best interests.'

You mean my presence, Harri thought, but she didn't say anything.

Elliot kept his eyes on Harri as she followed Mandy and Sabih out. They passed Ben Elmys, who was coming in through the front door, and Harri felt his eyes burning her with a judgemental stare. She'd brought these people to their home, and she felt very much as though this was a walk of shame.

But it's not, she thought as she stepped outside. She wasn't the one who'd done anything wrong. And she replayed the conversation she'd just had with Elliot. None of this was normal.

She glanced round and saw Ben shut the front door. Mandy joined Nessa, and the two of them walked towards the 3 Series parked down the drive.

'Sab,' Harri whispered to her former colleague, and he walked over. 'Cover me.'

He looked perplexed as she ducked round the Land Rover Defender and crouched by the back wheel. Sabih stood over her while she pretended to tie her shoelace.

'Are you coming?' Mandy called to them.

'Just a minute,' Sabih replied.

'I'm doing my shoelace,' Harri said.

She checked she couldn't be seen from the house, and produced the radiation detector from her bag.

'What's that?' Sabih asked.

'I'll tell you later.'

She switched it on and pressed it against the chassis over the back wheel. The display started dancing almost immediately, flashing numbers that were well beyond the normal threshold, but not quite at the level Dr Abiola had told her to look out for.

Harri gasped. She felt sick. Her worst imaginings were coming to pass.

'What?' Sabih asked.

Harri switched off the device and slipped it back in her bag.

'We need to get to the office,' Mandy shouted.

Harri stood and peered into the back of the Land Rover, but the privacy glass made it difficult to see anything clearly. She saw a lump beneath a blanket, but couldn't make out distinct shapes.

'What is it?' Sabih asked.

'I think I've found something,' Harri replied.

'What?'

'Any chance?' Mandy asked tartly.

'Coming,' Sabih replied.

Harri sensed someone watching her, and glanced up to see Ben Elmys and Elliot Asha in the upstairs window.

'H, what are you doing?' Sabih asked.

'I can't tell you now. Let's come back later,' Harri suggested. 'When there aren't too many eyes on us. I'll tell you then.'

Sabih nodded, his eyes landing then pulling away from the upstairs window. He and Harri started down the drive towards Mandy and Nessa.

'Sorry about that. Can you give me a lift to my car? It's parked in the next lane,' Harri said.

Mandy tutted, but Nessa smiled and nodded.

'I'm sure Mandy won't mind,' the younger woman said.

Before she climbed into Mandy's car, Harri looked back at Longhaven. Ben and the boy watched her, and she wondered whether Sabih was right. Had she simply been a pawn in whatever game Ben was playing? She got in the car, feeling dejected and betrayed, and wondered how she was ever going to be able to trust anyone ever again.

Extract from a transcript of a recorded safeguarding interview

Subject: Elliot Asha
Case Officers: Amanda Booker, Nessa Dooley

AMANDA BOOKER
Thank you for talking to us, Elliot.

ELLIOT ASHA
I have to, don't I?

AMANDA BOOKER
You don't have to do anything.

ELLIOT ASHA
Kids always have to do things.

AMANDA BOOKER
Do you understand why we're here?

ELLIOT ASHA
You're checking on me. Ben said you'd come, because
I'm adopted.

AMANDA BOOKER

We need to make sure Mr Elmys is providing a suitable home environment.

ELLIOT ASHA

I've lived here since I was a baby.

AMANDA BOOKER

You like it here?

ELLIOT ASHA

It's my home. That chair you're in, my mum used to sit me on her knee and cuddle me while we watched TV. My dad and I found a secret hiding hole beside that fireplace. Every happy thing that happened to me happened here. I don't ever want to leave it.

AMANDA BOOKER

No one will make you leave.

ELLIOT ASHA

But that's what would happen if you didn't think Ben was good at being a dad.

AMANDA BOOKER

Did he say that?

ELLIOT ASHA

No. I'm ten. I'm not stupid. I've had to grow up. I'm not really a kid any more, I suppose.

AMANDA BOOKER
You stopped going to school, Elliot. Why?

ELLIOT ASHA
I tried. After my dad . . . I tried, but my friends kept asking me about Mum and Dad. It made me cry, so Ben thought it would be better if he taught me.

NESSA DOOLEY
What has he been teaching you?

ELLIOT ASHA
Everything. Maths, English, science.

AMANDA BOOKER
He used to be a scientist, didn't he?

ELLIOT ASHA
Yes.

AMANDA BOOKER
He worked with your mum and dad, didn't he? Do you think they liked him?

ELLIOT ASHA
They loved him. He was their friend and my uncle. I've known him since I was a baby. They wouldn't have left me with anyone else.

NESSA DOOLEY
How often do you eat, Elliot?

ELLIOT ASHA

Three times a day. When he first took me from the home, he was a terrible cook, but he's studied Mum and Dad's recipes and learned how to make nearly all of them. He just can't get Mum's bolognaise. There was a secret ingredient she used and she never wrote it down. It's gone, I suppose. No one will ever know how it tasted. I miss them, you know?

AMANDA BOOKER

We know. That's natural.

ELLIOT ASHA

I see them everywhere. Look at that photo above the fireplace. They look like they're still alive. I just want them to come home. I want to go to the beach to look for them. It was my favourite place and theirs too. If they're anywhere, they will be there. Lying on the sand, watching the waves and the dolphins. But Ben says he won't take me. He says it's too painful. I loved playing in the sand, and they'd always be there, watching me. Making sure I was safe.

AMANDA BOOKER

Nessa, are you OK?

NESSA DOOLEY

I'll be all right.

ELLIOT ASHA

I'm sorry, I didn't mean to make you cry.

NESSA DOOLEY

You didn't. Don't apologize, Elliot. You're a brave boy.
You have nothing to be sorry for.

AMANDA BOOKER

Would you say you're happy with Mr Elmys?

ELLIOT ASHA

I don't know. We talk about Mum and Dad a lot, which
makes me sad and happy at the same time, because I never
want to forget them, but it also hurts to think about them.
I love him though – Mr Elmys. Not like Mum and Dad, but
in a different way, and he's kind to me and looks after me.
I'm not sure I'm happy. I don't think either of us are, but we
have each other. I wouldn't want to be anywhere else. Ben
is the closest thing I have to a dad, and this is our home.
Please don't make me go away.

Chapter 26

Are villains born? Or are they made?

Harri pondered the philosophy of evil as she sat in the car and waited for Sabih. She'd never believed in pure evil. Not in its truest sense. Most crime was mundane, a series of escalating events punctuated by a chargeable offence. Rarely had she encountered anything biblical, the forked-tongue, cloven-hoof malevolence of someone who sets out to harm another.

When she'd first met Ben, she'd found him sufficiently attractive and charming to dream of a life with him. He'd been warm and funny and they'd connected, but something had happened to change him. Some twist of circumstance had taken the man she'd fallen in love with and turned him into a murder suspect. He most definitely was a suspect. The evidence was starting to mount up. He had been at the hospital the night Elizabeth Asha's body had disappeared, had access to the missing Cobalt 60, and Harri had detected traces of radioactive material in his car.

She shuddered. A poisoner most certainly fell into a category of evil that stood apart from mundane criminality. It was callous, premeditated, and executed with calm reflection. Had Ben always been capable of such evil? Had Harri fallen for the sham veneer of a decent man? Or had something happened to set him down this road?

Sabih emerged from his little terraced house and locked his front door. He hurried along his footpath and got in beside her.

'All right, Kealty,' he said, fastening his seat belt. 'I've got some news for you.'

'Same here,' she replied as she put the car in gear and pulled away.

'You first,' he said.

'Dr Abiola didn't hire me to do background,' Harri confessed. 'That machine I was using by his car, it's a radiation detector. Keele is missing some Cobalt 60. It's a radioactive isotope. She thinks the readings I picked up were high enough for a residue of contact.'

Sabih exhaled sharply. 'Dammit, Kealty, you should have told me. So we've got a potential toxin? How would you like a motive? I spoke to the Ashas' lawyer. When they died, everything went in trust to the kid, but if anything happens to him, guess who inherits it all?'

'Benjamin Elmys?' Harri suggested.

'*Acha beta*,' Sabih replied. 'Absolutely. Ten per cent of the estate would go to the housekeeper. Ben Elmys gets the rest.'

Harri wrinkled her nose.

'Do I smell or something?' Sabih asked.

'No more than usual.' She flashed a cheeky smile. 'It feels wrong. He doesn't seem like the kind to kill for *money*. You've seen him, his place. He's hardly even on this planet.'

'Who can say why weirdos do the things they do? And he definitely scores high on the weirdo Richter scale.'

'Is that your professional diagnosis?' Harri scoffed.

'Do you really need a second opinion?' Sabih asked. 'Anyway, it's not my job to diagnose, it's my job to investigate and incarcerate.'

Harri smiled and shook her head.

'You're the expert on this guy,' Sabih said, and Harri's smile fell. 'You dated him. Was he this weird? Is that why you sacked him off?'

Harri grimaced. 'I didn't sack him off.'

'I'm sorry,' Sabih said.

'We went on three dates and he broke up with me. And no, he wasn't weird. At least not with me. I liked him. I liked him a lot.'

Sabih whistled. 'And now you want to lock him up?'

'I want to find the truth,' Harri corrected him. She still hoped that wouldn't involve Ben being locked up.

'So, what's the plan?'

'We go to the cottage,' she replied. 'See what he's got in that Land Rover.'

'If we find anything, I'm calling it in,' Sabih said.

She knew it wasn't up for negotiation. 'Deal.'

Chapter 27

Clouds lingered over the moon, wispy and faint, as though smudged by a heavenly hand. Harri followed the lane from the main road and drove through the patchwork landscape. To her right the high ridge of Hen Cloud and beyond it the massed cliffs of the Roaches. To her left, the silver shimmer of Tittesworth Reservoir.

She and Sabih had chewed over the investigation, but had fallen silent once she'd turned off the main road, as though even from six miles away their voices might alert Ben to their presence.

Harri switched off the headlights as they rounded the last bend before Longhaven, and she coasted to a halt in a lay-by about a quarter of a mile from the cottage.

'Ready?' she asked.

Sabih nodded, and the two of them got out. A dog barked in the distance, and a small creature shrieked a death cry from somewhere on the ridge. Harri shivered at the cool wind that touched her neck. She zipped up her black bomber jacket and thrust her hands into the pockets of her matching black jeans. Sabih was also clad all in black. They'd clearly had the same idea about being stealthy. He fell in beside her, and they walked swiftly towards the Ashas' cottage.

Harri glanced at her former partner and saw a familiar look

of anticipation. She missed this, but unless she found the man who filmed her chasing Alan Munro, she had to accept there was no way she was ever getting her job back.

They were about to start up the drive when the front door opened. Harri grabbed Sabih and pulled him down, and they took cover behind the drystone wall that marked the edge of the garden.

'What?' Sabih whispered.

Harri signalled him to look, and they peered over the top of the wall. She saw Ben dragging Elliot out of the house, and was suddenly aware of how loud everything was, her breathing, the crunching of loose stone underfoot, the pounding of her heart. She prayed Ben wouldn't hear, but she needn't have worried. He was too focused on the reluctant boy.

'I don't want to go,' Elliot protested.

'You don't have a choice,' Ben told him. 'Everything has its time and this is yours. You can't fight it. I told you one day you'd have to leave.'

'Please,' Elliot said pathetically. 'I don't want to go. This is my home.'

Harri looked at Sabih with concern. Where could this strange man be taking this child at such a late hour? Why was he talking about leaving?

'Come on,' Ben commanded. 'Get in the car.'

He badgered Elliot into the passenger seat before running around the car to get behind the wheel. The engine growled, the wheels spat up stones, and soon the red lights tore down the lane, speeding away from the cottage.

'Come on,' Harri said, and she and Sabih sprinted to her car.

A couple of minutes later, she was pushing the little hatchback to its limits. She raced along the winding road, and

Sabih held the hand grip and gasped at every violent turn. The Golf lurched around the bends, rocking onto two wheels in places, as Harri tried to close the gap.

When they reached the junction with the main road, Harri scanned left and right, before spotting a set of tail lights heading east. She pulled onto the main road, turning towards Buxton, and followed what she hoped was the Land Rover.

As Harri accelerated, Sabih took his phone from his pocket and placed a call.

'What are you doing?' Harri asked.

'What we should have done the moment we saw him acting like that with the kid,' Sabih replied. 'Checking someone's car is one thing. This is something else. That child might be in danger.'

He was right. Harri had thought about intervening at the cottage, but she'd been caught by surprise. And could they charge Ben for harsh words spoken to a child? Her instincts told her this was beyond harsh words, and a nagging dark feeling in the pit of her stomach signalled something bad was about to happen.

'Yeah, who is this?' Sabih said into his phone. 'Julia? It's Sabih Khan. I'm in pursuit of a suspect. Benjamin Elmys. We're on the A4015, heading towards Buxton. I need backup and a wagon.'

He paused.

'Hold on,' he said.

A hundred yards ahead, the tail lights glowed an angry red, and the vehicle slowed before turning left onto an overgrown track. As it made the turn, Harri saw the unmistakeable Land Rover silhouette before it vanished into the trees.

'He's heading north, towards Lud's Church,' Sabih said. 'Pinpoint my phone. Powell should have access. OK. Thanks.'

Sabih hung up as Harri turned onto the overgrown track. She killed her headlights and relied on the overcast moon to show her the way.

If Ben had spotted them, he gave no indication. He sped through the brambles and branches that reached across the track, and the Land Rover bounced around violently as it shuddered over the potholes that marred the surface.

Sabih fiddled with his phone, texting Powell and others. They'd send a couple of blues from Leek, which would take ten or fifteen minutes. She and Sabih just had to make sure nothing bad happened to the child before then.

Chapter 28

Ben pulled into a space beside the track, next to a gap in the treeline. Harri stopped a short way back. The trees in the forest beside them were misshapen giants, and the shadows they cast were black and endless, havens in which nightmares lurk.

Harri shuddered as she watched Ben jump out of the Land Rover. He ran to the boot, opened the tailgate, and grabbed a black backpack that was hidden beneath the woollen blanket Harri had seen earlier. He jogged to the passenger door and pulled it open. Elliot struggled against the man, and Harri could hear the poor boy's voice even at a distance.

'Let go of me! I don't want to do this. I want to go home!'

'What do we do?' Sabih asked.

Ben dragged Elliot out of the car, and Harri felt her anger rise, not just at him, but at herself. How could she have been so wrong about this man? She switched on the full beam headlights, and Ben froze in the dazzling glare. Elliot broke free of the man's grasp and raced into the woods.

'Elliot!' Ben yelled, before giving chase.

'He's a lunatic.' Sabih had said those words before, the night they'd encountered Alan Munro, and Harri saw something change in him. He needed to prove something to himself.

He jumped out of the car and sprinted after Ben. Harri

followed, and they ran through the gap in the treeline and were soon in the forest. The moonlight was blocked by thick canopy, and only a few fingers of shimmering silver managed to reach the mossy ground. This was all they had to guide them through the woods. Sabih opened up a gap and Harri followed, dodging broken branches, jumping large logs and scrambling over fallen trees. Leaves whipped at her face, and she heard Ben calling for Elliot ahead, but there was no sign of the boy.

'Ben! Stop!' Sabih yelled.

Harri saw Ben, maybe thirty yards ahead. He turned and registered their presence, but carried on running. Sabih leaped over a rotting tree trunk and sprinted on. Harri tried to follow, but her shoe got caught on a stump, and she tumbled over the trunk and fell onto the moist earth on the other side. She landed heavily and tears filled her eyes, but she fought the pain, got to her feet, and ran on.

Sabih was up ahead, not far from Ben, who broke the tree-line and raced into a clearing. Sabih followed and Harri was a few yards back. As she reached the clearing, an open circle perhaps forty yards in diameter, Harri saw Sabih was about halfway across, but to her surprise, Ben, who was almost at the other side, stopped and turned to face her former partner.

'Don't!' he yelled, but Sabih wasn't listening.

He tackled Ben, and knocked him to the ground. Harri picked up the pace as the two men rolled around exchanging wild blows. Ben's backpack bore the brunt of many of Sabih's punches, and Harri worried about what was inside. If there was any Cobalt 60 . . .

'Sabih!' she called out, but he didn't hear her.

He was lost in the heat of the moment, but Harri was

concerned he was also acting out the past, using Ben to rewrite his history with Alan Munro.

Movement in the trees caught Harri's attention, and she looked to her right and saw Elliot Asha crouched by the trunk of an ancient oak. His fingers were curled around calloused bark, and in the moonlight his face was as grey as a ghost. His eyes were on the fight, but when he sensed Harri watching him, his gaze shifted and met hers. He seemed sad beyond reckoning, and Harri couldn't hold his stare. She looked back at the two men scrabbling in the dirt.

Sabih slapped Ben and managed to get on top of him. He drove a flurry of punches into Ben's face, and Harri was taken aback by the ferocity of the blows and the look of furious determination on Sabih's face.

'You stay down, you lunatic!' he yelled. 'You don't hurt people. You don't do that!'

She'd seen Sabih take on suspects before, but this was different. He wasn't an angry person, and it took a lot to tap into his rage, but there it was. She had little doubt now he was picturing Alan Munro as he fought Ben, but a few more of those punches would probably kill the man.

'Sabih!' Harri shouted. 'Stop!'

He hesitated and glanced at Harri. His expression shifted and his fury subsided. He pushed himself up and stepped away from Ben, bewildered as though suddenly waking from a nightmare.

Extract from the court report of *R* v. *Elmys*

ROGER SUMPTION QC *for the Crown Prosecution Service*
And then what happened, Ms Kealty? After DS Khan
stood up.

HARRIET KEALTY
He stepped back . . . and . . .

ROGER SUMPTION QC
There's no need to look at the defendant, Ms Kealty.
Please don't feel in any way intimidated by him.

HARRIET KEALTY
I'm not. It's . . . it's just difficult for me.

ROGER SUMPTION QC
I understand, but the court needs to hear your account
of events.

HARRIET KEALTY
Sabih—DS Khan got up. He took a step back, and the
defendant, Mr Elmys, kicked him in the stomach. What
neither DS Khan or I knew, but what the defendant

probably did know, was that the clearing was at the edge of a ravine. DS Khan, Sabih, he . . .

ROGER SUMPTION QC
Go on when you're ready, Ms Kealty.

HARRIET KEALTY
He fell off the edge. One moment he was there, and then he was gone. He was just gone.

ROGER SUMPTION QC
There's some water beside you if you need a drink. Better? What happened then?

HARRIET KEALTY
I ran to the edge of the ravine. It must have been eighty feet straight down, and I could see DS Khan in the moonlight. He wasn't moving. I was crying. I was angry. Probably in shock. I turned to the defendant, who was on his feet, and I said, 'You did this. You did this.' And he said, 'I'm sorry. I'm so sorry. I'd take it back if I could. I'm so sorry.'

I heard a helicopter and sirens and he heard them too. He started backing away, so I said, 'No! Don't you dare go. Help me find a way down to him. Don't you dare leave me here alone.'

ROGER SUMPTION QC
Did he stay?

HARRIET KEALTY
No. He ran away.

ROGER SUMPTION QC
And the child?

HARRIET KEALTY
Elliot had come out from the trees. When the defendant saw him, he grabbed the boy and dragged him away. He left me alone. He left me alone there to face what he had done.

ROGER SUMPTION QC
And to be clear, the defendant kicked Sabih Khan over the edge?

HARRIET KEALTY
Yes. He kicked him over the edge. He killed him.

Chapter 29

Harri stood in the darkness and watched Ben Elmys take Elliot Asha into the forest. She wanted to go after them and snatch the child away from that foul man, but her friend and former partner was lying in the ravine. She had no idea whether he was alive or dead. He'd cried out as he'd fallen, and Harri tried not to think about the thud she'd heard, preferring to believe she'd imagined it. The odds of someone surviving a fall like that were . . . well, she couldn't bring herself to think about that. Her friend needed help. The sirens were some distance away, and the helicopter had banked south, probably looking for somewhere safe to land.

Harri gave up any thought of pursuing Ben and Elliot, and turned to carefully check the foliage around the edge of the ravine. She took her phone from her pocket and used the torch to search the undergrowth. She moved north and when she was a few yards from the spot where Sabih had fallen, she saw a flat slab. She pushed through the gorse and bushes. There were stone steps that descended into the ravine. They were damp, but the gritstone wasn't slippery, and she hurried down as quickly as her legs would carry her.

The ravine was about twenty feet wide, and its high walls were covered in lichen and moss that glowed an electric green in the moonlight. It was a few degrees cooler at the bottom, and the chill coupled with her gradual emergence from shock made Harri's skin tingle. Her stomach was churning and she felt the clammy grip of nausea threaten to overwhelm her. She ran from the foot of the steps along the muddy ravine floor to the spot where Sabih had landed, and when she saw his twisted body splayed like a broken toy and his blank unblinking eyes, she knew he was gone.

But she had to do something. She had to try to bring him back, so she ran to him, kneeled beside his body, checked his airway, and pounded out chest compressions. High above, she heard shouts and indistinct voices.

'Here!' she yelled. 'Down here!'

She was crying now, and her tears rolled down and hit Sabih's face like heavy rain, tracing little brooks of sadness across his lifeless skin.

'Help!' she shouted. 'Down here!'

Harri saw a pool of light materialize nearby, then another, and finally a third caught her and Sabih. She looked up and squinted into the glare of spotlights gathered at the edge of the ravine.

'Down here!' she yelled. 'We need an ambulance.'

She knew that wasn't true. There was nothing anyone could do for Sabih Khan.

Chapter 30

It was like looking up at heaven. Tiny crystal jewels had been embedded in the black stone that lined the domed roof, and the spotlights dotting the circumference were positioned to catch each gem and make them shimmer like stars. Below the ring of spotlights, clinging to the very bottom of the dome, was a band of white writing against a blue background. Harri couldn't decipher the script, but she got the impression the words were profound. The Arabic letters merged into each other to form the most glorious cursive patterns.

She stood at the very edge of a large balcony with the female members of Sabih Khan's extended family. Most were weeping, some sobbing quietly, and occasionally there was a lament which Harri couldn't understand, but whose anguish she shared. Beneath them, the men stood on thick red rugs, their unfurled prayer mats a myriad of colours and designs.

Hundreds had gathered to pay their respects to a fallen member of Stoke's Pakistani community and the mosque was almost full. Sabih had never spoken of his faith and his alcohol consumption suggested he hadn't observed it strictly, but it was clear from the grief and reverence of those in attendance that he was held in high regard by the devout. The close male members of his family were clustered around Sabih's father and uncles. DCI Powell and a group of colleagues from the station were gathered near the back of the mosque. Powell looked uncomfortable as he followed the congregation in the prayer ritual. Harri empathized and felt very much an outsider as she bowed, kneeled and prostrated herself, trying to mimic those around her. She didn't understand the ritual, but the prayer was a mark of respect and she wanted to do everything she could to honour Sabih.

She kept thinking back to that night, and wondering what would have happened if she hadn't called out to him. What if she hadn't intervened to try to stop him beating Ben? Would Elmys be dead, and a good man still be alive? She sobbed at the thought that she was responsible for the suffering of the gathered friends and family. Hundreds of souls traumatized by grief because she'd stopped Sabih. Because she'd involved him in the investigation. Because she'd taken him there that night. The guilt was almost too much to bear, and she shook uncontrollably.

She felt a hand on her back, and looked round to see Amina, Sabih's twenty-something cousin, smile reassuringly. Her eyes brimmed with sorrow, and there was nothing but anguish in her face, but she was trying to be kind and Harri couldn't cope with it. She didn't deserve kindness. She'd played a role in bringing all these people here, and she couldn't stop crying at the horror of it all. Amina embraced her and tried to soothe away a pain that would leave a permanent scar.

Harri prayed and wept through a disorientating fog of grief. She lost track of time and was consumed by flashbacks of the fateful moment. Guilt and remorse overwhelmed her, and she could find no way to escape them. She was surprised when the imam delivered his final words and left the pulpit.

The congregation started to disperse, shaking Harri from her waking nightmare.

'We're going to his parents' house to sit in mourning,' Amina said. 'Friends and family come to visit and pay their respects. You've welcome to join us. He spoke highly of you.'

The words were like needles. Harri didn't deserve to be held in high regard by the man she'd failed to protect. She deserved hatred. Punishment. Suffering for what she'd done.

'I can't,' Harri replied. 'I don't think I'm strong enough. Please know I have you all in my thoughts, but I can't.'

'It's OK,' Amina said, gently taking Harri's hands. 'I understand. He is with God now. He feels nothing but joy. Our sorrow is not for him, but for ourselves. He is beyond pain. He is in paradise, and his every moment is perfect.'

Fresh tears flowed, and Harri hated herself even more. How could this woman be so strong, when she was so weak? She wished she'd never found that book and never pulled on a thread she had no business unravelling. If she'd listened to Sabih, and left those people alone, he'd still be alive. She hated herself, but she hated Benjamin Elmys more. It was his fault they were all here. She wished she'd never met him.

'Thank you,' Harri replied, wiping her tears.

She left Amina with her family and joined the other mourners filing out of the mosque. She followed them downstairs, not really listening to their hushed conversations. When she got outside, Powell was standing on the pavement near the gates, looking lost. She took a deep breath to try to compose herself as she approached.

'Kealty,' he said when he saw her. 'That was rough. Are you OK?'

'Not really,' she replied, fighting to control the tremor in her voice.

'Whatever our past differences . . . well . . .'

She wasn't in the mood to give him absolution. 'Have you got any leads?' Harri asked.

Islamic custom dictated burial within twenty-four hours, but Sabih's interment had been delayed to allow for an autopsy. Benjamin Elmys and Elliot Asha had been missing for five days.

'Elmys doesn't have any real friends. His former colleagues have all been warned about harbouring him,' Powell replied. 'And we're watching the ports.'

'Just find him,' Harri said. 'That's all that matters now. He has to answer for this.'

Transcript of a video recorded by Ben Elmys Eleven Years Later

This video was discovered in Pilgrims Cave, near Lud's Church in the Peak District.

BEN ELMYS

I was there that night. I watched you and Detective Chief Inspector Powell talk. You couldn't see me, but I was there outside the mosque, hidden by the crowd of mourners. I shared your anguish. If there was any way to take it back, I would, but some things cannot be undone. We just have to live with them. They are steps on the path we must tread. I watched you from the corner, concealed by his friends and family. It was little comfort to see how much he was loved. Somehow that only made it worse, don't you think?

I wanted to reach out to you. To hug you and tell you it wasn't your fault, but, well, it wasn't practical. So I slunk away with a lump in my throat and tears in my eyes and I went back to my car, which was parked a couple of streets from the mosque. Elliot was asleep under a blanket in the boot.

I'd done the things I needed to do. The preparations had been made. So it was time to say goodbye and put Elliot somewhere he couldn't be hurt. Somewhere safe.

I drove to Ipstones and met Cynthia Hughes just outside

the village. I was worried the police might be watching her home, so we arranged to meet on a track we both knew. Elliot didn't need to see the drama of my arrest. I could sense her doubt, and there was suspicion in her eyes and an undertone of accusation in her words.

'Mr Elmys, where have you been?' she asked.

I told her I had some things I needed to do.

'The police are looking for you,' she said. She was unable to hide her disappointment, but that was so typical of Mrs Hughes, her feelings always shone through. She was far too honest. 'These things they're saying, please tell me they're not true.'

It still breaks my heart that I wasn't able to tell her otherwise, that she died being disappointed in me, but the truth was and still is that I'm responsible for Sabih Khan's death. So I didn't answer her question. I ignored it.

'You're going to need to take care of Elliot,' I told her, and I carried him from the boot of the Land Rover to the back seat of her car without waking him.

I told her I'd been keeping him . . . sorry you, Elliot, sedated. I apologize for that, Elliot, but you'd been through a great deal. Seen too much, and I needed you calm.

'What about you? What's going to happen to you?' Mrs Hughes asked me.

I gave her a sealed letter. 'Show this to the lawyer. He will make sure you have everything you need to raise Elliot,' I told her. 'I'm not going to be around.'

She broke down, but she didn't hug me. I think by that stage she was afraid of me, which is another sad little thought I carry. Everyone I ever loved had come to think poorly of me. Including you, Harri.

'Oh, Mr Elmys, I'm so sorry,' Mrs Hughes said.

And that was the last time I ever saw Cynthia Hughes.

I kissed you on the forehead, Elliot, shut the door and left you with the one person who loved you almost as much as your parents. It was very sad, but then so much of this is.

I drove into Leek, parked the car, and walked into the police station. It was late and there was no one around apart from an officer on reception. He asked if he could help me, and I still remember his look of surprise when I said, 'My name is Benjamin Elmys. I'm here to turn myself in for the murder of Detective Sergeant Sabih Khan.'

ACADEMIC SENTENCED FOR POLICE OFFICER'S DEATH

22 November

Local academic Benjamin Elmys (41) was today sentenced for the manslaughter of Detective Sergeant Sabih Khan.

Delivering the sentence in Hanley Crown Court, Judge Eustace Thomas said, 'Benjamin Elmys, I have reviewed the circumstances of this case and heard the sentencing recommendations. I've taken into account your late guilty plea and your previous good character. However, the crime you committed was extremely serious, the manslaughter of a serving police officer.'

Before he could pass sentence, the judge's remarks were interrupted by an outburst in court. A child, believed to have been the ward of the defendant, protested Mr Elmys's innocence and accused the prosecution's chief witness, former police officer Harriet Kealty (32), of falsifying her evidence. The child was escorted from the court upon the judge's instruction, and he resumed his sentencing, saying, 'I've had representations from Staffordshire Police, informing me that Detective Sergeant Khan was investigating the deaths of David and Elizabeth Asha and that you were a suspect. While I can't make a determination on that investigation, I can use it to inform my view that you had reason to wish the detective dead, and consider it as an aggravating factor. For those reasons, I sentence you to serve twenty-two years in prison.'

Jonathan Patel, a lawyer representing the Khan family, read a statement outside court. 'Sabih Khan was a much loved son and cousin. He was a devoted police officer who gave his life in pursuit of justice. While no court can ever undo the pain and suffering felt by his family, we are satisfied with the sentence handed down today. We would encourage those who would like to honour Sabih's memory to make a donation to Police Care UK. We hope the media will respect the family's privacy at this time and give us space to heal and move on from this terrible ordeal.'

Katie Harper, *Leek Advertiser*

Extract from Harriet Kealty's email journal

Justice was served today, but why does it feel so wrong? It brought me no satisfaction to see Ben led to the cells. He looked at me as he was taken away. I'd expected hatred, but there was nothing but pity. Why? Why did he pity me? And how dare he? I'm not the one doomed to spend at least eleven years in prison. I hope I never see him again. He used me, and I still don't understand how.

Elliot finally broke down, and disrupted the judge's sentencing with some shouting and crying. Cynthia Hughes dragged him out of the court after raised words from the normally placid judge.

I ran into them on my way out. I tried to apologize but Elliot was so angry.

'You're not sorry,' he said. 'You're a liar. He didn't push anyone. I saw what happened.'

'So did I,' I responded calmly. There were solicitors and court officials all around us. 'You're imagining things, Elliot. It doesn't matter what I said. Mr Elmys confessed.'

'So I wouldn't have to be a witness,' Elliot snapped back. 'So I wouldn't have to take the stand to tell everyone you lied. He did it to protect me.'

'You're not supposed to say anything about that, Elliot,' Cynthia Hughes chided him.

'Why?' I asked. 'Why wouldn't he want you to clear him? If he really believed he was innocent?'

Elliot didn't reply immediately. He stared at me with brooding hatred. Finally, he spoke. 'He was worried they might make me talk about it—' he clammed up.

'The secret,' I blurted out. 'The one you almost told me about at the house?'

'I should never have spoken to you. I should never have told you he was going to take me away. I should never have trusted you.' He turned his fierce eyes on me. 'You're a liar. He never hurt that man. You're a liar and I hate you. I never want to see you again.'

Those were his last words to me. Cynthia Hughes put her arm around his shoulder, gave me a courteous but cold nod, and took him outside.

I think back to that night and wonder about what really happened. It was so dark and chaotic. What did I really see? Did Sabih step back and fall? Or did Ben Elmys lash out and kick him over? I thought I knew the truth, but now I'm not so sure. Does it matter? I'm almost certain Ben had a hand in David and Beth Asha's deaths, and if he hadn't fought Sabih, my friend would still be alive, so he was responsible for his death.

Maybe, deep down, part of me wants to see Ben suffer for rejecting me? Does it matter? The man I loved was an illusion. The real man deserves to be locked up.

I could be kidding myself, though. Maybe punishing Ben Elmys for Sabih's death means I don't have to keep punishing myself. Perhaps the suffering of another is my absolution?

There's never going to be absolution though. The man

you loved proved to be rotten. Everything you'd thought about him was wrong. All those happy moments were tainted. He had been trying to use you in some way. To cover his tracks and compromise any potential police investigation?

It didn't matter, because whatever his motivation, he'd pretended to be someone he wasn't. Everything you thought you felt about him was built on a lie. He hasn't just killed your friend, and the memories of the good times you'd shared when you thought you were in love – he's murdered your hopes for the future. How will you ever trust anyone again? How will you trust your own judgement? How will you love anyone like that ever again? How will you ever be able to feel so deeply? You'll always hold something back, so no one can ever hurt you the way he did.

Chapter 31

The morning after the sentencing hearing, Harri woke up feeling no less troubled. Her dreams had been plagued by Sabih's death and she'd relived the horrific moment in so many different ways. Tonight, she'd been fighting him and had been the one to kick him over the edge, an experience that had seemed so real, she'd woken from the nightmare feeling physically sick.

She got up and went to the toilet. As she checked her reflection and waited for the nausea to subside, she realized today was the first time in a long while she didn't have any plans. They'd never found the missing Cobalt 60, and Ben had denied all knowledge of it. The university wanted to draw a line under the scandalous episode, and had terminated Harri's engagement a couple of weeks ago, shortly after the jury had passed its verdict. She needed to figure out what to do with her life.

She went to the kitchen and started making coffee. As she put her mug on the counter, she noticed an envelope had been slipped under her front door at some point during the night. She ambled over and picked it up.

There was no name or address, and when she opened it, she found a tiny USB drive with no markings. She went to the living room, sat on the couch, woke her computer, and inserted the drive into one of the USB ports. A folder opened almost immediately, and revealed a single video file.

Harri double-clicked it and her stomach flipped the moment she recognized the location. The camera was pointing towards a set of railway tracks. It was night, and she knew which night. She heard her own voice shouting off camera, and the image changed as the person filming shifted position. The camera swept over the railway tracks, up a steep embankment to take in what was happening in the road, which ran at a right angle to the camera's viewpoint.

Harri saw herself and Sabih Khan chasing Alan Munro, a dishevelled man in ripped jeans and a frayed T-shirt. He was known to them locally as a homeless person and sometime drunk, but he'd never caused any real trouble. At least not like that night.

Munro was holding a kitchen knife that glinted in the street lights. He'd been threatening people outside the Red Lion pub in Stoke, and Sabih and Harri had happened to be near by and were first on the scene. Munro had a history of mental health issues and had been living on the street for years, but he'd always been polite and respectful to members of the public and police. He'd always tell Harri how beautiful she was, but something had made him snap and become violent that May night.

The camera zoomed in, and Harri saw the wildness in Munro's eyes as Sabih caught up with him. She wished she could reach out to her old partner and tell him to back off. If he hadn't tackled Munro, and failed to apprehend him, maybe he wouldn't have been so eager to prove himself against Ben. Maybe he'd still be alive.

But she couldn't change the past. She couldn't reach out

to him, and she watched helplessly as Sabih grabbed Munro and they both went down. Munro was agitated and enraged and high on something, and the crack of his head on the road didn't faze him. He slashed at Sabih with the knife and caught him on the forearm. Sabih recoiled and it was all the opening Munro needed. He lashed out at Sabih, punching him and slashing, and soon Harri's partner was on his back.

'Get off me, you lunatic!' Sabih yelled between the cries and yelps of pain.

The road to the train station was quiet. A couple of cars had stopped, and the drivers were filming the violence on their phones, but no one was helping her partner. Harri recalled the moment she realized it was up to her, and she watched her past self step forward and extend her ASP – a telescopic baton that was intended to incapacitate. She swung at Munro and caught him behind the ear. He howled and dropped the knife, but reached for her again, so she fought him off with the ASP.

Adrenaline coursed through her and she remembered glancing over at Sabih, covered in his own blood. Was he dead?

Munro wouldn't go down, which wasn't surprising. Toxi-cology later found traces of PCP in his system. Munro managed to get to his feet and ran for the wall that separated the street from the embankment and railway tracks. He scrambled up and over the wall. She saw herself register the danger Munro now faced. There were train tracks down there.

'Help him!' Harri yelled at the nearest driver, pointing at Sabih. 'Call an ambulance.'

The guy in the grey Vauxhall Astra nodded, but Harri was already moving. She wished she'd stayed, and it pained her to see her former self running across the pavement. But she knew if Munro wasn't caught, he might hurt someone else. And if he strayed onto the tracks, he might hurt himself.

Harri sprinted to the wall and climbed over it to find a twelve-foot drop to the embankment. She made the jump without hesitating, which looked brave on camera, but Harri knew she'd been foolish. If she'd stayed with Sabih, her life wouldn't have been ruined, and he might still be here. An unfortunate fall of the dominoes.

The railway tracks lay forty feet beneath street level, meaning none of the witnesses in their cars could see what happened next. The only person who knew the truth was the person filming from the railway bridge above them, the man whose video she'd been desperate to find.

On screen, Munro leaped from the shadows beneath the railway bridge and attacked her, and the two of them lost balance and tumbled down the embankment, which was constructed of fist-sized jagged stones. The fall was brutal and Harri remembered how sore she'd been for days afterwards.

She and Munro came to a halt by the tracks, and he staggered to his feet. She was so dazed she could hardly move, but she forced herself to her knees, ready to defend herself.

Horror flashed across her face as she realized the deep rattle and rumble she'd heard as they'd fallen hadn't been the sound of their bodies clattering into the stones.

It was a train.

A fast freight train to London.

'No! Alan! Look out!' she cried, and she grabbed Munro's T-shirt, but he resisted her attempt to save him and pulled himself free.

The train was close now and Alan Munro had staggered into its path, his eyes wild, not of this world.

She tried to get to her feet to reach him, but she couldn't move quickly enough.

The video caught the moment of impact, but the full gruesome sight of Munro's body breaking, rupturing, and bursting was concealed by the camera angle. Harri remembered it though and it was a moment she would carry with her forever.

The video did prove, contrary to the assertions of Munro's family and the incident investigators, that Harri had not pushed Munro into the path of the train. It proved what she'd said all along: that she'd tried to save him and his death had been a terrible accident of his own making.

On screen, Harri saw her past self look directly at the camera. She'd caught sight of the recording light after the train had thundered past. It was screeching to a halt some distance down the track.

'Hey!' she yelled. 'Wait—'

The camera zoomed out and started backing away, then the screen went black.

By the time Harri had dragged herself back up the embankment and pushed her way through the growing crowd of bystanders and first responders, and run round the corner to reach the railway bridge, the camera operator was long gone.

She looked at the tiny USB drive in awe. This was the footage she'd spent months trying to find. She hadn't seen the camera operator's face; the lights on the railway bridge had been out, but she'd launched a public appeal, posted endlessly to social media, and had even given an interview to the local paper. This video was shot by the person Powell and the disciplinary committee had refused to believe existed. They concluded she'd used excessive force in beating Munro in the street. They hadn't accepted her argument her actions were proportionate to the danger, in light of how high he'd been. They said the footage shot by the men who'd stopped in their cars indicated she'd lost control of her emotions. They argued there were reasonable grounds to believe she was motivated to avenge her partner's humiliating beating and that she pushed Munro into the path of the train during a struggle.

This was the video of the night her life had been ruined by a false claim of manslaughter, the allegation that had set the wheels in motion for her dismissal. She'd never faced criminal charges because the evidence against her wasn't sufficient for conviction beyond reasonable doubt, but there was enough smoke for a vindictive Detective Chief Inspector to ensure the investigation went against her. That's exactly what Powell did, and the panel recommended her dismissal.

Only Sabih kept his faith with her, perhaps feeling guilty that if he'd stood up to Munro, she wouldn't have had to. This was the incident that had set her on her road to nowhere.

Harri pulled the USB drive from the port and studied it with a growing sense of excitement. This tiny thing would change everything. She could prove her innocence. She could get her job back.

She could reclaim her old life. Her only regret was that Sabih wouldn't be by her side when she did. Her partner was gone, and that took the shine off her redemption.

Chapter 32

So there we are.

Benjamin Elmys, the man I thought I knew, the man Beth and I had entrusted with our son, the man I'd come to call brother, suspected of our murder and imprisoned for the death of another. And our boy, left in the care of a killer, now shunted on to his next guardian, our former housekeeper, Cynthia Hughes. I can hardly bring myself to think about the suffering my son endured and the trauma of being abandoned in such circumstances.

My days are numbered. Or so goes the cliché. I look back on my crooked, broken path and long for things that can never be. If you're reading this, the chances are you're familiar with my work. My publishers tell me I have a loyal fan base, and the messages I receive from around the world certainly wouldn't make liars of them.

Laurie from Manhattan wrote to me a few years ago and asked why so many of my novels involve the abduction of a child. Have you ever been looking at a painting only to have someone sidle up to you and say something that makes you see it completely differently? Laurie's email was just such a sidle. I'd been writing books without ever really thinking about them, but when I look back through the catalogue of twenty-three thrillers that forms my modest contribution to literature, I realize many of them, particularly the early ones, involve a missing child.

Have you ever seen an ouroboros? It is a snake with its own tail in its mouth. A symbol of the eternal, the cycle of death and rebirth. Writing is a little like that. Writers learn about themselves through their words, and that education feeds our work, making it richer. Our lives leave an impression on the page, but the page marks us, and each word we write prompts change, so in the end it is impossible to tell whether the writer or the imagined world is most altered by the process. Like the ouroboros, the end and the beginning, cause and effect, cease to matter.

Perhaps that's why I'd never reflected upon my subconscious choice of subject matter. I was too close to see it clearly, and it took a stranger with a broader point of view to notice.

They say there are people who feel no love. Sociopaths, psychopaths, pitiless souls. They look like the rest of us, but they're very different. I can't imagine being such a vessel – having form, but being empty, experiencing nothing when looking down at my newborn son. I wouldn't have been able to feel anything as I watched his eyes, wide and unfocused, taking in the uncertain forms of the world, his other senses alert to the sounds and textures of the delivery room: the urgent voices of doctors and nurses, the metallic smell of disinfectant and surgical solutions, the touch of my hands against his buttery smooth skin.

As it was, I experienced nothing but the most profound love for Elliot in the moment of his birth and felt more complete than at any other time in my life. A firstborn child. Life created. Magic made mundane by frequency, but still magic nonetheless.

Sometimes I wish I was an empty vessel, that I wasn't able to feel. Sometimes, in the darker hours, I dwell on what was, and long to be free of the memories of the life I left behind. Was it cruel to leave Elliot? Yes, but it was as cruel on me as it was on him. I had no choice, or at least I didn't realize the choice I was given. Not until it was too late. I struggle with it every single day. I pray to a god in whom I don't believe to help me change the unchangeable, but what's done cannot be undone, at least not by me.

This isn't an appeal for pity. It's not supposed to be therapy on a page. I just want you to know that guilt rots my waking moments and that I am as tormented as you are likely to be, when you read what comes next.

Some regrets are so large they create their own gravity, and all emotion is drawn towards a singularity of pain. I spent a long time there, caught in a crushing, dark storm of depression, and I'm afraid if I think about my young son too long, I will return to that Hell.

When I went back to my early work and read the words I'd written so long ago, I realized my reader knew more about me than I did. Laurie was right. The absence of a child was a common theme in my first books. In my second novel, *The Constant Child*, I wrote:

We are bound to the past, links in a chain that stretches into the infinite unknown. The death of a parent is natural. It is the passing of a soul into history, another link that ties us to the ancient beginning, but the loss of a child breaks that chain. It is unnatural and abhorrent, for the child's loss is felt in the past and future.

The child is mourned by the souls of their dead ancestors because the chain of which they are a part will go no
further. All the hardship those ancestors endured, all the
suffering, all the love that forged new links was for nothing, because their story is now at an end.

The child is lamented too by all the future souls who
will never be born, who are doomed to exist only in the
netherworld of imagination, in the minds of those who
ponder what might have been.

And while the ghosts of our ancestors and the spectres
of an imagined future mourn, the loss is felt most profoundly of all by the child's parents, who miss hair to
tousle, a smile to brighten their day, and a warm body
to hug.

When we read, it is sometimes easy to imagine the words
have simply materialized on the page. We can lose sight of
the author, and if we do catch a glimpse of him or her, we
may consider them a dispassionate chronicler of events. This
is far from true, and among the handful of authors I know
well, there are few who aren't as moved by their work as any
reader. Tears are shed, anger boils and laughter erupts even
on the tenth reading.

As I look back on my earlier work with wiser eyes and see
my words in the context of what my life was, I can't help but
shake with the sadness of it all, but most of all I see echoes of
what happened to my son. I had laid out his suffering without
ever consciously intending to do so. But you're not here for
my sorrow.

You want to know about my son.

The child I left behind.

Dear Elliot,

I'm sorry there was no other way. Lord knows I've tried to live a different life, but this is the one I'm fated. I hope Mrs Hughes gives you this, and even if she doesn't, I know there will come a day when you'll sit down and read it, and all the other letters I shall write you. I intend to send you a letter every week I'm in prison. I want to continue your education. It's essential, and even though I know you're angry with me for leaving you, there will come a time when you will turn to my words for guidance, so it is important I set them down. One day you will understand and remember me fondly.

These letters are almost as important for me as they are for you. I have eleven long years stretching ahead of me, time that will pass slowly and painfully without a useful outlet. My words are essential for both of us. Remember that.

I spent two weeks in Stafford Prison after the trial, before being transferred to Long Lartin. It is a bleak place in the middle of green fields of nowhere. They say it is the second most secure prison in Britain, after Belmarsh. There are patrol dogs and high wire fences everywhere, and I am incarcerated with rapists and murderers. I'm afraid of what my future holds here. I know there is cruelty and suffering in store, but I mustn't dwell on that. I know I will get through it, and while eleven years might seem an eternity, all things pass. All pain fades and sadness wanes. Brighter days will come. I cling to the notion that one day we will see each other again.

And then there's her.

She came to visit me on my first day. She still doesn't believe it, but we are connected. A prison officer, a young woman called Anya, took me to the visitors' room, which is in a satellite building off the main administration block, and I found her waiting for me. Despite everything that's happened, I still love her, and I hope one day the love I knew she had for me will be rekindled. I long for her to look at me the way she did when we first met, I long for another kiss, but for now she greets me with the suspicion one would reserve for a murderer. There wasn't any small talk.

'Don't you think it's time you started telling me the truth?' she asked.

I smiled, which only annoyed her.

'Something funny?' she asked.

'I've only ever told you the truth,' I replied.

She shook her head in disbelief. 'Why did you confess? You could have put up a defence.'

'Who would have believed me?' I replied. 'Besides, I had my reasons.'

'The secret?' she asked.

'The secret,' I conceded. 'You won't find out today,

but in time you'll know what it is and why it must be
kept.'

'In time?' she replied. 'There is no more time. I get to
move on. You're going to be trapped in here for at least
eleven years.'

'I don't want us to fight,' I said.

'We're not a couple,' she snapped. 'Just tell me one
thing. Is he your son?'

I hope it's not a question that ever troubles you, my
dearest Elliot, and I shall tell you what I told her.

'Why is the world so sordid? We never see beyond
our own limited perspectives. We can never look at the
world through other people's eyes.'

I knew exactly what she was suggesting; that I'd had
an affair with your mother, that your father had found
out and killed her, been overcome with remorse and
taken his own life. The tawdry imaginings of people
who don't understand what we've been through.

'The uniform suits you,' I said.

She was in her full dress uniform. Perhaps in an
attempt to intimidate me or to show me how much
she'd moved on.

'The day after your sentencing, someone sent me
a video I'd spent months looking for. The footage
exonerated me. I got my job back.'

'I'm happy for you,' I told her honestly.

'But you don't know anything about it?'

'Why would I?'

'Don't you think the timing is strange?' she remarked.

'Perhaps, but there are such things as coincidences.'

'Like us meeting?' she asked. 'Months before I started investigating you for murder.'

'That was no coincidence,' I replied. 'That was love.'

'It was an illusion built on lies,' she snapped back.

'It was real,' I assured her. 'One day you'll understand.'

She shook her head and sighed. 'No one's interested in your cryptic little games any more. You've lost.'

'In that case, if you feel anything for me, anything at all, even the tiniest fragment of pity, please don't come here again,' I said.

'Why?' she asked.

'It's too painful. I've got a long time ahead of me. I need to forget what lies outside these walls,' I told her. 'We'll meet again, Harri.'

I didn't wait for her to respond. I got to my feet and asked Anya to take me back to C-Block.

I glanced over my shoulder as we left, and saw Harriet Kealty in her beautifully pressed police uniform, rising from the table, totally perplexed.

I knew it was the last I'd see of her for a very, very long time.

I don't think she is likely to contact you, but if she does, remember what binds us. The secret once broken can never be remade. It is ours and ours alone, and I hope that no matter what happens, you will honour that. I know you will.

I discovered the therapeutic power of poetry as a child. It helps me make sense of the senseless, and brings the magic of chaos to order. The mystery of interpretation, someone once told me, is that we can

project ourselves into the spaces between the words
and find room to imprint our own meaning. Our souls
flourish in those spaces.

Someone wrote a poem for me once, and I'd like to
share it with you.

> *Life's colour dancing on fragile wings*
> *Flower to flower*
> *Beautifully elusive*
>
> *Clearly seen, floating on*
> *But closer gazed*
> *Gone*
>
> *Those ethereal wings*
> *Churn a storm*
> *Of winter wind and hail*
>
> *That chips and flakes*
> *The stone king's face*
> *And all he thinks and knows*
>
> *And on the heather*
> *Royal purple blooms*
> *Inviting you to come again*

If we list the biological characteristics of a flower,
do we diminish its beauty? I think the same is true of
poetry. If we tear the verse apart, all we're left with are
words, but sometimes one can't help but analyse. This
work has played on my mind for years. Am I the stone

king? Is it about humility? Or love? Or truth? Sometimes I think it was just meant to torment me, to give me something to do, like a sudoku puzzle, infuriating, yet strangely addictive. I shall devote at least some of the years ahead to try to understand its meaning. If you have any insight, do please write to me. About this, or anything else. I would very much like to hear from you.

    With love,

      Ben

Part Two

The Man

Chapter 33

Elliot Asha had grown into a fine man.

His soft brown hair flashed with hints of gold in the bright sunshine. His muscles shifted beneath his Lycra shorts as his legs carried him along the cobbled street at speed. His oversized cotton rowing shirt swung from his broad frame. At six-one, he stood taller than most of his crew. The eight of them joked and jostled each other as they dodged the tourists clustered at the bottom of Bear Lane. They raced up to the High Street, which was thronging with crowds, crossed the busy road, dodging traffic, and turned onto Turl Street. They ran along the old street, past the souvenir shops on one side and the imposing sandstone college walls on the other.

'Bar?' someone at the back of the group suggested.

Elliot's books were in the library and he'd gone to the training session with every intention of returning to his studies, but he was thirsty and the lure of a cold beer on a sunny afternoon proved too strong to resist.

They slowed to a walk by the college gate, which had been built like the bailey of an old castle, and one by one they stepped through the small doorway that was cut into the huge double gates.

Founded in 1427, Lincoln was one of the oldest colleges in Oxford. Located in the heart of town, it was built around three quadrangles, with All Saints Church as a sentinel that stood guard at the southern mouth of Turl Street. A small Oxford college, Lincoln was known for its good food and friendly atmosphere. There was a rumour it had been one of the principal university hubs for recruitment into the intelligence services, and college legend had it that John Le Carré had modelled George Smiley on a former tutor, Vivian Green.

Elliot loved the rich history of this six-hundred-year-old institution, and as he walked the large flagstones that formed the lodge floor, he reflected on how he'd changed in his two and a half years at Lincoln. He'd arrived there a naive boy, and over time, as though he'd imbued the magic and tradition of the place, had become a man. Simply being part of such a long and ancient story had transformed him and given him a perspective that transcended the boundaries of his own life.

'Mr Asha,' a voice called, and Elliot turned to see Pip, one of the college porters, beckoning him from the service window in the lodge office.

'I'll catch you up,' Elliot told his crew, who hurried around front quad towards Deep Hall, the ancient bar that was tucked beneath the oldest parts of the college.

'Sorry to bother you, sir,' Pip said. He was a kind old man with ruddy cheeks and wild grey hair and even though he had seen decades upon decades of young men and women pass through these gates, he somehow managed to make them all feel special. 'Professors Hoyt and Gardner were looking for you. I said you were likely at the river, and they asked me to send you up to Professor Hoyt's room when you got back.'

Elliot didn't bother to ask what they wanted. He had a suspicion he already knew.

'Thanks,' he said.

'You're welcome, sir,' Pip replied, before sliding the window shut.

Elliot headed into front quad, which was formed by four sets of college buildings linked together in a square, set around a perfectly manicured lawn. Professor Hoyt, the head of the physics department, had rooms in the building on the northern edge of the quad. It was covered in ivy which was positively alive in the sunshine. Elliot walked towards the old archway that led to the staircase where Hoyt's rooms were located, and as he started up the steps his good mood ebbed away faster than water draining from a canal lock.

He was expecting a hard time.

Extract from the journal of Professor Lindsay Hoyt, Professor of Physics, Lincoln College, Oxford

Printed with the kind permission of her family.

The Icarus Theory curses physics. We spend so much time pursuing truth, trying to understand the essence of reality, we lose touch with it. We reach for knowledge that would have been beyond us in our natural, primitive state, and once exposed to it, some minds are burned. I have known many Icari and some might say I am an Icarus myself, although I would dispute such an assertion. I am eccentric where others are disturbed or depressed. My oddities do not compare with the absence of mind of Heisenberg, or the lack of empathy of Oppenheimer, or the obsessive compulsion of Erdős. I'm positively rational and grounded in comparison, but of all the minds I've ever encountered, the one that troubled me the most was Elliot Asha.

He was an Icarus, and I believe he had flown higher than any of us, and it had cost him his ambition. He was twenty-one and his mind had already been scorched. Most people didn't see it, but I knew because I could tell when a person had seen beyond the constraints of life and perceived some new reality. Michael – Professor Gardner – and I had called Elliot to my room early in Trinity term of his final year.

He came in without knocking, which suggested either pathological overconfidence or nihilistic indifference to social convention. I suspected the latter. His nihilism was evident in his work and attitude. He was only concerned with pleasure, not effort. My assessment was underscored by his attire: crumpled rowing kit. Pip had been right. Elliot had been wasting his time at the river.

'You wanted to see me,' he said, and Michael and I cut short our conversation about him.

'Have a seat,' I replied, and he chose my favourite armchair, an old Laura Ashley floral pattern I'd inherited from Mother.

Michael and I were at opposite ends of a leather couch, separated from our student by a coffee table that was covered with my papers and notebooks.

No one said anything, and for a moment all I could hear were the voices rising from the front quad, drifting through the open sash windows.

'Professor Gardner and I are concerned,' I began. 'We're worried about the effort you're putting into your work.'

Elliot gave me a look I cannot easily describe. It wasn't contempt, nor was it pity. It might have been disinterest but there was too much emotion for it to have been that.

I dream of a world of robots where circuits are dismantled and motherboards analysed so we're all absolutely clear who feels what at any given time. I can describe the orbit of a thousand suns in mathematically perfect formulae, but I still to this day don't know how that young man felt. I doubt he had much respect for us though.

He picked up my Mont Blanc StarWalker fountain

pen – a most indulgent gift to myself – and a notebook, and flicked through it absently as I went on.

'You have a brilliant mind, Elliot, but you're just not present.'

As if to prove my point, he started doodling.

'Why did you come here? Why pick physics?' Michael chimed in. 'Was it your parents?'

Elliot didn't reply, but the pen froze for a moment, and he concentrated on his doodle intently. He might have been furious. I don't know. Everything about him was so contained.

We knew about his parents, of course. Few in our world didn't. They were accomplished scientists and their deaths had been grave tragedies. It was hard to imagine what the loss might do to a child, but perfectly reasonable to believe he might have come here in an attempt to live up to what he imagined their expectations of him might be.

'Are you bored?' I asked. 'Is there something that might rekindle your love of the subject?'

'I'm not bored,' Elliot replied without even glancing up from the notepad. 'Have you ever wondered why we do it? A dog looks up at the stars and sees beauty or spots or perhaps nothing at all. We look up and we have to dissect and pull apart and explain. Why can't we just accept things as they are?'

These were the jaded words of a much more experienced scientist. He was too young for this. I'd heard similar from the mouths of grey-haired physicists near the end of their careers.

'It is in our nature to seek truth,' Michael remarked. 'That is our beauty.'

Elliot flashed a cynical half-smile.

'Truth,' he scoffed. 'Someone once made me a promise. It

wasn't kept, but if it had been, it would have made lies of all our truths.'

'Why?' I asked.

He looked away, troubled. He was a cracked soul, damaged by his past, and it was beyond me or Michael to put him back together. I regretted inviting him up. Broken toys should be left by the side of the road.

'If I told you, it wouldn't come true, but it hasn't come true so I can't tell you,' he replied.

'We didn't bring you here to talk riddles,' Michael said. 'Or muse about the nature of truth. We want you—'

'Am I being sent down?' Elliot interrupted, using Oxford's gentile term to describe an expulsion.

'Of course not,' I replied.

'Are my grades not satisfactory?' he asked.

'You know they are,' I conceded. 'Satisfactory, good, even, but they could be exceptional.'

'Then why am I here?'

'We feel you could be doing so much better,' I replied. 'You have a brilliant mind. If you apply it, you could achieve greatness.'

'You want me to be more beautiful? Is that it? You want a more comprehensive deconstruction of the stars?' He shook his head.

'We want you to fulfil your potential,' Michael said.

'There's only one thing I want, and none of you can give it to me,' Elliot countered. 'Can I go?'

He got to his feet but waited until I nodded.

Michael and I were silent as we watched him leave, and when he'd gone we discussed him for a while. After thirty minutes we decided to let time and fate take charge and hope Elliot Asha rediscovered his love of the subject. Michael went to his next tutorial, and I leaned across the coffee table and picked up the discarded notepad to see what Elliot had been doodling.

This journal will only be published posthumously to spare me the embarrassment of the confession I'm about to make.

Three years after this encounter, the members of the Swedish Academy awarded me the Nobel Prize in physics for my work on the Hierarchy Problem. It was the defining work of my career. I explained how particles at the electroweak scale are less impacted by gravity than those at the Planck scale.

My confession is this: the work was not mine. At least not entirely. I found the key equations in my notepad. Elliot Asha had written them while we were imploring him to be a better scientist. The truth is, he was above us all and I have never stopped wondering what else he might have discovered if he'd lived an uninterrupted life. His equations weren't the whole story, but he'd solved all the principles that I later became so famous for. I felt sick with excitement and the guilt of temptation, and agonized over what to do. I knew that notepad contained riches and glory that weren't mine, but I'm ashamed to say I listened to temptation.

I resolved to spend a few weeks building out his work into a proper theory, after which I planned to offer him second author on publication if the work proved robust. But that was the day he left, and despite all the rumours surrounding his death, no one ever really found out what happened to Elliot Asha.

So I took his work as my own, and am forever grateful and profoundly ashamed.

Chapter 34

Elliot was annoyed when he left Hoyt's room. They didn't know him. They didn't know what he'd been through. He didn't measure his life by their yardstick. He hadn't come to Oxford to study physics out of love. He'd come because it was easy. For all his many faults, Ben had given him a grounding in the subject that was beyond compare, and Elliot had never lost his ability to see solutions others considered impossible. He'd left Hoyt one such example as a riposte to her criticisms of him as a scientist. It was a solution he'd puzzled out while considering the abstracts of gravitational theory and causal dynamics. She would make a fuss, of course, and want him to publish, but what did it matter if the stars were deconstructed a little further? He preferred them beautiful and mysterious.

He was no longer in the mood to join his crew, so he headed for the library to collect his books. He walked through the lodge and turned left up Turl Street, aiming for the old church that had been converted into the college library.

With each step his mood soured. Nothing was ever enough for these people, and while they would always ask more of him, none of them could help him achieve the things he wanted. Despite what he'd said to Hoyt and Gardner, he was interested in truth.

Ben had made him a promise once, and he was desperate to know if it was true.

Elliot approached the wrought-iron church gates, which were set in a high fence, and he opened the one on the right. He stepped into the old stone churchyard and walked towards the grand library.

He pulled one of the huge wooden doors, stepped into a tiny antechamber, produced his library keycard from his pocket and ran it over the reader beside the glass security gates. The sensor beeped and he pulled one of the gates open and stepped inside.

The librarian wasn't at her desk, so he climbed the wooden steps into the main vaulted chamber. A run of long, broad tables formed a spine down the centre of the room, and a dozen students occupied well-spaced chairs. High shelves flanked the central table and between each pair were carrels, many of which were unoccupied. Elliot nodded at a few familiar faces. As captain of boats, he was well known within the college, but not always well liked because of some of the rowdier antics of the rowing crew.

His books were where he'd left them, in a carrel at the very rear of the church, but the space next to him was no longer empty. It was now occupied by Jessica Sealey, a girl he'd had a crush on since fresher's week. The cloud of his encounter with Hoyt and Gardner lifted at the sight of her, and he forgot his anger.

Their timing had always been off. She'd been with someone, and then he had, and despite what seemed an obvious mutual attraction, they'd managed to go almost three years without getting together. Had she seen his stuff? Had she asked around to find out where he was sitting? Or was it coincidence?

His heart tripped into a higher gear as he walked behind her and took his seat. There was no way he was leaving until she did.

She removed her headphones and said, 'Hey. Good session?'

'Yeah,' he replied, wishing he'd gone back to his room to shower. 'Studying hard?'

What a stupid question, he thought immediately. *Studying hard?*

She smiled. 'Yeah.'

The headphones went back in, and she returned to her books. He'd have to do better than that to win over this otherworldly woman. Her skin glowed, her red hair tumbled and her brown eyes shone like stars. She seemed more elfish than human, and if she'd told him she was really from Lothlórien, he might have believed her.

He opened his book on optical measurement of subatomic particles, but couldn't concentrate on a single word. He pretended to read the pages, but in truth he was just turning them so as not to appear weird.

They spent hours sitting side by side as though locked in a competition to see who would betray their union first. Night fell, and the massive stained-glass windows sprang to life with rich colour, illuminated by spotlights that hung outside the building. Glazed saints performed wondrous deeds all around them.

Elliot heard a steady stream of people leave until he was sure he and Jessica were the only people in the building. He checked his phone. It was a little after ten, but the sidelong glances and lingering looks told him he needed to stay.

Finally, when the grand old church was still, and he felt he couldn't breathe air that was so heavy with expectation, she removed her headphones and said, 'So, I was thinking we could go and hang out in my room. I have some wine.'

'OK,' he replied instantly, and a moment later he kicked himself for not playing it cool and taking his time to respond.

But she didn't care and was grinning at him almost as foolishly as he was at her.

They left their books and walked through the library side by side. Their fingers touched and he was shaken by tremors of excitement, which developed into a full-blown quake when she took his hand. They said nothing as they passed the high shelves laden with books, and still no words came as they skipped down the stairs and hurried into the churchyard outside. The cool night was still, as though the world was holding its breath.

The gate was always locked after ten, and students had to get out through a maze of corridors that ran through the college. A door in the north-east corner of the churchyard offered access to the corridor, and they were about to start along the path that lay between ancient gravestones when Elliot sensed movement out of the corner of his eye.

There, beyond the high wrought-iron fence, on the other side of Turl Street, was a face he hadn't seen for years, and the time that had passed wasn't enough. Standing across from him was the man he'd once loved, but over the years had come to hate.

The man whose face he had almost forgotten: Benjamin Elmys.

Chapter 35

'Elliot?' Jessica said. 'Are you OK?'

Her concern was evident, and she tried to pull him towards the door in the corner of the churchyard, but Elliot was transfixed.

Not tonight of all nights. Had it been eleven years already? How dare this man come back into his life? Ben was watching them from the mouth of the alleyway that ran between the old Mitre building and the parade of shops that lined the west of Turl Street. He looked as though he was enjoying the dismay his reappearance had caused.

Elliot had never visited him, nor opened a single one of the weekly letters he'd written. Instead, he'd spent years in therapy trying to come to terms with the wreckage of Benjamin Elmys. This man might have murdered his parents, and as he'd matured from child into man, Elliot had promised himself he would find the truth one day. He felt years of suppressed anger rise within him, and realized today might be that day.

'Elliot?' Jessica asked again.

'Why don't you go to your room? I'll meet you there in a few minutes. There's something I have to do,' he replied, and he squeezed her hand reassuringly.

She looked completely baffled, but he didn't know how to

explain it. The loss of his parents hung over him every day, their ungiven love, their unlived lives haunting him. He still wore his mother's necklace, a circular silver pendant with an embossed relief of a half-moon and a cluster of stars above the word 'Beth'. When all other memory was faded, he would always recall the feeling of his father's embrace the night he'd given it to him. If this was an opportunity to avenge his parents, he would not pass it up. He ran along the path towards the fence, and when he glanced over his shoulder, Jessica was watching him in total bemusement.

His mind wasn't on her any more. He was fixed on Benjamin Elmys, the man who'd once held himself out as some kind of surrogate father, the man who'd filled Elliot's head with mad imaginings. Ben simply stared at him, and there was something about the impassive gaze that made Elliot hate him even more. As he clambered over the fence, Elliot saw Ben Elmys turn and head into the alley.

'Hey!' he yelled. 'Stop!'

Elliot dropped onto the road. He sprinted down the alley and went through a patch of total darkness before emerging into a service area that contained a few bins. The foul-smelling space was a dead end apart from a fire door that led to one of the neighbouring pubs. Elliot tried the door, but it was locked. He kicked it in frustration. Ben must have had his escape route planned. His intention was clear. All he'd wanted to do was show up and give Elliot a sinister message: I'm back in your life.

Evil bastard, Elliot thought. *One day you'll pay.*

Frustrated and angry, Elliot walked back up the alley onto Turl Street. He looked at the churchyard and saw it was empty. Jessica had gone. He would find her and try to explain.

He jogged along the street to the main gate and stepped into the lodge. He nodded at Dean, the night porter, who was watching a TV show in the small office. Elliot walked through the post room, which was lined with hundreds of pigeonholes, and when he glanced at his own, he saw something inside it.

He reached for the solitary envelope and pulled it out to see his name typed on the front. He didn't need to open it to know who it was from.

He went to the porter's window and gently tapped on the glass. Dean turned the volume down on his iPad.

'Sorry to disturb you, Dean, but did you see the man who delivered this?' Elliot asked.

'No, sir. Must have come before my shift,' Dean replied. 'Sorry, Mr Asha.'

'Thanks.'

Dean closed the window and returned to his TV show, while Elliot stepped away from the counter and opened the envelope. Inside there was a typewritten message.

If you'd read my letters, you'd know it's time. The past has caught up with you. Your future is fated.

Beneath the message was one of Ben's poems.

If it's in your mind, it's in your heart
You see it, hear it, own it
That dream again, the one where you're dying
To be reborn, renewed, refreshed
The other side of night
Returning from elsewhere

To what will be, beginnings, endings
Come to us all, a tree from earth, a seed from sky
Rising
Falling
On and on
That dream
Again

Elliot leaned against the ancient stone wall. He felt nauseous and realized his hands were trembling. This man. This evil man, who'd done so much harm, had now targeted him. Elliot's mind raced and painful memories collided with frightful imaginings.

Elliot staggered out of the lodge and up Turl Street towards his room on Bear Lane. He felt sick, tired, and alone.

He never did go to Jessica's room.

Chapter 36

Elliot hadn't been home for months. He steered his BMW E Series off the main road, and drove down the familiar little lane that led to Ipstones. He knew every nook and turn, having travelled the route twice daily on the school bus. The trees had grown, but not much else had changed in the years since he'd first moved to the village.

He didn't remember arriving at Ipstones. He just woke up one day and was living with Mrs Hughes. He recalled crying a lot. He'd missed his parents terribly, and the pain had never really left him. There were no graves, his mother's body had never been found, and his father's had been taken by the sea, so he never had closure. There were so many unanswered questions, and Elliot puzzled over them constantly. It was a way of being close to them, he supposed. He could never feel their embrace, but he could try to keep them alive in his memory. And the more he thought of them, the more he came to hate Ben Elmys, the man he was convinced had some role in their deaths.

He parked in a space by the old church, and walked back along the road to the little cottage he'd shared with Cynthia Hughes. He let himself in, and was immediately greeted by the musty smell of a house that hadn't seen a living person for months. The place was still and silent. Cynthia's rosy face, constant humming of show tunes, and the smell of her baking had been absent since she'd passed away at the end of his first year at Oxford. He'd spent the summer straightening out her affairs and coming to terms with the fact he was utterly alone. Tears and self-pity had been his only companions that bleak, rainy summer, but as he'd started his second year, the pain of her passing had faded.

He still didn't like to come home, though. He hadn't cleared the house, and there were reminders of Cynthia everywhere. The tacky, kitten-festooned 'Home Sweet Home' sign by the front door, the collection of Edwardian china figurines, the family photos of Cynthia as a child with her older brother and parents. Elliot passed the mementos of his guardian's life and went into the kitchen to reclaim a set of keys from the odds-and-ends drawer.

Minutes later, he was on the road again, this time heading for a house that had once been full of love and laughter, but was now associated with loss and suffering. The dark clouds that had been spitting mockingly all morning finally threw down their worst, and the roads were coated with a slick wash of heavy rain. This was how Elliot remembered Longhaven, the cottage where his mother had become sick with cancer, where he'd received news of his father's death, the place that had been his home until he was ten. There had been happy times, bright moments with the parents he longed for every single day of his life. But those happy memories had been overwhelmed by a fog of misery.

Time was friend and foe. The years had made his suffering fainter, so he didn't feel as though he would immediately cry at the thought of his mother and father, but equally, the passage of time was the enemy of memory. He used to recall exactly how his mum smelled, and what her hair felt like when she hugged him. He used to be able to remember the flush of contentment he'd experience whenever she smiled at him. When he was younger, he could recall the sound of his father's voice, the smell of his aftershave when he carried Elliot upstairs to bed. Now those details were gone, and his absent parents were just ideas, vague ghosts that haunted his memory. He tried to clasp specific moments, like the night his father had given him his mother's necklace, but his mind was fallible, and he was afraid it would eventually fail his parents and forget them altogether, and that was a prospect he simply couldn't bear.

Elliot turned onto Ash Ridge, the winding lane that led to Longhaven, and he followed it through the wild open countryside that stretched from the foot of Hen Cloud, the inland cliff formation that had sparked his imagination as a child. His father had often used the gritstone towers that loomed above their family home as inspiration for stories, but like the memories of his parents, the details of those tales were lost and all Elliot recalled were vague snippets of pirates and dragons lurking in hidden caves.

Elliot saw the cottage as he rounded the bend and it looked as miserable as ever. Cynthia Hughes never felt she had the authority to sell the place, so she had rented it out, but it had stood empty ever since her death. Elliot wanted nothing to do with it and had abandoned it, perhaps as pathetic retaliation for his own abandonment. As he neared the building, all the old feelings surged. He wanted to feel his mother's loving embrace and hear her tell him everything would be OK. He longed to be with his father and ask why he'd abandoned his only son.

A lump grew in his throat as he thought of all the things he would say to his parents, all the moments that were stolen from him, and how fate, ill fortune, or the malevolence of one man had conspired to leave him utterly alone.

Elliot parked on the lane and jogged towards the cottage with his hood up, trying to shield himself from the worst of the rain. He pushed open the creaking gate and hurried up the drive. The dead house exuded loss. There were times when Elliot wondered whether he should have it torn down, but now he thought there was no need. The years and the elements would do the job. The windows were intact, but the pointing in the brickwork was crumbling and coming away in places. Any paint had been attacked by the seasons and was faded and flaked, and there were splits in all the door and window frames.

Elliot walked around the back of the house and took out the keys he'd retrieved from Cynthia's – his – kitchen, but he didn't need them. When he reached the back door, he saw it was ajar.

Where else would a recently released prisoner go? Elliot asked himself.

Something had told him Ben would come here. He prayed the man was still inside. A confrontation was overdue.

He pushed the door and crept into the damp utility room. He entered the large kitchen and found only empty units, a rusting Aga and the ghosts of his past, bubbling memories of the weird lectures Ben used to deliver over hastily prepared meals of beans on toast.

Elliot went on, and moved through the rest of the house, but it was empty and there was no sign of Ben Elmys anywhere. Elliot lingered in his old bedroom at the front of the house. It had been converted into a study by one of the former tenants, but was now empty. His eyes welled up as he imagined all the family moments that were fading with time. Of his mum and dad tucking him in, reading him bedtime stories, a tender happy history being consumed by passing seconds. His strongest memories were of his months with Ben, and even they seemed faded, patchy and unreal.

There was always one interaction he could recall clearly; the night his dad had given him his mother's necklace. He pulled it from beneath his hooded top and studied it now, tracing the embossing with his fingertip. Elliot remembered how he had tried to be brave when his dad had given it to him, but once he was alone, he'd clasped the necklace and cried most of the night. He had put it on the next day and hadn't taken it off since. It was a permanent connection to his lost parents, and for all the faded memories, Elliot thought the night his father gave him the necklace was something he'd never forget. The following morning was the last time he'd ever seen the man.

Elliot went downstairs and drifted through the old dining room, and the living room, where Ben used to make him listen to weird recordings. He was about to leave when he noticed a brick by the fireplace was askew. Elliot recalled his father showing him the secret hiding place that lay beyond, and he went over and pulled the brick out. He reached into the small cubby hole and felt a piece of paper.

He unfolded it and read the distinctive typescript, as rain drummed the window.

> *Fluttering on a wind that isn't there*
> *The kite floats along the corridor*

Light beyond
Dark behind
A girl skips after it
Chasing
Hands reaching
Fingers stretched
And sprung
Ready for the moment
Hungry for the catch
Always on and on
The kite floats along
On a wind that isn't there
Hurry Harri
Your time has come

Elliot's stomach knotted, and his heart raced. He knew where Ben Elmys was going.

Harriet Kealty was in grave danger.

Chapter 37

Harri loved the morning briefings. Every time she stood in front of the men and women she commanded, it reminded her of how far she'd come. There had been a time in the distant past when she'd thought her career was over, but the discovery of the video had seen her reinstated. Powell had taken early retirement after questions were raised about his failure to properly investigate the incident, and his role in Harri's dismissal, and after a year as his interim replacement, Harri got his job permanently. She'd been running the serious crimes unit for more than ten years, and her stewardship had nudged their clearance rate up by a couple of points.

'Blues are expecting trouble at the Stoke match on Saturday, but I want everyone to stay focused on the Heinemann investigation. We need to find him and bring him in,' she said. 'Let's go people.'

It was her trademark sign-off, something she'd borrowed from an old American TV show.

The briefing broke up and she slipped out of the room before her subordinates. She crossed the detective pool and went into what had once been Powell's office, but was now very much hers. She shut the door as her team went back to their desks and the day's hubbub started.

She sat in her high-backed chair and turned to look at the

jagged rooftops of Hanley, which stretched into the distance on the other side of her large window. A brooding sky hung over the city, and flecks of drizzle streaked the glass. It was a miserable day, but this was her home, and the familiar scene brought her contentment, if not happiness.

She had the job, which kept her intellectually stimulated and busy, and that was a lot more than most people could hope for. But she still had a gap in her life, which she tried not to think about. Sometimes when she was out and saw couples holding hands, or families with children, she couldn't help wonder what was wrong with her, and why, after all these years, she hadn't been able to find someone to love her.

Her depth of focus shifted, and she caught sight of her ghostly reflection in the pane. She had aged well, despite the stress of the job, and thought she was still reasonably attractive, but other than a few brief physical relationships, she had lived a solitary life.

She often thought back to the Elmys investigation, to the white-hot feelings of love she'd had for him. No one could ever hope to measure up to that profound emotion, but he'd ruined her. She could never trust anyone again. Her mind sometimes wandered to the sour old woman who lived in Barmouth with her dog. At the time, Harri had sworn she would never end up like – what was her name? Abbott? Allen – Margery Allen, that was it. But now, as the years had ground down her optimism, Harri had to admit a solitary end was a distinct possibility. And if that was the worst life had to throw at her, it wouldn't be so bad. She, too, could buy a dog and do lots of fast walking.

Harri exorcized her melancholic thoughts with a sigh and turned to face her desk. The job was all the comfort she

needed for now, and her morning routine after the briefing was a ten-minute trawl through her email inbox. As she
brought her computer to life, she noticed the post had come
early. There was a small parcel in her tray.

She examined it and found a typed name and address
label, but no stamp. She tore away the brown packing paper
to reveal a white cardboard box. She removed the lid. The
inside of the box was padded with dense grey precision-cut
foam and at the centre was a beautiful crystal cube about four
inches wide. At the heart of the cube was a two-inch glass
ball filled with what looked like stars. It was shimmering as
though it contained a whole galaxy. The ball was like a living
gem. Harri had the vague sense she'd seen something like it
before, but couldn't remember where.

She checked the box and packaging, but found no note or
any trace of who'd sent her such a beautiful gift. She would
ask Marcus, the guy who ran the internal mail, to see if there
had been a delivery slip. In the meantime, she put the cube
on her desk, next to the well-thumbed copy of *Happiness:
A New Way of Life*. She kept the book front and centre, to
remind herself and the detectives who worked for her that in
the hands of the right investigator, even the smallest clue, the
most tenuous thread could have far-reaching consequences.

Chapter 38

Elliot followed the police officer up a flight of stairs. He noticed the man's shoes were scuffed and worn, a far cry from the high shine he'd imagined were part of a regulation uniform. The officer swiped a keycard over a reader and unlocked a glass door that opened onto a large office. Elliot trailed the uniformed officer across the space, aware he was being watched by the men and women at their desks.

'This is the serious crime unit,' the officer explained.

Elliot nodded and waited while the man knocked on the door to an office. He could see Harriet Kealty through blinds that hung on the other side of a glass partition.

She nodded, then the officer came out and led Elliot into Harri's office.

A window took up most of the exterior wall and offered a view of the rain-soaked city. Two chairs faced a desk, behind which sat Harriet Kealty, now Detective Chief Inspector Kealty, according to the plaque in front of her.

'Thanks, Mason,' Harri said, and the officer withdrew and closed the door. 'Have a seat,' she suggested. 'It's been a long time, Elliot.'

He took one of the chairs by her desk.

'How have you been?' she asked.

She hadn't changed much. Ben used to talk about her and

how beautiful she was, and time had done little to dim her looks. Elliot could understand the attraction and, despite their age difference, felt himself drawn to her. He remembered feeling nothing but hostility towards her because Ben had told him she would eventually split them up, but over the years he'd realized she was just trying to bring an evil man to justice and she'd put herself in harm's way to do so. She was brave and selfless.

He cringed at the memory of the last time he'd seen Harriet Kealty outside the courtroom, the day Ben had been sentenced. He'd been horrible to her.

'I've been well, thanks,' he replied.

'And Mrs Hughes?' Harri asked.

He frowned. 'She passed away a couple of years ago.'

'I'm sorry to hear that.'

'Thank you. She was a good woman, and very kind to me,' Elliot remarked. 'I miss her.' And he did, but not like he missed his parents. Their loss was a festering wound that would never heal.

They sat quietly for a moment, listening to the muted sounds of the detectives beyond the partition.

'Did you know Ben Elmys has been released?' Elliot asked.

'No,' Harri replied. He sensed her sudden concern. 'Has it been . . . it can't . . . where has all the time gone?'

'He sent me letters from prison every week. I never read them. Some went straight in the bin, others were gathered for a ceremonial burning,' Elliot revealed. 'He came to Oxford yesterday. Hand delivered one.'

He produced the envelope and gave it to her.

' "If you'd read my letters, you'd know it's time. The past has caught up with you. Your future is fated," ' he recited as

Harri read the letter. 'I haven't seen him for eleven years, but I know him and I know he's planning something.'

'I can have a word with Thames Valley Police, have them check on you,' Harri suggested.

'I'm not worried about me,' Elliot said. 'I'm worried about you. I look back on my childhood, and my memories of my parents are marred by Ben Elmys. He was always hanging around. He's an obsessive. Those months I lived with him, he wouldn't stop talking about you. He wrote poems for you. Said it helped him cope with things. He said you would betray him, but that he would forgive you. He said he'd complete you, heal you, and he dreamed you and he would spend eternity together. It was your destiny to leave this world, that's what he'd say.'

Elliot saw his words had shaken Harri and he felt guilty for making her afraid, but she needed to know the truth if she was going to protect herself. 'I found this in the cottage.' He pulled the poem from his pocket and handed it over.

Harri read in silence until she got to the last couplet.

'"Hurry Harri, your time has come,"' she read. 'When did you find this?'

'Today,' Elliot replied. 'He left it somewhere only I would look.'

'He's served half his sentence and will have been released on probation. I'll call his probation officer and find out where he's living. I can send a couple of officers round to see what he's up to. Let him know he's being watched,' Harri suggested.

She rearranged some papers on her desk while searching for her phone, and revealed an object Elliot recognized. He looked at it in disbelief.

'Where did you get that?' he asked, pointing to the galaxy

of stars shimmering inside the sphere that was contained within the crystal cube.

'It came in the post today.'

'It's from him,' Elliot said.

'What? No.'

'I'm telling you it's from him.' Elliot picked it up and studied it reverently. The light inside the sphere ebbed and flowed as though it was alive.

'I thought I dreamed it,' he said.

'Dreamed what?'

'When you've lost faith, and all seems broken, the last beacon of hope will break the rock of despair,' Elliot whispered, eyes still fixed on the sphere.

'Why do I recognize that?' Harri asked.

'It was on the iPod he made me listen to as a kid. Said it was training, but it was just nonsense, the mad ramblings of a lunatic.'

'What was he training you for?' Harri asked. 'What was the secret?'

Elliot wavered. What did it matter after all these years? Ben was never going to honour his part of the deal, so why should he keep the man's confidence?

'Come on,' Harri said. 'You almost told me that day at Longhaven.'

Elliot was about to answer, but something inside tugged the words out of his mouth. Desperation? Hope? Even after all he'd experienced, he couldn't bring himself to betray their secret bond. It meant too much to him.

'Is he your father?' Harri asked. 'Were he and your mother having an affair?' She looked at the ball in the cube. 'Is that how he poisoned her? Is that why he sent it to me? Is that Cobalt 60?'

'I don't think so,' Elliot replied. 'But I think it is the key to the secret.'

'Which is?'

'I can't tell you. Not until I see where this thing leads.'

He started for the door.

Harri got to her feet. 'You're not leaving with that. It belongs to me.'

'Fine. I think we're meant to go together,' Elliot replied. He couldn't believe what he was holding, and kept looking at the ball as though it might suddenly disappear.

'Meant to?' Harri asked. 'If you think I'm walking into a trap set by a crazy—'

Elliot cut her off. 'Come with me. Come with me, and I promise I'll tell you the secret before the day is out. Come with me and by sundown you'll know why this man has such a hold over me.'

Chapter 39

Elliot wouldn't tell Harri where they were going. He drove them out of Hanley on the Leek Road, which took them into the rolling hills north-east of the city. The rain stopped, but the grey sky shifted and swirled as though the clouds were being pummelled by an angry god.

'Did he ever talk about your parents?' Harri asked as they came to the outskirts of Leek.

Elliot nodded. 'All the time. He was constantly telling me what good people they were. How they didn't deserve what happened.'

'Did they ever find your mum's body?' Harri immediately regretted asking when she saw the flash of anguish on Elliot's face. 'I'm sorry. That was insensitive of me.'

'No. They never did,' he replied.

They drove through the centre of town in silence, passing the old antique shops and takeaways that lined the route. They turned right onto Buxton Road, and were soon in open countryside again.

'He spent a lot of his time talking about you,' Elliot recalled. 'You were an obsession.'

'We dated for a while. I thought I loved him, but when I started investigating him it got weird,' Harri confessed. 'Scary even.'

'Did you ever get married?' Elliot asked.

'We could both do with sensitivity training.' Harri smiled ruefully. 'No, I didn't.'

'He always said you wouldn't. He told me you were destined to be together. If not in this life, then in the next,' Elliot revealed.

Harri shuddered. It was the kind of talk she'd heard from unhinged lovers, stalkers, and serial killers and she didn't feel good about this man being at large. She hadn't thought about him for years, but it all came flooding back: their dates, the feeling of completeness she got being with him, the pain of the break-up, the night he'd cornered her in the lift, the strange poems, the walk on the ridge the day the social workers came to assess Elliot.

'Did he think I was pining for him?' Harri asked angrily. 'A man who was responsible for one death and probably murdered at least one other.'

'You said he was responsible for one death. Do you mean Sabih Khan?' Elliot asked. He hesitated before adding, 'What happened that night?'

Harri didn't answer.

'I dream about it sometimes,' Elliot said. 'I see them fighting. Sometimes he kicks out at your friend. Sometimes your friend just stumbles back and falls over the edge.'

Harri flushed with shame. Her skin burned with the sudden exposure of the past. She'd almost forgotten this young man had been there that night as a child.

'What really happened?' Elliot asked.

Harri took a deep breath. 'I don't know,' she confessed. 'I really don't. I was angry. Upset I'd lost my friend. I'm not sure what I saw any more.'

'Your testimony sealed his fate.'

'I know, but if he was innocent, why did he confess and plead guilty at the last minute?'

'It's like I told you that day outside the court. He didn't want me taking the stand. He changed his plea to protect me, so I wouldn't have to testify,' Elliot replied. 'What did you really see?'

'I thought . . . I don't know what I saw, but I thought he needed to be punished.'

Harri had given Ben all the motivation he ever needed to hate her. It was her testimony that had locked him away for eleven years.

Elliot frowned. 'When I was a kid, he seemed to be right about everything. I believed in him. Some beliefs are hard to shake, no matter how old you get. You know monsters aren't real, but when it's dark and you hear a strange noise, what's the first thing that springs to mind? It's never the mundane, is it? We always go back to our basic beliefs, no matter how irrational. The creature under the bed.'

Harri looked down at the galaxy sphere inside the crystal cube. It was resting on her lap on the copy of *Happiness: A New Way of Life*. She'd brought the book with them to avoid having to touch the cube in case it was toxic.

'What is this thing?' Harri asked.

Elliot looked at it, but didn't reply.

'What if we're wrong?' he asked a few moments later. 'What if he was telling the truth? What if he's a good man?'

'He can't be,' Harri protested. 'He can't be good.'

'But what if he is? What then? What does that say about us?'

Harri didn't like the question, but she hated the answer even more. She refused to voice it, and the two of them went on in silence.

Chapter 40

Harri had assumed they were driving out to the cottage, but they passed the lane that led up to Hen Cloud and Longhaven, and continued along the Buxton Road.

'Where are you taking me?' she asked.

Elliot gave her a grim look but didn't reply. She knew the answer the moment he turned left onto the narrow track that led to the forest where Sabih had died. Her stomach stung with the release of nervous acid, and she realized how stupid she'd been. There was no guarantee these men weren't working together. It was very possible Elliot had been indoctrinated as a child – there was no telling where his true loyalties lay. Had she been lured here for revenge?

'Pull over,' she said. 'I want to get out.'

Elliot ignored her. 'The night your friend died, after we ran away, Ben took me somewhere. I was in a mess, and to this day I'm not sure what was real and what was nightmare. I was just a child. I'd seen a man die. My parents were dead. My whole life felt like a bad dream. He took me to despair.'

'Pull over,' Harri repeated as Elliot's little car barrelled along the bumpy track. 'I said, pull over.'

He looked at her in puzzlement. 'What? Why? You don't think . . .' he trailed off. 'I would never hurt you.'

Harri wasn't reassured. The distant look in his eyes, his tone of voice – she was reminded of Ben.

'Please,' she said. 'Stop the car, Elliot. I'll come back here properly with a team of officers.'

The track was much more overgrown than the first time she'd driven it, and thick branches whipped at the windscreen, creating an ominous, irregular beat.

'I can't,' Elliot said. 'It has to be the two of us.'

Harri saw the shimmer of tears in his eyes, which did not reassure her. He seemed in a state of distress, and she was trapped in the small car with him.

'He told me,' Elliot continued. 'He told me I'd be the one who'd show you the truth. The place we went that night, after he snatched me and we ran. The place he takes me to in my dreams, he calls it the rock of despair.'

Harri looked down at the cube and thought back to the words Elliot had spoken in her office: the last beacon of hope will break the rock of despair. She'd heard them when she'd broken into Longhaven and listened to Elliot's iPod.

'At least let me call for support,' she suggested.

'For what?' Elliot asked as they drove further into the ancient forest. 'You don't trust me. You're worried I'm working with him and that we've lured you out here for revenge? Is that it?'

His tone was uneven, and Harri was concerned about upsetting him further, so she let her silence speak for her.

'Trust me. I've grown up hating this man. If I was going to take revenge on you for anything, it would be for failing to find out whether he had anything to do with my parents' deaths.'

He paused.

'But I have no desire for revenge. I just want to know the truth. It's the only way I can lay the past to rest and move on with my life. I need to be free of this man and the nightmares he's given me. I just have to find a way beyond what he did to me and my family.'

Elliot's pain was evident, and Harri almost reached out to comfort him.

'You wanted to come,' he said. 'I didn't force you. You came of your own choice, but if you really want me to stop, I will.'

He looked troubled, but Harri didn't believe he was dangerous.

'Do you want me to stop?' he asked, and when she didn't respond, he said, 'I don't think you do. I think you're just like me. You want to know what this man has done. You want to know what he really is.'

Harri nodded. He was right. Even after all these years, she was still desperate for the truth.

Chapter 41

The difference between life and death is a single step, Harri thought as she stood at the very edge of the cliff and peered into the ravine.

She remembered being afraid to look down after Sabih had fallen. Perhaps age had hardened her, or maybe she was less concerned by the prospect of her own death and was untroubled by the thought she might follow her friend. She could picture him now, his body on the mud-covered rocks below, broken, twisted and lifeless.

A step, a breath, a heartbeat – such transient, insignificant things were all that stood between life and death, separating light from endless night. She looked at the cube she carried on the book. She held it like a tray, and for a moment she thought about dropping it so it would smash on the very spot Sabih had fallen.

'I don't think you need to hold it like that,' Elliot said, and she glanced over her shoulder to see him smiling uncertainly. 'I don't think it's dangerous. I can carry it if you like.'

Harri shook her head. She felt there should be some memorial to mark the place where her friend lost his life, but she couldn't bring herself to drop the cube, so she stepped away from the edge. She took the cube in her left hand and slipped the book into her coat pocket.

'We should find the way down,' Elliot said, and he started searching the undergrowth a short distance from where Harri was standing. 'Ben brought me back here the night Sabih Khan died, after you and all the police and ambulance people had gone.'

'It's over here,' she told him.

She walked past him and pushed through the bushes until she found the first stone step. She would never forget her journey down to Sabih's body. It had been a descent into Hell.

They walked the old weathered steps, following countless others who'd worn away the stone over what might have been centuries. Who built the steps – and why – were secrets lost to time, but they had clearly been constructed long ago.

Elliot hesitated at the bottom and got his bearings.

'I think about that night. About what I could have done differently,' Harri said. She looked at the spot where she'd found Sabih's body. 'If I hadn't shouted his name, would he still be alive?'

'Would Ben be dead?' Elliot wondered.

They considered their questions silently, while the leaves rustled high above them, and an unseen stream babbled over rocks some distance away.

'I don't think any of us could have done anything differently,' Elliot said. 'We all make mistakes. We have regrets, and sometimes we do things we think are right, but time makes fools of us all. Our intentions are good, our outcomes bad.'

Harri nodded. She seemed to have had more than her share of bad outcomes, but Sabih's death was by far the worst.

'It's this way,' Elliot said.

He walked past the spot where Sabih had been found, and moved into a narrow gully. Harri followed, treading carefully to avoid slipping on wet rocks. They went through a four-foot gash that looked as though it had been etched in the rock by ice many thousands of years ago. The walls of the slabs on either side were sheer and tall, and Harri started to feel claustrophobic as they went on. The cut appeared to come to a dead end, but there was a dogleg turn that went off to the west. Elliot started down it and Harri took a deep breath and followed.

'Where are we going?'

'To the rock of despair,' he replied, as though that explained everything.

The gorge they were in was perhaps two feet wide, and the ground sloped down, sinking lower and lower, so the tops of the cliffs loomed higher and higher above them. The gorge narrowed and they had to turn sideways to squeeze through.

'What happens if we get stuck?' Harri asked as they edged on.

'I guess we stay here until we lose weight,' Elliot replied with a dark smile.

Another seemingly dead end, but this time Harri spied a tiny opening at the bottom of the rock face. Elliot dropped to his belly and crawled inside.

'Come on,' he said. His voice echoed out of the opening as his feet vanished into what looked like a stone mouth.

Harri's heart pounded and her palms grew moist as she dropped onto her front. She clasped the cube in her left hand and used her elbows to drag herself into the small aperture.

'How did he find this place?' she asked as she moved into darkness. She wanted to hear another voice to know she wasn't alone.

'I think it's something of a local secret,' Elliot replied from some unseen place. 'My dad brought me here ages ago. When I was little.'

Harri tried not to think of the millions of tons of rock suspended above her, or the ease with which she could be entombed and never found, and instead focused on following the sound of Elliot's dragging feet. She moved into complete darkness and for a moment couldn't see even the faintest outlines of form or shape, but the void didn't last long and soon she was rewarded with dim light. She crawled into Elliot's shoes.

'Are you OK?' she asked, fearing he was stuck.

'Yes. Just give me a second,' he replied.

He hauled himself out, and light suddenly illuminated the tiny tunnel. He leaned into the mouth and said, 'This is it. We're here.'

He helped Harri pull herself out of the opening. They were at the bottom of a well. It was a rough circle, perhaps twenty feet in diameter, cut into a solid rock cliff whose top was some two hundred feet above them. The walls were slick with run-off from an unseen stream, and they were so deep there was nothing but lichen on the surfaces. The only notable thing in the well was a nine-foot diameter boulder that was pressed against the north wall.

'This place is called Lud's Church. Puritans used to come here to worship in secret to avoid persecution. Legend says the authorities dropped this boulder from the top of the well to block the entrance to Pilgrims Cave, so they called it the Rock of Despair because it prevented them from being near their god,' Elliot said. 'Give me the cube.'

Harri hesitated, before handing it over.

Elliot looked at it reverently.

'Now we see whether my dreams were real. Whether the promise can be kept.'

Elliot threw the cube at the boulder, and the sudden movement made Harri flinch. It struck the huge rock and shattered, and shards of crystal glinted as they flew everywhere. The glass ball broke next, smashing into a multitude of tiny pieces. The stars inside scattered over the rock, but rather than simply glitter on the craggy surface, the most marvellous thing happened.

The stars unfolded to create tiny hexagons of energy, and the hexes multiplied, spreading across the surface of the rock to form a mesh of shining geometric shapes. When the mesh was complete and the rock was encased, there was a flash of energy and the rock and shimmering hexagons vanished to reveal a large cave mouth.

Harri looked at Elliot in astonishment. If he shared her disbelief, he didn't show it. Instead, he seemed at peace. Were the stars some kind of caustic or corrosive substance? Was that how Ben and David had disposed of Beth's body?

Harri was startled when Elliot grabbed her arm and pulled her forward into the yawning cave mouth.

'Come on,' he said. 'We don't have long.'

She allowed herself to be led into the darkness.

'Move,' he urged, pulling her further inside.

Harri couldn't understand why he was so concerned, but then to her dismay there was a thunderous crack and a great tremor, as though reality was being rent asunder, and the huge boulder materialized, covering the cave mouth and plunging them into total darkness.

Chapter 42

Harri was stunned. She could hear Elliot beside her, but she couldn't discern even the faintest shape.

'What just happened?' she finally managed.

'I'm not sure.'

'I've got a torch on my phone.'

'There's no need,' Elliot told her.

Harri heard him moving in the darkness, and soon afterwards there was the click and thud of a large switch locking into place, and two lines of LED lights came on, illuminating a long tunnel that ran deep beneath the cliff. The lights reminded Harri of a runway, and she couldn't shake the feeling they would take her somewhere terrible.

'What is this place?' she asked.

'Ben brought me here the night DS Khan died,' Elliot replied. 'I was so upset I wasn't sure what was real and what wasn't, but he said he wanted me to see it, that it was important I knew it existed. I came here once, about a year after I'd moved in with Mrs Hughes. I wanted to see if it was real, but I couldn't get past the rock. For years, I thought I dreamed this place, but it seems not.'

Elliot started down the tunnel, and Harri followed. The LED lights were attached to bare stone that had been worn smooth, perhaps by an underground river. They were connected to each other by thick cabling, and at an interval of every five fittings the cable ran into a glowing cylinder about six inches long and one in diameter. The cylinders were filled with what looked like the same stars that had consumed the boulder. Harri touched the nearest cylinder and felt a gentle warmth.

'It's some kind of power source,' she said. 'Did he build this? If so . . . why?'

'I don't know. The night we came, he said he had to hide something, that the police would be coming for him,' Elliot said.

They continued along the tunnel for another sixty feet, and Harri bristled with nervous energy that intensified with every step. They rounded a bend, and the tunnel stretched ahead about twenty feet or so, but the lights ended abruptly and whatever lay beyond was shrouded in darkness.

'What's in there?' Harri asked.

'I don't know,' Elliot replied. 'This is as far as I got. He made me wait out here while he went inside.'

They moved forward tentatively. Harri traced the fingers of her right hand along the smooth rock that formed the tunnel walls. Moisture gathered in the lines left by her fingertips, and droplets ran down the wall in her wake. Watching them distracted her from the looming darkness, and the sense Ben Elmys was lurking in there, ready to do her violence. Then, the damp stone was gone, replaced by black air.

'We need a torch,' she said, reaching for her phone.

As if in reply, more lights came on, illuminating a chamber the size of a large church. There were many rocky shelves and outcrops in the vaulted space, and the furthest recesses were lost to shadow.

'Motion sensor,' Elliot observed, pointing to a device fitted to the wall near the tunnel mouth.

Harri noticed a large television screen positioned on a stone plinth off to their right, and she moved towards it. As she approached, the screen flickered to life. Elliot joined her.

'Hello, Elliot,' Ben Elmys said as his image appeared on screen. 'Harriet. Thank you both for coming.'

Ben did not look like the same man she'd sent to prison. The eleven years he'd spent inside seemed to have left deep marks. His eyes, which had once been so filled with fire, were subdued and thoughtful. His brown hair was flecked grey, and his face was etched with the marks of sorrow. He was still handsome, and if anything, the loss of his manic edge seemed to make him more attractive, more human. He seemed in spirit more like the man Harri had first met and fallen in love with.

'Is this a video link?' Elliot asked. He shouted into the cave. 'This isn't funny, Ben. Come out. Tell us how to move the rock. You know we're trapped here.'

Harri felt a rush of panic. The thought hadn't occurred to her until Elliot spoke, but he was right. There was no way they could move that huge boulder.

'You still don't really trust me, do you, Elliot?' Ben asked on screen. 'Do you think I'd ever bring you somewhere that wasn't in your best interest?'

'Why don't you come and talk to us properly?' Harri asked tersely.

'Harriet. Sweet Harriet. If I was here, I would come to you, but I'm long gone.'

'Then how can you answer me?' Harri asked.

'Stop playing games, Ben,' Elliot said.

'Does your phone work in here?' Harri asked, checking her device. She didn't have any signal.

Elliot looked at his and shook his head.

'I know this is difficult for you both, but it's better this way,' Ben said on screen.

'Better for who?' Harri asked, her temper rising.

'For Elliot,' Ben replied. 'And for you, Harriet. If you'll indulge me, I want to tell my story. When I'm finished, you'll understand everything.'

Chapter 43

'I was thirty-two when I came home, eleven years older than you are now, Elliot. I came back for the job at Keele. Dr Abiola had heard about the particle work I'd been doing in Sydney, and had interviewed me by phone, and then I did a panel by video conference.

'They must have liked what they heard, because they offered me a research position and lectureship with a view to tenure if everything went well.

'It was raining the first time I arrived at the university. I turned up in the wrong place, the main administration block, near that weird modern church and the library that looks like it belongs in small-town America.

'I didn't realize Dr Abiola and her team were based in the science park. I got soaked running back to the little Polo I used to drive then, and arrived late for my first day, looking like a drowned cat.

'Dr Abiola was very gracious. She's always been far too polite to confront people directly. She showed me to her office and I used her private bathroom to dry off. Afterwards, she took me on a tour of the faculty, and I met your mother. She was standing at a bench in her lab. She was wearing a tinted visor and was busy fixing a circuit board.

'I thought she was the most beautiful person I'd ever seen,

and was so moved by the moment I couldn't speak. I think Dr Abiola inferred I was infatuated with Beth, but she was wrong. There's no way she could understand the profound connection I felt for your mother, nor why it mattered so much to me.

'"Beth Jennings, I'd like you to meet Ben Elmys," Dr Abiola said. "Dr Elmys has joined us from Sydney."

'Beth shook my hand and I felt charged by her touch.

'"When I heard you were coming, I took a look at some of your work," she revealed. "Your theories on block determinism are fascinating. The idea our fates are set seems quite bleak, don't you think?"

'"Dr Elmys isn't here for his philosophy," Dr Abiola said. "We're interested in his particle work."

'I must have been looking at your mother like a love-struck suitor, because she smiled at me uncomfortably and said, "Are you OK, Dr Elmys?"

'I snapped out of my daydream and nodded sheepishly.

'"Please call me Ben," I replied. "I'm fine, thanks. You're too kind. What are you working on?"

'I knew, of course, but I wanted to hear her speak. It brought me such pleasure simply listening to her voice.

'"It's a side project I'm trying to finish in my spare time. A holographic projection system so we can get inside complex machines and spot problems before we build them. See how they work, what their tolerances are."

'"Sounds fascinating," I replied. "How far off are you?"

'"A ways," she replied.

'"I've been researching optical diffusion as part of my work," I said. "I might be able to help."

'"I'd like that," Beth responded.

' "Well, you two don't need me to help you get along," Dr Abiola scoffed.

'It was then that your father came into the lab. Some people think we were rivals for your mother's affection, but that's a lie. We liked each other from the moment we met, and seeing him made me just as happy as being with your mother. I finally felt I'd found people who understood me, who were on my wavelength. I'm fairly certain your parents felt the same way too.

' "I didn't realize you were busy," David said. "You must be Benjamin Elmys. I've read your stuff. It's next level."

'He offered me his hand and I shook it with nothing but genuine warmth. I looked from David to Beth and back again, and for the first time in what seemed like an age, I felt as though I was somewhere I belonged.

'Maybe truth exists on different levels, and perhaps they could sense the deepest of all truths; that we were always destined to be together. They never said anything, at least not to me, but I like to think they knew.'

Chapter 44

'From that moment on, we were inseparable. I didn't know anyone else in the area, so your mother and father sort of adopted me. We became friends. More than that, really. We were family. I was there when your father picked out their engagement ring. I was best man at their wedding. I went with them for the second viewing of the cottage that was to become your home. If they ever tired of me, they never showed it. They welcomed me into their home like a child, or maybe a pet, I never could tell.

'They looked after me with all the kindness I could ever ask for, and I tried to repay it, but no matter what I did, it never seemed enough. I hope they took something from our relationship, though. I like to think they enjoyed my company and that there was a sense of completeness, the feeling that together, we somehow made a whole. They gave me something I hadn't felt for a very long time, not since I lost my own parents. They made me feel welcome. They gave me somewhere to belong.

'And then you were born, and I was almost as proud and amazed as David and Beth. I mean, think about it. As a species, we can choose to create life. We can breathe being into a collection of cells and from such simple biology emerges creatures who can hold the universe in their minds. We can dream the stars, picture the beginning and end of time, relive countless histories, both real and imagined. My path means I'm unlikely to ever have children of my own and I doubt I'll ever get to find out whether I would have made a good dad.

'I hope our time together wasn't too much of a disappointment, Elliot, and that you'll forgive my failings. I only ever wanted the best for you.

'I was there for your birth. I wasn't allowed in theatre, but I was waiting in the corridor for news from your father. I almost burst with joy when he came out and told me everything was OK. I held you soon after you were brought up to the ward, and I'm not ashamed to say I cried. David and Beth were perplexed, but they humoured me. They couldn't understand what I was feeling. Our connection coursed through me, it made my soul shiver and I knew the moment I saw you that we had great things to achieve together. You were so tiny and perfect and I marvelled at the miracle of life and the magic of the universe bringing us together.

'I've known you your whole life. Every step, every word, every fall, every tear, every smile, I feel it all so deeply. And your parents could see that love, which is why they asked me to be your guardian in the event anything happened to them. How could I say no?

'I remember the day we went to their lawyer's office. It was a sombre occasion. They joined the lawyer in cracking jokes and making light of the need for such preparations. They were young and healthy and your mother was so strong as you squirmed in her arms.

'I was the only one who wasn't smiling and joking. I was the only one wrapped in a cloud.

'Because I knew what had to happen.

'Beth was diagnosed when you were seven. They tried to keep it from you to begin with, but eventually she became too sick, and it became too much to hide, so you finally knew what I'd known sitting in that lawyer's office all those years ago: she was fated to die.'

Chapter 45

Readers, Ben has his version of what happened, but it's tainted by his role in events. I'm Beth's husband and Elliot's father, and I think it important you hear the truth from me.

Is it the whole truth?

What does that even mean?

Can truth be broken into fragments and parcelled out to create nuggets of belief? If parts of the truth are torn off, does it become a lie? How badly does it have to be dismembered before it is sufficiently disfigured for the transformation to take place?

We'll leave Elliot and Harri listening to Ben in the cave. He talks to Harri about the walk they took along the ridge, and the night he saw her at the mosque, and tells her and Elliot the story I'm about to tell you. I will give you my version of events. Since I am the author of this book and believe readers deserve completeness, I will endeavour to make it the whole truth or as close to completeness as is humanly possible. Any disfigurement will be an oversight. It is not my intention to mislead, even if the truth makes you think less of me. I hope it won't, but I suspect that at least some of you will hate me for what I've done.

Chapter 46

Beth was diagnosed when our son, Elliot, was seven.

Ben waited in reception with Elliot while we discussed Beth's treatment plan with her consultant, Dr Kelly Jackson. He kept our son company while we talked through cold hard alternatives with the doctor who was to be our guide through this horrific new reality. People like to imagine cancer patients as brave fighters, but I know from bitter experience some of them are just as scared and emotionally traumatized as one might imagine them to be. Beth and I spent many tearful nights trying to rationalize the ill fortune that had touched us out of so many billions. We wanted to understand why it was our fate to suffer, but of course there are no good answers to those kind of questions, so over time you learn it's pointless to dwell on the why, and simply get on with the how.

We tried not to live in the negative, but faced with such uncertainty it is impossible not to explore every outcome. We pictured life without her and as her condition worsened, we discussed the things she wanted of me if she was taken from our family. She was worried about Elliot and wanted my assurance he'd be raised to be a happy, loving, kind, consider-ate man. She wasn't concerned with ambition or attainment. For her the only measure of success in life is happiness. She made me promise I'd do my best to make that my priority, and of course I gave my word. It pains me to know I broke that promise, and not a day goes by that I don't regret my failure. I did the one thing that would guarantee Elliot would never be happy. I left him, and it is my eternal shame that I can't reach out to him and explain why. I can seek absolution in this book, but he will never read it. You might hate me, you might pity me, but your thoughts amount to nothing when all I want is my son's forgiveness.

The leadership team at the university were good, and gave me all the time I needed to support Beth. Ben was with us day and night, running errands, looking after Elliot, constantly mothering us as though we were his children. He was without a doubt the best friend we could have had, which is one of the reasons why the truth was so hard to deal with. If he hadn't lied to us –

I can hardly bring myself to imagine the alternative.

We raised money for a new T-Cell therapy from America, and I'll never forget the night we held a candlelit vigil outside Longhaven. Hundreds of people came, and most of the university staff, many students, and much of Leek turned out to support us and share what they could afford. I was so emotional I could hardly talk, and Ben had to tell everyone what the night meant to us. He spoke in touching terms about Beth, and I could see the love shining in his eyes. Over the next few weeks, we made the $250,000 target.

She lived eighteen months longer than the original prognosis, but finally she was taken from us.

Ben and I were with her the night she died. She had a private room in the Royal Stoke Hospital, and we took turns to sit vigil. Towards the end, neither of us could bear to leave, so one would sleep in a chair in the corner of the room, while the other sat with Beth and held her hand.

I was sleeping when Ben woke me to say Dr Jackson thought it was nearly time. I've written millions of words, but I still cannot find a way to describe the emptiness that spread from my core and engulfed me. Those words don't do it justice. None can. It is a visceral experience beyond the confines of language. These words on the page are intended to evoke emotion. They connect my brain to yours, but sometimes they aren't enough and I have to ask you to reach for experience, to trawl the depths of memory to understand how it felt.

If you've lost someone you love, you will know. If not, I envy you your innocence. It is an anguish so deep, so primitive, it burns, but this animalistic sense of loss is combined with a consciousness that understands the notion of time and can conceptualize the permanent absence that will blight the rest of our lives. It is our unique curse to grieve for what was and lament what might have been. All those shared moments never to be realized. A son motherless. A husband robbed of the light by which he steered.

I went to her bed, and Ben and Dr Jackson stepped back to give me the pretence of privacy. Beth was on the edge of consciousness, but I like to think she knew it was me who held her hand at the end. Her fingers were as light as dry twigs and her skin was paper white, almost translucent. Blue veins lurked beneath the surface, transporting broken blood back to her ailing heart with each erratic beat. We'd been warned to expect Cheyne–Stokes breathing, and her breaths grew shallower and shallower with each rise and fall of her emaciated chest, and then finally she took the breath we'd been warned about. A long draw that was different from all the rest – deep, raw, and final, as though her body was saying goodbye.

And then she stopped.

She was gone.

I cried.

I wept like never before.

I wanted whatever foulness had taken her to reach out and take me too. I had known death was coming, but it is one thing to imagine something so profound, quite another to live it. Ben and Dr Jackson led me out. I don't really remember much beyond that. They took me somewhere. Words were spoken, but I didn't hear them.

My beloved Beth was gone.

She died as I held her hand.

That's all I really remember of that night.

Chapter 47

The days and weeks that followed were some of the most difficult I've ever experienced. I spent them in a daze, but even though I was numbed by grief, it didn't stop the memory of Beth cutting me to the bone. Our home was full of pictures of the three of us. Her side of the bed still smelled of the coconut shampoo she liked. Her trainers lay in the hall, caked in mud from the last time she'd walked the ridge.

When we picture the death of a loved one, I believe we imagine the trauma, the sense of loss, the all-consuming grief, but we don't consider the relentless mundanity of life. Meals need to be cooked, and the food to make them must be purchased. I found myself breaking down in the crisp aisle in Tesco because I happened to catch sight of Beth's favourite flavour, sea salt and cider vinegar. I'd start crying while driving because the radio played a song she liked, 'Tiny Dancer' or 'Space Oddity'. Melodies of grief. Moments of bereavement. Looking back, I have no hesitation in saying I was a wreck. I wanted nothing more than to abandon my life of pain and join her.

But I couldn't. I had to be brave for Elliot. I was trapped by obligation. I had a child depending on me, and as dark as things were, I tried to keep sight of how much he needed me. I attempted to comfort him, but where I was a wreck, he was sullen and withdrawn. The death of his mother had wounded him as profoundly as it had me. I tried to reach him, but it was difficult because I found the time we spent together so very painful. I wanted to lessen his suffering, but there was nothing I could say or do, so I bumbled on, delivering a poor impression of a father.

I wonder now if I found my son painful to be around because I saw so much of her in him. He had her eyes and mouth, and the same softness of skin, and his smile always reminded me of Beth. It's a poor excuse but he was a living ghost of his mother, and I think I might have been too weak to cope with the breathing reminder.

The hospital didn't inform me they'd lost Beth's body immediately. They waited three days and finally told me after their internal investigation couldn't find any sign of her. They added anger to my emotional storm. I couldn't stop picturing Beth somewhere horrible, all alone in some rotten place. What if she was alive? What if I'd imagined her death and she was trapped somewhere, weak and desperate for my help? The loss of her body almost drove me beyond the brink, and I became obsessed with the idea she was still breathing somewhere and was calling for me. I hardly slept because my nightmares were plagued by this picture of her in need.

Somehow I managed to cling on and, over time, the nightmares faded. The hospital promised to find her, but it never did, and a month after she died, Elliot, Ben and I finally said goodbye to Beth at a small memorial we held in St Leonard Church in Ipstones. Mrs Hughes came too, because she lived so close, but we told friends and family we would have a proper funeral once the body was recovered. This was just a ceremony that would allow Elliot and me to express our grief, say

farewell, and begin the process of piecing together our shattered lives. Like repaired china vases, we would never be quite
the same, and would carry blemishes for the rest of our days,
but I owed it to Elliot to try my best to fix what had been broken.

I'd like to pretend I was the one with the strength to see
that we needed to find a new normal, but it was Ben. After
the service, we went up to the ridge and walked the ancient
rock formations behind Longhaven. We were silent for a long
time, and Elliot shuffled ahead of us with his head bowed and
his hands in his pocket, as dejected as I'd ever seen him. Had
the service finally convinced him she was never coming back?

I know I had trouble believing it. I saw her everywhere,
even in the black peaty soil around us. She'd been an avid
runner, much better than me, and we'd jogged these paths
together. I could see her now, alive with the rugged beauty of
the place, taking great enthusiastic breaths as her strong legs
propelled her along. That's how I wanted to remember her.

'She used to love running up here,' I remarked.

Ben sighed and gave a sad smile. 'I know it's hard, but
you've got to start living again. There are things you need to
do with your life.'

'What things? What matters now? I can't move on. The
memories are all we have left,' I replied pathetically. 'If we
don't stay here, in this moment, they will fade and she doesn't
deserve that. We're the only people keeping her alive. Up here.'
I tapped the side of my head, and then placed my palms over
my chest. 'And in here. The pain is unbearable, but I have to
learn to cope with it. I have to stay in this moment, because if
I move on, she'll be gone. That's how she'll die. We'll kill her
by forgetting. Each day, we'll think of her less, and soon we
won't know the sound of her voice, or the smell of her hair.

We won't be able to remember her face, she'll just be a vague shape, then an idea, a thought, and finally just a name we think fondly of. I won't do that to her.'

My voice had been rising throughout. 'I can't, Ben. Don't make us.'

Looking back, it's fair to say grief had made me mildly hysterical.

He took my arm and pulled me to a halt. We gazed at each other for a moment, both with tears in our eyes, and then he gave me a hug. We'd never been tactile, but in that moment I understood his love for me. He wanted to take my pain away.

'I know what Beth meant to you,' he said as he stepped back. 'I loved her too, but you can't lose yourself in grief. You need to get back to work. Elliot needs to go back to school.'

Elliot had stopped a short way ahead and he wheeled round at the word. 'I'm never going to school ever again. I'm never leaving Daddy. He needs my help. When I'm not with him, he cries.'

His words were like tiny daggers. He was being brave and putting on a front. He thought it was his job to look after me. That's when I knew we had to find a new way to live. I'd made a promise to Beth to do whatever I could to make Elliot happy.

It is not the job of the son to look after the father.

It is never the job of the son to look after the father.

'You have to go back to school, little man,' I said.

'No!' Elliot replied, before running away.

'Elliot,' I called after him, but he ignored me and kept going.

'All this grief isn't good for either of you,' Ben said. 'I know how much you loved her. We all did. But you need to get your lives back. Elliot needs to move on, and so do you.'

I look back on Ben's words and realize he never once lied to me. He never lied, but he never quite told the truth, and I still can't decide whether by keeping so much concealed he crossed the line into dishonesty. Did he dismember the truth? Or merely sculpt it? I don't know whether to find him guilty or if I should forgive his good intentions. I struggle, not least because it was his economy with the truth that ultimately took me from my son.

Chapter 48

That night, I had no idea what Ben was going to do to us. I went to see Elliot in his room. We hadn't spoken since he'd run off. We'd had beans on toast for dinner, eaten in silence, and he'd taken himself to bed without even saying goodnight. I wanted to try to mend some of the broken pieces of our lives, so I knocked and entered to find him lying curled up in bed. He was wearing his favourite dinosaur pyjamas, the ones he and Beth had picked out together. He had his back to me and I saw him bring his hand to his face. I'm pretty sure he was wiping his eyes.

'How are you doing, little man?' I asked.

He ignored me.

'Little man, how are you doing?' I tried again. I sat beside him and put my hand on his shoulder.

He shuddered and said, 'Bad.'

'I know it's hard, but Mummy wouldn't want to see you like this. She loved your smile, Elliot. She loved to hear you laugh. She never liked to see you sad.'

'I miss her so much, Dad,' he replied.

'Me too.'

A lump rose in my throat and I started to well up.

'Me too,' I croaked.

I sat there for a while, fighting my emotions. I can't say

how many minutes passed, but I stroked my son's shoulder, trying to reassure him. I felt him tremble, but I couldn't bring myself to look at him, because I knew the sight of his tears would destroy me. I railed against a universe that could be so cruel. Were we so important that our happiness had to be stolen? Could we not have gone unnoticed by fate?

We were insignificant creatures whose existence was of no consequence to gods or man.

What had we done to deserve this?

Even as those anguished thoughts overwhelmed me, I knew how pointless they were. Our insignificance was the very reason fate was blind to our happiness.

This was just one of those things. One of those terrible, ugly, brutal things.

'It is what it is,' say the gods, and the universe shrugs and moves on.

In a hundred years our suffering and tears and laughter and happiness will all be forgotten, replaced by another generation whose existences are equally transient and meaningless, and yet deeply meaningful and significant to them and those they love. Our ability to know we are nothing while perceiving we are everything has driven some mad, and it almost broke me during those dark days.

But it didn't. I took deep breaths and stroked my son until I felt able to continue.

'I've got something for you,' I said at last. 'I thought you might like to have this.'

I pulled Beth's silver pendant and chain from my pocket, and Elliot turned round to look. His eyes were raw and streaks of long fallen tears marked his cheeks. I almost broke down, but told myself I had to be brave for him.

'Your mum always wore it. When you were a baby, you used to play with it all the time. Here,' I said, and I leaned down and fastened it around his neck.

The silver glinted in the light of his bedside lamp. He held the pendant and studied the moon, stars and the word 'Beth' closely.

'She'll always be with you, little man,' I said, and I pulled him into a hug.

He sobbed and I did too, but I held him and stroked his back until he fell asleep.

Chapter 49

Elliot went back to school the next day. I took him on my way to work. Ben was right, we had to get back to some kind of normal, but it wasn't easy.

I held the little man's hand all the way through the car park. His village school was tiny, the sort of twee Victorian red-brick building that might have featured in a BBC costume drama, but we managed to make the distances seem vast because we walked so slowly. I don't think either us of wanted to be parted from the other. We were all we had in the world. Some of Elliot's friends passed us on the way, and they asked him to run in with them, but he didn't want to let go, and neither did I.

The school had three classrooms, a teacher and assistant for each, and a bubbly friendly head, Mrs Furnival. Of course, she knew what had happened to Beth and how hard it had hit us, and she watched us approach the entrance with a look of surprise.

'Hello, Elliot,' she said. 'Welcome back. Everyone's missed you.'

'Good morning, Mrs Furnival,' he replied flatly as he turned to me.

I dropped to his level and he threw his arms around my neck.

'See you at three,' I said. 'I love you, little man.'

'Love you too, Dad,' he replied, before going inside with his friend Asif.

'How's he doing?' Mrs Furnival asked.

'Pretty much as expected.' I felt tears coming, but I didn't want to make a scene.

'And you?' she added.

I nodded and managed to force out, 'OK. Thank you. Please take care of him.'

She gave me a sympathetic look, and I hurried along the path back to the car park. I got the now familiar glances of pity from some of the other parents, but no one stopped me. Perhaps I looked too much of a mess?

I made it back to my car and roared out of there. I cried most of the way to Keele. I can't remember what started me off, but once I got going, I kept fixating on Elliot all alone in that school. He had friends and teachers, but none of them knew him the way I did. None of them understood him or what he was going through. Only I knew that. Our grief had formed a connection so profound no other could match it. What if something happened to me? What if I lost the strength to continue? These thoughts panicked me. Despite everything, I'd never considered the new reality: I was a single parent. One doing everything once done by two.

I told myself to stop being so pathetic, that millions of people managed and that I would too.

My own brand of tough realism worked, and by the time I'd finally crossed the green hills and rich fields of Staffordshire and reached the science park, I'd stopped crying.

I pulled into my usual space in the shade of a great oak tree, and started towards the building where I worked, but something stopped me from going inside. Instead, I slumped on one of the benches that were scattered around the manicured gardens.

I sat and watched leaves tumble across grass that danced in the breeze. The blades were like little fingers reaching up to trap the errant leaves, but they couldn't be caught and rolled on, only to collect in an ugly pile in the shadow of a low wall, prisoners of the wind that had freed them. I felt there should be some significance in their journey, but my nihilism was so absolute, I couldn't be bothered to search for it. So I sat and watched the leaves tumble, taking cruel joy in the knowledge their journey would bring neither benefit, nor meaning. Just an end.

'Dr Asha? Are you OK?'

I looked up to see Angelika Beale, one of Dr Abiola's PhD students, standing over me.

'We've missed you. I was so sorry to hear about Beth.'

I smiled, but it was largely because I had to do something with my face to avoid crying at her kind words.

'Thank you,' I managed.

'Can I walk in with you?' she asked.

I hesitated. I looked at the leaves. Maybe there was meaning in them? Maybe I just had to keep going until I hit a wall?

'Sure,' I said.

I got to my feet and this relative stranger kept me company as we walked inside. She prattled on about something or other. I wasn't really listening and I think she knew that. She smiled politely when we parted, and I hurried through the building, eager to avoid other sympathetic people who might tip me over the edge.

Within minutes, I was in my office with the door locked,

looking at the daunting pile of paperwork and correspond-
ence on my desk.

The first thing I did was put the framed photograph in my
drawer. It was a picture of Beth, Elliot and me outside the
cottage, and I simply wasn't strong enough to face it. Once it
was out of sight, I took off my coat, sat in my chair, and tried
to figure out where to begin.

Chapter 50

An hour later, there was a knock at my door. I thought about pretending I wasn't in, but I heard Ben say, 'David?'

I sighed. 'Come in.'

The door opened and he entered, somewhat furtively now that I think about it.

'This doesn't feel right,' I remarked, raising my hands in a gesture of surrender. 'It's too soon.'

Ben nodded, but didn't reply. He seemed troubled, and struggled to meet my gaze. If you asked me to describe him now, I'd say he was agitated, and even though the fog of grief coloured my perception, I could sense something was wrong. He was shuffling from one foot to the other and had his eyes fixed firmly on the floor. I'd never seen him like that before.

'Are you OK?' I asked.

'Are you OK?' he countered. 'What does that even mean? Am I suicidal? Am I happy? Have I been though a personal hell?'

I thought I knew what he was talking about. 'It's not easy for any of us.'

'No, it's not,' he replied coldly.

I couldn't understand the hostility in his eyes. Not then, anyway.

'I can't think of a good way to ask this, so I'm just going to do it.'

He bit his lip and I got the sense he was in tremendous pain. The turmoil seemed to spill from him and fill the room, and for the very first time in all the years I'd known him, I was afraid of what he was going to say next.

'I . . . I don't . . .' he stammered.

He sighed and shook his head in frustration.

'What? What do you want to tell me, Ben?' I asked fearfully. If it was something bad, I wanted to hear it. I was afraid, but I needed to know. It pains me to say I went to a dark place and thought he was about to confess to an affair. 'Tell me.'

He finally looked at me, but he wasn't the man I'd known for so many years. In place of my quiet, thoughtful, true friend was someone who looked quite unhinged. I got to my feet slowly.

'What would you do to get her back?' He rattled off the words like a child.

'What would I do . . .' I trailed off.

I didn't know whether grief had finally broken him, or what was going on inside that mind of his, but I wasn't in the mood for one of his philosophical enquiries. Beth wasn't the subject of a thought experiment. I grew quite angry that he felt entitled to abuse her memory so.

'Yes. What would you do?' he said.

'What kind of question is that?' I snapped.

'One that needs to be answered,' he replied calmly. His nervous energy dissipated and was replaced by a resolve I was more familiar with. 'We both know the answer, but I need to hear you say it.'

'Anything,' I replied. I was exasperated and resented him

for prising the word from me. And I hated myself for answering, although not as much as I would in future. I should never have replied to that damned question, but I didn't know any better and I went on. 'I'd do anything. I'd sacrifice anything. I'd suffer anything,' I said with tears in my eyes. 'That a good enough answer for you?'

He looked at me unflinchingly.

'Yes,' he replied thoughtfully. 'There's something you need to see.'

Chapter 51

I followed Ben along the corridor that connected our offices. A young student I vaguely recognized passed us, and Ben waited until she was out of sight before he opened the door and led me into his office.

'Can't be too careful,' he muttered, adding to my growing concern for his state of mind.

The room was plunged into darkness when he closed the door, and I realized he'd stuck sheets of card over all the windows, blocking out the world and giving him complete privacy.

'Ben?' I said hesitantly, feeling that discomfort many experience in the presence of someone who's in the grip of acute mental illness.

What was this? Had Beth's death been too much? Did he need help?

'Wait, wait,' he replied hurriedly.

He fumbled around his desk and switched on a lamp, but it really didn't make things any better.

There were piles of paper everywhere and stacks and stacks of books. Used fast food cartons and empty cans and bottles littered the place, which had changed drastically since I'd last seen it.

'Ben, what is this?' I asked. 'What's happened?'

He hurried round the desk and opened the small cupboard beneath it.

'Were you serious?' he asked. 'Would you do anything?'

There was a mania in his eyes that frightened me, and I didn't reply. I was too busy thinking about who I could call for help. Security? Dr Abiola?

He lifted a flight case onto the desk. It was a perfect cube made of brushed aluminium. He unhooked two clasps that sealed it.

'I need to be sure,' he said. 'Were you serious?'

I felt I had to humour him. 'You know how much I loved Beth.'

He nodded and opened the lid. Inside, black laser-cut foam protected three spheres. Each of them was approximately two inches in diameter and they were filled with sparkles of light that reminded me of stars. They swirled, moving like constellations in the night sky.

'What are they?'

Ben pocketed two and grabbed the third, before approaching me.

'Whatever happens, you must do exactly as I say,' he told me.

'Ben, I don't want—' I began, but shock knocked the breath from my lungs.

Ben squeezed the sphere until it shattered. The stars spread over his hand, covering it, before multiplying and sweeping down his arm. The first stars unfolded to form hexagons of light that connected to create a mesh. I tried to back away, but he grabbed my wrist and held me tight.

'Ben,' I cried. 'Please.'

'Exactly what I say,' he repeated as the stars spread across his torso.

I tried to free myself but he held me like a vice and I watched in horror as the stars travelled up my arm, covering me. The process accelerated, and I knew I didn't have long. When Ben was covered, there was a surge of energy that illuminated the mesh, and he vanished. What was this? Why was he doing this? Was it murder? Was he killing us? I looked at the wisps of ethereal smoke that were all that was left of Ben, and felt nothing but hatred for him.

And then I, too, was gone.

Chapter 52

Everything was black as though I was in the deepest, darkest night, and for a moment I thought oblivion had taken me, but then I realized I was still breathing. I pressed my fingers into my palm and felt my digits and hands were where they should be.

'Give me a second,' Ben said.

I heard shuffling and then a click, and I was dazzled by a bright light.

My eyes adjusted. Ben stood in the same clothes he'd been wearing, black trousers and a navy blue sweater, but rather than his office, behind him loomed high steel shelving that supported bottles of bleach, soap, and other cleaning products.

I grabbed him by the collar. 'Where are we? What just happened?' I asked.

'Come on,' he said, cutting me off. 'We don't have much time.'

He opened the door to what turned out to be a cleaning supplies cupboard, and we went into the corridor beyond. I followed warily, but the moment I stepped out, I was unnerved by the familiarity of the place. The corridor was eight feet wide with a dark-grey linoleum floor, grey walls to the halfway point, a black rubber dividing bumper and white uppers and ceiling.

We were in the Royal Stoke Hospital.

'This way,' Ben said, hurrying on. 'Quickly.'

I was stunned. Speechless. He jogged back for me, grabbed my wrist, and pulled me forward.

'Come on.'

I was dazed and put up no resistance. We went through a set of ward doors and I caught sight of an exterior window. At first I didn't register what was wrong, but when I realized, my mind rejected what it was seeing.

'This isn't possible,' I remarked, gesturing at the bright street light that illuminated the darkness outside. It had been daytime only moments ago.

'We don't have time to address the limits of your understanding,' Ben said. 'We have to hurry.'

He pulled me through another set of doors into the oncology wing. I'd always found it terrifying. Not like an overblown slasher film – it was far too real for that. This was the kind of quiet place where real horror happened; people were torn from their loved ones by a foul disease that darkened the lives of everyone it touched.

I staggered on in disbelief. How had Ben done this? How were we here? We had travelled without moving. I started to question myself. Was this some sort of lucid dream? I couldn't fault my perception. I felt as though I was awake.

I'd been in this corridor many times and I'd never expected to come back, but what made my return worse was the sense of dread that Ben had done something unnatural in an attempt to achieve the impossible.

We stopped outside what had been Beth's room, a few feet

from the door. Ben looked directly at the closed-circuit security camera that hung in the top corner of the corridor. He had one of the glass spheres in his hand, and seemed to squeeze it softly. The light on the camera went out and he turned to me.

'Come on,' he said, 'Look.'

He urged me forward to the door to Beth's room. It had a narrow strip of glass cut in one side, and I looked through the window, beyond the wire that criss-crossed the pane. I gasped, and my mind reeled as I tried to take in what I saw. Even now my pulse races, my stomach churns and I feel light-headed and dizzy at the thought of that moment.

I looked into my wife's room and I saw her lying in bed. I saw myself asleep in a nearby tan leather armchair. I watched Ben cross the room and gently wake me. I rose with tears in my eyes and looked at Dr Jackson, who nodded sombrely.

Impossible.

Chapter 53

'How did you do this?' I asked Ben softly. And then with a sense of anger, 'Why did you bring me here?'

I grabbed Ben by the collar and pushed him against the wall.

Somehow we'd travelled to the night Beth died.

'How?' I demanded.

He ignored me, and craned his neck so he could see through the slice of glass.

'We don't have time for you to evolve, David,' he said. 'You need to be better than this. You need to be a scientist. Follow the evidence. How do you think I've done this?'

I looked through the window to see my former self holding my wife's hand. I watched the moment of her death all over again, and my eyes brimmed with sorrow. The loss was brought back to me, and I lived through that awful anguish twice. I hated the man I'd once considered my best friend, but while I was suffering I could only sense excitement and anticipation from Ben.

I saw myself being led from the room by Dr Jackson. I watched them go through a side door, followed by Ben. On his way out of the room, the Ben who was from the past glanced in our direction and gave an almost imperceptible smile. The gesture sent a shiver down my spine and I looked at my companion in astonishment.

'What is happening?' I asked, but he just freed himself from my grasp, pulled the door open, and rushed into the room.

I followed and approached the bed in awe. I had never expected to see Beth again. She looked so fragile, so empty. I felt my grief rising, but with it came anger.

'Why did you do this?' I demanded. 'How could you be so cruel?'

There was no answer. Instead, Ben ducked under the bed. I glanced down to see him disconnecting cables and tubes.

'What are you doing?'

'We have to take her,' he replied.

'We're taking her—*We* took Beth?' I staggered back in disbelief. 'We took her?'

I steadied myself against the bed and looked down at Beth. I stroked her face. She was still warm. I tried to make sense of what was going on, but my brain fizzed and buzzed with raw energy and countless questions, a jumble of ideas that led me nowhere.

Ben stood and continued disconnecting lines and tubes.

'Don't try to get your head round this, David. Now is not the time,' he said. 'It will only slow us down. This is going to be difficult for you to accept, but we can save her.'

I couldn't believe what he was saying.

'We can do it, David, but I need your help.'

Voices approached, and we both froze as a couple of medics flashed past the side door. Once they were gone, Ben leaned in and whispered, 'No one can see what happens here. It would jeopardize everything.'

He finished disconnecting Beth's tubes.

'Hold her hand,' he said.

I looked down at Beth's fingers. They were skeletal, so different from the colourful soft digits that had clasped my hand countless times over the years. I remember thinking, *If there's a chance I can have you back, I'm willing to do whatever it takes.*

What a fool I was.

I slipped my fingers under hers and took hold of her hand.

'Good,' Ben said.

He produced one of the spheres from his pocket and crushed the glass, which shattered to tiny slivers. The stars ran down his arm and coursed over him, and then travelled over Beth and me, accelerating as they swept over all of us. They expanded into hexagons and covered us in the geodesic mesh of energy, which flared brightly.

A moment later, we were gone, and when the orderlies entered the room a split second after we vanished, they were perplexed by the empty bed and lack of a body, beginning the great mystery that has remained unsolved until now.

Elizabeth Asha's body was taken by us.

Chapter 54

Now.

This word.

This one.

This word right here.

What is it?

When you read these words, what are they?

Tiny sparks of electricity travelling as fast as light, coursing through your brain. Neurons firing one to the other, transforming information, converting it into knowledge and sensory experience.

Our bodies?

Information manifest as genetic code. An error in sequencing can cause ill health. A correction can cure it.

Information is at the heart of what we are. Code the right cellular structures and you can create the primordial ooze that is the precursor to life. Ben had found a way to break things down to their most fundamental state – information – and he had devised a way to insert that code into a different temporal phase of reality.

He had solved the problem of time travel by looking at it as a question of information rather than one of energy or matter.

Hold on to a moment.

Now.

This one.

No, this one.

We can't. Everything we experience as the present is either near past or near future, and yet we perceive time happening to us. We feel the present as a real thing, but it is artifice, a sense of perception to give us a feeling of progress. We create that illusion and imprint our perspective on the universe, but what if all moments in what we perceive as time have already happened? What if we are simply following paths laid down for us?

These questions still keep me up at night as I try to make sense of my life. I used to be a physicist. Then I became an author, but my quest for truth has turned me into a philosopher, perhaps a poet.

The transit itself was magical. As the stars broke me down, my senses changed so my every experience was amplified. The energy was like an electrical charge pulsing over my body. I was able to perceive colours beyond anything I'd ever thought possible. I'd never seen them before or since, and they were so far outside the normal spectrum there is no common frame of reference that would allow me to describe them. It was as though they were the colours of life itself. They went beyond sight and touched a part of my soul that perceived them as part of me. Red means nothing to someone who sees the world in monochrome, and I would not only have to invent new words but impart a new experience to convey the richness of those hues. Imagine all of life as colours, every friend, every family member, all the creatures in the universe, and you'll come close to what I experienced, and they tinted the world around me as I disintegrated.

I registered a regular beat that might have been the sound

of a heart or drops of water falling on a lake. As the milli-seconds passed it grew louder until I became convinced I could hear the sound of the universe in its anticipatory state, an instant before it came into being, and that the beat was a countdown.

The rhythm warped into a deep monotone and signified the build-up of a phenomenal amount of energy. Shock had robbed me of the ability to note the experience of my first transit, but the second journey left a profound mark on me.

When the last of myself was gone, there came an instant between non-being and being that seemed to last an eternity. Were we passing through a place without time? Were we at the heart of all things? There was a void, and emptiness that was more than darkness, more than blackness, because dark and black are elements of reality, and this was something else. An unreality, a nothingness that is hard to even con-ceive, let alone explain. If reality is day, then this was night. It was non-existence, and in the brief moment I experienced it, I was without desire or suffering. I look back on it and think that was as close to contentment as I will ever get. I was beyond space and time.

Then suddenly, as Ben's poem described it, I was on the other side of night and I saw it all.

I was conscious of galaxies being born and dying, of stars fading in the turning aeons, of the relentless draw of singu-larity, but from wherever I was, they all seemed small and insignificant. I was part of the whole and for a moment that seemed to last for eternity, I felt acceptance and peace as I passed through the very eye of reality itself.

Then I was.

I came into existence somewhere else. At some other time.

There was no reconstruction process. I simply manifested elsewhere, like a rapid and sudden birth.

I still held Beth's hand, and Ben had the other.

'Where are we?' I asked, a little dazed.

'Somewhere they can help,' he replied. 'Come on.'

Chapter 55

We were in a small room. A strip window ran the length of one wall, near the ceiling, allowing hazy light to fill the space. Wherever we were, it was daytime, and there was a warmth to the light that suggested summer. The walls were bare, devoid of power sockets or switches, just plain white panels made of a translucent plastic. Behind me was a thick door with an air seal.

Ben picked up Beth's body. She seemed so insubstantial it was as though he was hardly carrying anything.

'There's a keypad on the left,' he said. 'Just touch it and press the open button. It shouldn't be locked.'

I did what he asked. There was a three-inch square cut into the wall beside the door, and when I touched it, a display appeared, showing a red lock button above a green open. I pressed the latter, and the air seal deflated and the door slid back.

I walked into a corridor constructed with the same material as the walls of the previous room. I looked in both directions. Circular hatches capped either end. There were a dozen or so air seal doors flanking the corridor.

'What is this place?' I asked Ben as he emerged from the room carrying Beth.

'An isolation unit for infectious diseases.'

He turned right and I followed him. When we reached the hatch at the other end of the corridor, a sensor registered our presence and the aperture opened like an old camera shutter. Ben ran on, but I only managed to take a couple of steps beyond the aperture before I came to a halt.

We were on a glass bridge that connected two skyscrapers. The building we were leaving was a sleek glass and steel structure. The one we were heading towards was a contoured building made of translucent white plastic.

Both structures towered over the ground, rising perhaps as high as two hundred storeys. We were about two-thirds of the way up. Beyond the glass walls of the cylinder was a city unlike any I'd ever seen. Buildings, just like the one we were leaving, rose into the sky in elegant contours to create a beautiful skyline that contrasted with the jagged teeth of most cities I was used to. There were holographic billboards, advertising products I didn't even understand. The sky was full of aircraft, personal drones that carried people from landing pads which protruded from the buildings. There were vapour trails high in the sky, but they didn't traverse the atmosphere. They were heading straight up. I looked across the city and saw the source of the trails – a spaceport – and the physicist in me was overwhelmed as I realized humankind had achieved an ambition that was as old as our species. We had touched the stars.

Everything seemed to shine beneath a golden sun.

'Ben,' I finally managed. 'Is this . . .' I trailed off.

'Yes,' he replied. 'Come on.'

I marvelled at what I saw.

The future was dazzling.

Chapter 56

'Help,' Ben said, running through the aperture at the other end of the bridge. 'Someone help us.'

I snapped out of my astonishment and ran after him. I entered a sleek lobby. Everything in it was curvilinear and geometrically complex. Even the chairs were designed in honeycomb shapes that shouldn't have been possible. Self-supporting structures that had to have been 3D printed.

A nurse and doctor came through a door on the other side.

'She needs help,' Ben said as they rushed over.

The nurse – a tall, muscular, rakish man in his mid-thirties with a windswept California tan and straw-blond hair – ran to the wall by an unstaffed reception desk and pressed a panel. It retracted to reveal a small closet, and he pulled out a platform that had no wheels. As he removed it from its holster, it powered up and hovered at waist height. He ran over, pushing the high-tech gurney ahead of him.

'Put her down,' he said. He had an American accent.

Ben lowered Beth onto the stretcher.

'Run diagnostic,' the doctor, also American, said. She was a slim woman in her forties and exuded intensity as she craned over the gurney.

It came alive with holographic imagery of Beth's vital signs, scans of her major organs, and analysis of her bloodwork, and the doctor studied them all.

Ben and I followed the medics into a bay off the lobby. The dome-shaped room was constructed out of the same translucent plastic we'd seen elsewhere in the building, but the moment we stepped inside, the walls came to life with an extremely realistic forest scene. It was as though we were outside. There was a rocky brook nearby and water babbled over pebbles. Birds flew between the branches, chirping and whistling, and the wind ruffled the leaves. It was an unnerving experience to be suddenly thrust outside, but when I acclimatized to the simulation I found the environment soothing, which was the point I suppose.

The nurse pushed Beth into the centre of the dome and stepped back while the gurney diagnostics linked up with a larger system, and more data appeared in the air above my wife.

'How long has she been gone?' the doctor asked.

'Two or three minutes,' Ben replied.

It felt like an age, but he was right; it was only minutes since I'd watched Beth die for the second time in my life.

The doctor studied the displays. 'We've got a cardiac arrest. Code blue. We need to restart.'

The nurse produced two pads from a small drawer in the gurney and pressed them onto Beth's sternum.

'Charge,' the nurse said, and the hologram displayed the two pads accumulating energy. After a few moments, he gave a command. 'Release.'

The hologram showed the pads discharge their energy into Beth, and a second or two later, the holographic representation of her heart started to beat.

I looked at Ben with tears in my eyes, and he smiled at me. I didn't register it at the time, but when I reflect on that moment I realize there was a tremendous sadness about him.

'We've got a pulse,' the doctor said. She examined the hologram above Beth. 'I'm also seeing stage-four lymphoma. How did it get this bad? What treatment has she had?'

'Chemotherapy,' I replied. 'We also tried T-Cell engineering.'

'Chemo?' she asked. 'T-cells? No one's used that for a hundred years.'

'They've been overseas,' Ben lied.

'Prep five CCs of Kryopeptide,' the doctor instructed the nurse. 'Do you consent to its administration?' she asked me. 'I assume you're this woman's partner.'

'Yes, I'm her husband,' I said, wiping my eyes. 'What is Kryopeptide?'

'It's a synthetic peptide delivery system that administers a gene edit to directly target cancer cells. It's perfectly harmless. Do you consent?'

'Yes,' I replied. 'Please do whatever you can.'

She manipulated the hologram, and replayed footage of me giving my consent. I looked around the room for a camera, but saw nothing other than the projection of the forest. The sun shone through trees and the dappled light fell on the tiled floor around us. It was a beautiful scene made more wondrous by what was happening.

The nurse touched part of the forest and a small patch of wall returned to its normal state. A plastic panel opened to reveal a robotic arm and a tiny reactor. It looked like an advanced version of peptide synthesizers I'd come across in the genetics lab at Keele. The robot's tiny octopus-like metallic tendrils could be seen through a reinforced window in the small machine as it finished creating a dose of Kryopeptide. A green light flashed and a hatch opened at the top of the reactor.

'It's matched to her genotype,' the nurse said as he extracted a vial from the device.

'Good. Let's administer,' the doctor said.

The nurse attached a needle-less syringe to the vial and returned to Beth. He pressed the device against her neck and pushed a button, and the liquid in the vial permeated her body.

I edged closer and watched in amazement as her eyelids started to flutter. Was she regaining consciousness?

The hologram showed the Kryopeptide spreading through her body.

'She'll be in remission within an hour,' the doctor said. 'It will take a couple of days for the damage to be repaired at a genetic level, but after that she'll be completely cured.'

Colour started returning to Beth's face. I staggered and the nurse caught me.

'I'm sorry,' I sobbed. Never had I dreamed such a thing would be possible.

I wondered if I was hallucinating, if this was all a delusion brought on by grief. I turned to Ben for reassurance and confirmation.

But he was gone.

Chapter 57

I stepped into the lobby and caught sight of him crossing the glass bridge to the other building. What was he doing? He had to see what he had made possible. He had to be there when Beth woke so he could experience the joy of the life he'd saved.

'Ben,' I called out.

He glanced back, his face expressionless, as though he'd been hailed by a stranger. The aperture on this side of the bridge closed, obscuring him.

I ran across the lobby and the lens opened as I approached. There was no sign of Ben, so I hurried across the bridge, through the aperture at the other end, and into the corridor beyond. He was nowhere to be seen, so I jogged on and finally, when I reached the isolation room where we'd arrived, I saw him through a window in the air-sealed door. He had his back to me.

I ran over and touched a small panel on the wall beside the door. I pressed the open button, but a red light flashed, informing me it was locked. I banged on the window.

'Ben?' I said. 'Open the door.'

There was no response.

'Ben? What are you doing?'

I wasn't even sure he could hear me through the thick door,

so I hit the glass again, and this time he turned around. His eyes shimmered like the endless sea. They were full of rich, heavy tears. I saw the last of the three spheres in his hands. He was studying it intently.

'What are you doing?' I asked. 'Ben?'

'You have to stay here,' he said. His voice came through a speaker built into the ceiling.

'What are you talking about?'

'You have to stay here,' he replied emphatically, and he raised his head and looked me in the eye. 'It's the only way.'

'What are you talking about?' I banged on the glass again. 'Open the door.'

'It has to be this way.'

'No! What about Elliot?' My voice was shredded by anguish. Why was he doing this? 'Please, Ben. Don't.'

'I have to,' Ben replied, his tears falling fast now. 'Remember what you said? You said you'd do anything to bring her back. Sacrifice anything.' He choked on the words and took a deep breath. 'This is the price.'

'Not my son!' I yelled, hammering frantically. 'No. Not Elliot. Let me in. Take us back. Please.'

Ben shook his head. 'I can't. That loss. The loss of both of you. He carries it forever. It inspires him to do something truly amazing.'

'You don't have to do this!' I kicked the door. 'You can't.'

'I have to. If you go back, none of this can happen. Time isn't what you think it is. This is the way it was. This is the way it has to be.'

I wept freely, thinking about my son, alone and abandoned. I pictured him lost, trapped an age away from us, and as I imagined him frightened and alone, grieving for us, my angry blows grew weak and pathetic.

I wanted Beth.

I wanted her so much, but not like this.

'Please,' I begged Ben. 'I never even got to say goodbye.'

'You do,' Ben replied quietly. 'One day you do.'

He reached beneath his top and produced something small and shiny. I looked closer and realized it was the necklace I'd given Elliot, the one that had belonged to his mother.

The stars and moon and the word 'Beth' gleamed at me, shining as brightly as the truth.

'You were right. She is always with me. You both are.' Ben pressed his fist to his heart.

My legs went weak and my head spun as the dazzling glare of realization hit me. Everything came together in a single moment of profound revelation.

'Elliot?' I asked, barely able to form the word.

My son.

A grown man I had known for years as my friend.

My son.

I saw it all. The resemblance. The rumours Elliot was his child. Our connection. The love I felt for him. I looked at Ben and I saw myself. I saw Beth. This was our boy.

This was our boy grown.

He nodded.

'I'm sorry.' He choked the words out. 'I'm sorry. Look after her. I have to go.'

'Please,' I said, finding my strength. I battered the door with my fists. 'Please. Take us with you. Please.'

He stared at me for a moment, and I saw raw pain. My

words had affected him deeply, but they weren't enough. He shook his head.

'Goodbye, Dad.'

He crushed the sphere and as the stars coursed over his skin and along his arms, I gave a cry of anguish and collapsed against the door. I looked up and saw my boy being consumed by time.

'Goodbye, little man,' I cried. 'Goodbye, son.'

And then he was gone.

I don't know how long I stood there crying.

'Sir?' a voice said. 'Excuse me, sir?'

I turned to see the nurse in the aperture. He looked at me sympathetically as I wiped my tears.

'Your wife is coming round,' he said.

I followed him, staggering back over the glass bridge. The city didn't look so beautiful. It seemed complicated, alien, and frightening. My legs felt as though they might give out as we crossed the lobby and went into the medical bay where the forest simulation was still running.

The colour had returned to Beth's face, but I could feel mine had been drained by grief. I took her hand and squeezed gently. Her eyes flickered and fluttered open.

My Beth. My beautiful Beth. As overjoyed as I was to have her back, I was grieving for my son and struggling with the sacrifice he'd made. I wouldn't learn the full extent of it for many, many years, but it was already beyond comprehension. He had given everything to save his mother.

Beth focused on the strange world she'd woken to, and took in the trees and the sunlight falling between the leaves.

'David?' she said weakly. 'Where am I?'

I had no idea. I couldn't even tell her what year it was.

She looked at me and must have mistaken my tears of grief for ones of joy. I suppose some of them were.

'It's OK,' she said. She squeezed my hand, and it was a boon to feel her strength returning. She soon realized something was wrong. 'What's the matter?'

How was I supposed to answer?

Chapter 58

Harri and Elliot stood in the cave, having heard Ben's video recording. He told them the same story you've just read, but from his perspective. I've listened to the recording so many times, but it doesn't give me enough. I want to know how he felt knowing he was leaving us behind, to understand how he felt about the sacrifice he'd made, but he explained it to them in very mechanistic, practical terms, perhaps to dissociate himself from the huge emotional implications of what he'd done.

Elliot was shaking with grief and anger, and Harri was shell-shocked.

'So now you know,' Ben said on screen. He put his fingers to his eyes and removed the amber contact lenses he'd worn for so many years, revealing Elliot's electric-blue eyes.

'Oh my god,' Harri remarked.

'You could have brought them back,' Elliot responded coldly. 'Bring them back. I want my mum and dad. Bring them back to me.'

'And if I did, what would that do? Would you devote your life to unlocking the secret of time travel? I know you, Elliot. I am you. An older you, who has already walked the paths you're yet to tread. I know you've already started working on a theory, a theory you've never shared with anyone. I know what you're capable of.'

Harri looked at Elliot and saw, from the surprise on his face, that Ben's assertion was true.

'Part physics, part biology, tapping into the coding of the universe,' Ben went on. 'The language and data sets that give the cosmos order can be rearranged, just like a computer program. I know you can already see that. You're not like other people. You perceive time differently. It is not a chain of events; it is a simultaneous moment, all occurring now, all having occurred, all to occur. It is a happening and the potential to happen and, with the right key, one can move between moments. Would you even be thinking that way if your parents were still around? Our love drives us to do incredible things.'

'No!' Elliot said. 'I don't want this. I want them back.'

On screen, Ben smiled softly.

'You'll see them again, Elliot. When you come back from Australia, twenty-one years ago. Or eleven years from your current age. You'll see them again and share their lives as a friend and you'll save her. You'll tread my path and then you'll know you had no choice. You save Beth. You save our mother.'

Elliot trembled. His whole body shook as he struggled to absorb a new and troubling reality. Harri reached out a soothing hand and rubbed him gently on the back.

'Time travel?' she said to the screen. 'The world needs to know—'

Ben cut her off. 'And what would the world do with this technology? What do people do with anything of true value? Nations would go to war for it. It must stay secret. How much evil would be committed in the name of setting things right?'

On screen, Ben, or the older Elliot as Harri had started to think of him, hesitated. 'If you could travel in time, what would you do? What better purpose than to save a life?'

'Sabih's life?' Harri asked. 'Or was he not worth saving?'

Ben looked pained. 'I've been back to that moment countless times. I can never save him.' He looked at Elliot, and Harri wondered where Ben really was. How could he see them and respond to what they were saying? 'Those research trips, when I left you with Mrs Hughes, I was trying to undo my one great regret. No matter what I try, Sabih Khan always dies that night. No matter how hard I try, there is no way out for him. Just like the rest of us, his path is set.'

Ben fell silent, and for a moment the three of them said nothing. Harri saw Elliot struggling for composure. She was finding this difficult, but she couldn't imagine what it was like for the young man who was coming to terms with what was expected of him. There were differences in the two men, but now she knew the truth, the resemblance was too profound to ignore.

A resemblance Ben could have used in other ways.

'The cliff at Arthog,' Harri remarked. 'That wasn't David Asha, was it?'

On screen, Ben shook his head. 'Margery Allen saw me. I had to tie up loose ends, removing the remotest possibility anyone ever gets near the truth. David's sudden disappearance would have raised questions, so I gave him closure. Probably the most difficult thing I've ever done. It doesn't matter how many times I've used these transits; it takes a lot to convince yourself one will save you from a fatal fall. But it was necessary. The resemblance was good enough for Margery Allen to believe she'd seen David jump, so when the police showed her his photo, that's who she thought she saw. Your investigation tied up all the loose ends.'

'And if I don't do this, I'll create a paradox,' Elliot remarked.

Harri sensed resignation in his voice.

'It's never not been done,' Ben said on screen. 'But if it were possible to break the chain of events, I imagine the consequences would be profound.'

Elliot hesitated. 'How? How do I do this?'

'You leave now,' Ben replied.

A light came on further into the cave, illuminating an old backpack. Harri recognized it as the one Ben had been wearing the night Sabih had died. Next to the backpack was a sphere, one of the transits.

'There's a passport, identity papers, academic credentials, and bank cards in the name of Ben Elmys. The real Ben Elmys died in the car accident with his friends, but I altered the official record to show he was the sole survivor. This will be your name from now on.'

Elliot walked over to the backpack. He picked it up and pulled out something about the size of a shoebox. It was made of metal and covered in digital input panels, some of which were cracked.

'This is how you make them, isn't it?' Elliot asked.

Ben nodded. 'Yes. It's called a forge. It creates the spheres. I call them transits. It was broken during my fight with Sabih. You can reverse engineer the technology to help you build a new one.'

'The missing cobalt?' Harri asked, gesturing at the device.

'Yes,' Ben replied on screen. 'I took it from the university and used it to power the forge.'

Elliot picked up the transit that was next to the backpack. 'And this?'

'One of only three transits that now exist. The last three I created before the machine was broken. It will take you to Sydney, thirty-one years ago. Inside the bag you'll also find all the letters I wrote to you from prison. The ones you destroyed. I wrote two copies of all of them, because I knew you would never read the ones I sent you. They will tell you everything you need to know about your path.'

'What about me?' Harri asked.

'You'll be given a choice, but not until Elliot leaves. He can't know what you're going to do. The temptation to look for a shortcut or an easier path would be too great. Moving in four dimensions requires paranoia about security and time-line constancy.'

'Do we meet again?' Elliot asked.

Ben shook his head. 'You won't see me, but you will meet your childhood self. Be kind to him.'

Elliot studied the sphere. 'I just crush it?'

Ben nodded. 'The nanoparticles create an energy field. It will recode your genetic information to manifest you in Sydney thirty-one years ago. One last thing. There's a letter with instructions about the minor plastic surgery you need to have, and the contact lenses, so our resemblance isn't absolute.'

Elliot took a deep breath.

'Are you sure you want to do this?' Harri asked. She was in awe of the bravery and sacrifice of this young man.

'What would you do?' he asked. 'If you had the power to save the life of someone you loved, how far would you go? What would you sacrifice? I miss my parents every single day.

All I have is memories. If I get to see them again, and save them . . .'

Elliot slid the backpack over his shoulder and crushed the sphere. The stars rushed up his arm, expanding to become the geodesic mesh that flared brightly.

'Goodbye, Detective. I'll see you again in another time,' he said, before he vanished.

Chapter 59

Harri looked at the space Elliot had occupied, and marvelled at what she'd just witnessed. Part of her refused to believe any of this was real, but the larger part of her couldn't refute what she'd seen and heard.

Her assessment of Ben had changed through the telling of his story. A boy who had suffered terrible loss. A man cast as a villain, who endured prison rather than break his fate, a soul alone, raising himself, trapped in a loop in time to save the life of his mother and free his father from grief. No wonder he'd seemed unhinged. No wonder he couldn't tell her the truth.

Her initial assessment of him on their very first date had been right. He was a good man, the noblest of souls, and she regretted all the evil she had believed of him and all the hurt she'd caused.

She realized everything she'd thought about him had been wrong. He was no villain. He'd suffered grief, loss, prison, vilification, and he'd done it all for the happiness of others. She'd been so wrong about him. And so right about him. Her initial impression had been true. He was greater than good, he was heroic beyond any normal measure. He was the man she'd first fallen in love with, and he was so much more.

'You'll have to accept my apologies,' Ben said on screen.

'Now Elliot is no longer here, I have no memory of what happens, so my timing will be off and I can no longer answer any questions.'

'What choice do I—' Harri began, but the video cut her off.

'There are two transits left,' Ben said, and a light illuminated two stone plinths. There was a sphere on each. 'The one on your left will bring you to me. The other will send the boulder that blocks the cave ten seconds into the future. Long enough for you to escape. Know that if you come to me, you'll be leaving your life behind forever. We'll be together in another place, another time.'

Harri approached the two plinths. They were about six feet apart, and she stood between them.

'Do you know what happens? Do you know which one I choose?' she asked.

There was no answer, and when she looked at the screen, she saw Ben was stuck in a loop, repeating his last movement – a slight turn of the head. It was the end of the recording.

Harri walked to the right plinth and pocketed the sphere and then grabbed the other one.

She hurried through the cavern into the rough stone tunnel to the giant boulder. She pulled the sphere from her right pocket and threw it at the giant rock. She watched it dematerialize and quickly ran through the tunnel mouth into the well.

Seconds later, the boulder thudded back into place with a thunderous crack. She looked up at the sky. Patches of blue broke through the cotton-wad clouds. She reflected on the times she'd been with Ben and considered all the unkind thoughts she'd had about him. If she'd known. If only she'd known. She thought of all the years wasted, time they could have spent together. She looked at the crawl space that led to the tiny tunnel that would take her home, and questioned what waited for her. An empty flat? A job? What mystery would ever compare to this?

No crime could measure up to the adventure that lay before her.

The moment Ben had presented her with the choice, she'd known what her answer would be. She'd taken the other sphere to use on the rock because she didn't want to leave any trace of his technology to be found by others. People who might come looking for him and the wonder he'd invented. There was never any doubt in her mind. She wanted to be with him.

She removed the last transit from her pocket and squeezed until it shattered in her hand. Whatever encased the stars looked like glass, but it broke harmlessly. The energy spread over her skin, electrifying every inch of her body, and a moment later, she was gone.

Chapter 60

Harri felt as though she'd been born again.

She materialized after passing through a realm beyond the physical and took a moment to get her bearings. She was in an alleyway behind some grey stone buildings. She tasted salt in the air, and heard the cack and caw of birds. There was a road to her right and she ran towards it.

A rusty old Ford Capri drove by as she emerged from the alleyway, and she heard Prince's 'Purple Rain' blaring through the open windows. She was on a provincial high street, and saw an estate agency, ice cream shop, and a pub called the Eagle and Child. A couple of puffy-faced men in shabby suits were heading for the pub, and she hurried to intercept them.

'Excuse me?' she said. 'Where am I?'

They both stank of cigarettes and neglect, and looked at her with bloodshot eyes.

'Hen night?' the bald one asked.

'Something like that,' Harri replied.

'Barmouth, love,' he said. 'You're in Barmouth.'

Harri's heart soared. She knew exactly where Ben would be.

'When?' she asked. 'What year is this?'

'Blimey,' the grey-haired man remarked. 'Must have been quite a party. It's 1989, doll.'

'Thank you,' Harri said, and she ran south along the high street, leaving the two bemused men in her wake.

She sprinted by shops, pubs, and restaurants, dodging tourists with lollies and cones. A boy with a Walkman almost collided with her, but she danced around him and ran on, passing a newsagent with a poster of Charles and Diana in the window. She rushed along memory lane, and the past that was now her present flew by in a blur. She raced by Margery Allen's block and down the steps to the wooden railway bridge that crossed the estuary.

She whirled through the turnstile, and darted across the bridge without pause. She slowed when she climbed the grassy slope that led to the clifftops on the other side. The sea wind whipped her face and the sun beat down, but nothing could temper the thrill that electrified her. She was breathless and tired, but still she pressed on, and when she rounded the curve of the cliffs, she saw the Elsewhere House, where she knew he'd be watching and waiting for her.

Elsewhere. Just like he'd said in the poem. Elsewhere.

She accelerated, and as she neared the building, the front door opened, and Ben Elmys stepped out to greet her.

The sight of him stopped her in her tracks. She couldn't believe he was real, that this was actually happening. He came to meet her, his relief visible.

'I'm sorry,' he said. 'I'm sorry I didn't tell you the truth. I couldn't tell anyone. It's been so difficult.'

Harri took his hands. 'You don't need to apologize. Do you remember what I told you that day we walked up Maer Hills? You're not alone any more. Neither of us are.'

Harri pulled him towards her and they kissed. When their lips touched she felt complete, and all the love she'd ever had for him came flooding back. They were bound by an experience so unique and profound, she was hardly able to fathom it. All she knew was that it had provoked a storm of swirling emotions that fell calm when she looked into his crystal blue eyes.

'I'm the one who should apologize. I'm sorry,' she whispered. 'I'm so sorry.'

'You have nothing to be sorry for.'

'I lied,' Harri confessed. 'I lied and I sent you to prison.'

For years, she'd tried to convince herself she'd seen Ben kick Sabih off the top of the ravine, but deep down she'd known it wasn't true. She'd lied to herself and committed perjury in court and sent an innocent man to prison because she wanted someone to suffer for her friend's death, and she couldn't blame herself. 'You've been through so much, sacrificed so much, and you did it for love. You did it for your mother and father. You didn't deserve any of this.'

'A man died,' Ben replied. 'I set that in motion, and no matter what I tried, I couldn't fix it. Even if I didn't push him, what I started caused his death. I needed to pay a price for his life. For my own peace of mind.'

He was an honourable man. A good man.

'I still don't understand how can you forgive me,' she said anxiously.

'Harri,' he paused and looked at her with all the love and longing she'd seen in his eyes the first time they met, 'you've been there for me ever since I was a child. You came to help me. To find out what happened to my parents. They live in here.' He touched his chest. 'That's where my mum and dad are. They're always with me, watching over everything I do. That's what you told me. You tried to make me feel better, because you're good and decent and full of love. Everything you did, you did with the best of intentions. Any wrong you did me was because I didn't tell you the whole truth. I couldn't. You're decent, smart and beautiful, and you have a kind heart. Fate put us together, Harri, and I don't know what I would have done if it hadn't. You remember that day you came to Longhaven? "Where do I put all the love I have for them?" That's what I asked you. I know now. I've known for a long time. You fill the space in my heart. You make me whole.'

Harri couldn't stop the tears from coming, but she was beaming so brightly she felt as though her entire face was a smile.

'I love you,' he went on. 'I've loved you since the moment we met in the cafe. You were everything I'd hoped for. Everything I'd ever dreamed of. My life is fractured, distorted, broken, the pieces of my existence scattered across centuries, but one moment has kept me sane. This moment. The prospect of standing here with you in my arms. I love you, Harri. I always will.'

She cried with a sense of contentment that had eluded her for years.

'I love you too,' she said, but the words didn't seem big enough to contain her feelings for him, so she leaned forward and kissed him, and he held her in his arms and for the first time in forever, everything felt right.

She wished the moment would never end, but time wound on and eventually she took a breath and wiped her eyes.

'So what happens now?' Harri asked.

Ben put his arms around her waist.

'I don't know. My younger self never sees what happens once he leaves the cave and goes back in time. This is the first time I haven't known what's going to happen since I was twenty-one. I'm blind to the future. I suppose we figure it out together.'

He gestured at the cliff and the wide open sea and big sky. 'This is ours.' He turned to the Elsewhere House. 'And if you like it, this is our home. Where we can really get to know each other.'

'Anyone who would do what you've done, sacrifice as you have, endured what you've endured – I already know everything I need to know about you. I loved you the moment we first met,' Harri said. 'Someone once told me something beautiful: "You are my star. You light up the darkest day." Now I understand what it means. You *are* my star and you do light up the darkest day.'

Harri pulled him in for another kiss. When they parted, they were both beaming.

They could hardly contain their happiness as they walked into the Elsewhere House together.

Dear Dad,

I sit here writing this letter with so much behind me, and very little in front. I remember the day when Harri and I met outside the Elsewhere House, when we saw each other for who we really were and understood the truth for the very first time. That's when she fell in love with me again. We spent that night in the bed we would share for many years, and for the first time since the time in Oxford when Jessica Sealey invited me to her room, I felt wanted.

I was loved.

I woke the next morning. We'd forgotten to close the shutters, so the sunlight roused me soon after dawn. She was already awake and had been watching me and playing with my hair.

'You know the most infuriating thing about this?' she said. 'We've wasted so much time. I wanted you from the moment I met you.'

She kissed me, and it felt as good as it had the previous night.

'Why did you ask me out?' she said.

'I had to,' I replied. 'I knew it had to happen because Ben, the older me, always talked about it when I was a child. And I knew from when I was older and we watched the video together in the cave. I knew it had to happen. And part of me was intrigued. I wanted to see what you were really like.'

'So why did you break up with me?' She was unable to hide her hurt.

'I couldn't face it,' I responded. 'Knowing what was to come. I was falling for you, and the pain of what was to happen – Sabih's death, prison, losing Elliot – it would have all cut that much deeper if I'd loved you and lost you too. We always only ever had three dates. We always only ever have three dates. If we'd had more, or I'd explained why it was over, would you have pursued the investigation so tenaciously? Your investigation tied up all the loose ends. It was necessary to protect the secret.'

I'm not sure she ever fully understood how to think in four dimensions, the idea that what happens had to have happened, but she smiled sympathetically and kissed me again.

'The video of the arrest?' Harri asked. 'The one that got me reinstated. Was that you?'

'No,' I replied. 'I don't know who that was.'

'And this book?' She leaned over the edge of the bed and reached for her coat, which had been discarded on the floor. She pulled a copy of *Happiness: A New Way of Life* out of her pocket. 'The thing that got me started.'

I shook my head. 'Nothing to do with me.'

She put it on my bedside table.

'Why this place?' she asked. 'Why this time?'

'I had to take myself out of the equation,' I replied. 'The temptation to intervene in a timeline is intense, so I brought myself to a time when I couldn't meddle. You used the last transit getting here and the technology hasn't been developed yet that would enable me to build more. This time is sufficiently familiar so as not to be completely alien to us. And as for this place . . . well, it's beautiful.'

'That's true,' she said. She kissed me again and got out of bed. 'I'm going to take a shower.'

She went into the en suite bathroom, and I turned to gaze at the breakers cresting beyond the edge of the cliff. As I watched the sea rolling and swelling, I noticed the book she'd brought with her. *Happiness: A New Way of Life.* She'd left it on a notepad I kept by the bed to capture any poetry that strikes me in the lucid dreams I have between sleep and waking.

I smiled, wondering what a book could teach me about happiness. I had everything I'd ever dreamed of. I might not be with them, but my parents were safe and *I was with the woman I loved.* I picked it up and flicked through it absently.

I saw something that set my heart racing, and immediately went back to the offending page.

'Where did you get this book?' I called to her.

'It was in the used section of Nantwich Bookshop,' she replied.

'Did you see anyone else there when you bought it?' I asked.

I found the page I'd been looking for and saw the words

I want to live
Help
He's trying to kill me

I picked up my pen and wrote on my pad.

'Yes,' Harri replied through the door. 'There was an old man there.'

I looked down at my words. The handwriting was a perfect match for what had been written in the book.

The handwriting in the book was mine.

I'd written the message in the book that had started Harri's investigation.

'We spoke,' Harri said.

I had a terrible feeling of dread and had to resist the urge to cry out.

'It was very sad. He'd lost his wife. She'd died suddenly,' she added.

I was consumed by fury at the fates. I was trapped in this time without the tools or technology to build another device. I knew the old man was me, and the wife he'd spoken of was Harri. I looked at the book, at the breaking waves, at the closed bathroom door, and felt nothing but despair.

And then a sudden acceptance washed over me. Every story has an end. I have been through many transits and there is a calm one feels at the heart of time. Beyond the noise of the real, in the moment between worlds, there is peace. I held on to that. The stillness beyond suffering and desire. I was fifty-three and Harri was forty-two. Unlike Mum, Harri would live a full and natural life and that would have to be enough.

We might only have thirty or so years together, but I was determined they would be happy ones. I tore the page off the notepad, scrunched it up and put it in the bedside cabinet.

She poked her head round the door.

'Everything OK?' she asked.

I couldn't help but be cheered by her smiling face.

'Yes,' I replied. 'Everything's fine.'

I was determined to make every second count.

'You coming in with me?' she asked.

I nodded and followed her into the shower.

We made the most of our time together, growing old in that house, laughing, living a simple life as the world passed us by, but that was the day I knew my part in the story wasn't over.

Many years later, I bought the book from the library after Mum had borrowed it. I wrote the inscription in the book the day Harri and I met in the bookshop.

The day I told her about her own death.

I could hardly speak when I first saw her. She was a living reminder of brighter days, of a past when we had been young together. I had wanted so much to reach out and touch her, to hold her close, but I was an old stranger to her, not the man she loved in another time.

I could tell she was humouring an old, grieving man, but being with her was a blessing after having experienced the trauma of her death.

I hope you find this letter. If you do, I'm sure it will be strange for you to read these words, to know your son grieved for a wife he would meet again, but that is my life, a broken journey through time with nothing where it should be.

It turns out I'd lied to her without knowing it that day. It was me who videoed the fight with Alan Munro and his death. I went there that night, as a shuffling old man, just to see her, because it was one of the few times I knew exactly where she would be, and I wanted to be near her. When I realized I was the only one on the railway bridge, I filmed the altercation, an old man watching his wife in her prime, capturing the evidence that would prove her innocence.

I delivered it to her flat the day after my younger self was sentenced, exactly when she'd told me it had been delivered the day she came to visit me in prison. I slid the envelope under the door, knowing she was inside. The woman I loved. The woman I'd grown old with. I leaned against the door and listened while I caught my breath. Even the slightest sound would have been something to take with me, but there was just silence, so after a while I shuffled on.

Sometimes it's hard, Dad. Sometimes I struggle.

Time.

Time.

Time.

My friend and foe. A friend who let me save Mum. A foe who tied me to a fate, unable to deviate from my path without destroying the intricate structure I'd created. I'm not sure I could even if I wanted to.

But you mustn't worry about me. Harri and I had many good years together in the Elsewhere House and for a long while, I was as happy as any person has any right to be. I want you and Mum to know that.

I don't want you worrying your son was miserable. It was difficult for a while, but I found comfort in the end. I only hope you and Mum live many happy years together and have the joy I had with Harri.

If you go to the well we found that day we went exploring Lud's Church when I was about seven or eight, there's a boulder, the Rock of Despair. Find a way to move it and you'll discover the rest of my story in there. It might bring you both some comfort.

I'm an old man now, Dad, and I write this alone as I near the end of my journey. I don't think I have long, but I want you to know that I will try to find what joy I can in such time as I have left.

After all these years, I still have Mum's necklace. I'm looking at it now. I think when the time comes, I'll take it with me so when I sleep the long sleep we'll always be connected. I am with you and you are with me.

Always.

Throughout this, my poetry has helped me comprehend what I have faced. I think this poem might be my last.

And the end nears
The sun
A heavy fruit
Ripe with stories
Seeds unspoken
Time unseen, unknown

The darkening forest
Reaches up
Crooked fingers
Long buried dead
Claw the heavens
Demanding more
Time unearned, unspent

In the distance
Lies the darkness
Crooked fingers
Now gone
Space and soil
For those to come
Time unknown, undone

With love
Your son,
Elliot Asha

Chapter 61

I found that letter with the others, behind the loose brick beside the fireplace in the living room at Longhaven. They prompted this book. I've spent years researching my son's life, finding out what happened to him after we transited. I used a robotic excavator and was able to tunnel through the boulder and discovered the cave and the computer that stored his video files. I saw the same footage Harri and Elliot did; concealed motion-activated cameras captured the day they came to the cave. I was able to access Harri's email journal, and the court and police records to provide me with enough information to try to do my son's life justice. I've shifted through time as I've told this story, moving from past to future, through perspectives, to try to give some impression of what it must have been like to be my son, living and thinking in four dimensions with nothing in his life where it should have been.

Beth and I were marooned two hundred years in the future. Temporal refugees without a thing to our name. Or so I thought. Elliot left some money and the cottage in trust to an Elizabeth and David Asha, but we could never bring ourselves to live in it. So I maintain it as a museum of our lives and visit once a year to be reminded of his sacrifice. Beth comes with me to the Peak District, but she has never once accompanied me to Longhaven.

Too painful, I suppose.

When Harri didn't come back, her colleagues thought she and Elliot had been murdered by Ben Elmys, a man recently released from prison and set on revenge. The police searched for him, but of course he was never found. None of them were, and rumours swirled about their disappearances, but everyone assumed Elliot and Harri were dead. Case closed. No loose ends for anyone to pull on. The secret safe. The secret of time.

I often think about the implications of what Elliot did, and have spent many years researching time. Is he a paradox? Some might say so, but they'd be wrong. We perceive time as a continuum, but block theory dictates it must be extant. All moments must exist and always have existed for other physical properties such as gravity or atomic bonds to be true. The block theory of time, that all moments exist at once, changes how we consider paradox. If moments are as real as rooms in a house, we can move between them, be active in them and affect physical reality without what we would typically consider to be causation. Cause and effect cease to matter if all we're doing is travelling between spaces.

Our minds are bound by their limitations. Elliot's wasn't. He saw the universe differently. We imagine ourselves travelling from one moment to the next, but are we? Where is the past? Point to it. Where does it exist other than in our minds or the collective memory or some artificial record of history? And where is the future, other than in our anticipation? And the now? The now we experience is the new past, and as it drifts away, it becomes the distant past.

Time is an illusion our minds create to give us a sense of direction. Elliot knew that and invented a way to break free of our bonds. I've tried to tell this story before, to close friends. Given my profession, it's dismissed as fiction, but even those who give it a degree of credence struggle to conceptualize time in this way, and when they find it difficult, I talk about stories and storytelling. A tale can be told from beginning to end, going neatly through the middle, or the author can chop and change, taking the reader through time as best suits the purpose of the story. In the real world most of us are like characters, destined to play out our lives in the chronology we're given, but Elliot found a way to become something akin to an author, to rearrange events to suit him. I'm not sure my explanation helps, but it gives people a new way to think about time and ultimately it doesn't matter what others think. What's important is that Beth and I know the truth about our son.

And now you do too.

Beth and I had three more children. We named them Ellie, Ben, and Harri, after the people who made their lives possible. We have never told them about their older brother and all he did for us. They don't know about the sacrifice that made their lives possible. I suppose they will learn the truth when they read this book.

Honour your brother in your acts and deeds, children. Hold him dear in your memories. Think of him when you look at your own children. What he did echoes through the ages in the good that you do, and all the good that is done by those who come from you.

His legacy is boundless.

I don't like to think of my boy alone, for even though it seemed he had company for a while, he raised himself. He shaped his destiny. He made choices as an adult that forced a life upon him as a child. I don't like to dwell on my boy alone, lost, afraid, hurting. Seeing the universe so differently must have been nothing but a source of torment.

I don't like to linger on that. I like to picture him as a brave spirit. I prefer to think of the years he spent with Harri, living in the Elsewhere House, happily growing old together.

He died shortly after meeting Harri in the bookshop, at the age of eighty-four, in a bed and breakfast not many miles from Longhaven. As far as I can tell, it was two weeks after he wrote me the letter that contained his last poem. There was no notice of his death, just a note in the church record that an Elliot Asha had passed away at the Three Horseshoes Guest House. He was buried in the churchyard at St Leonard in Ipstones, next to the grave of Anna Cecilia, mentioned by Harri in her journal.

I'm proud he chose to be buried using his real name and when Beth and I visit his grave each year, we can just about make out the faint outline of the letters in the weathered stone. Anna Cecilia's inscription is almost gone.

I haven't much more to say. Beth is calling me. We came here as refugees, and what career options are available to a person with no assets and little talent beyond the ability to spin a yarn? Our skills as physicists were useless in our new time. We were like Victorian railway engineers dropped in the world of silicon chips. So she retrained as a historian and I became a writer. There is a steady demand for historical fiction and as a refugee of the time of war, espionage, sickness, and poverty, I can draw on a lot of personal experience that is alien to my contemporaries.

So I've written my stories, and Beth has taught, and together we have built a life here. It is a world of wonder and possibilities compared to the time we came from, and not a day passes we're not grateful for the sacrifice our son made.

It took a long time for us to get over the loss of Elliot and to understand and accept what he'd done, but eventually we realized that if we didn't learn to move on, we would have been torn apart by grief, and all his suffering would have been for nothing. So, to honour him, we have lived a good life together and raised a family. We have a house by the sea. It's not an elsewhere house, but it's our home, the place where we raised Elliot's brother and sisters, and where they now visit with our grandchildren. Each time we see them, every photograph we look at, we cannot help but think of Elliot and the sacrifice he made. None of them, none of the blessings we have in our lives, would have been possible without him. We're supposed to suffer for our children, but he took such pain for us and he bore it alone. It troubled me for a long time, and I know Beth struggled too. When we'd had three more children and the pain still hadn't stopped, we realized we needed help to get through it. So we went to a therapist, telling him we'd lost our first son. One of the exercises he had us do was to write a short story about what we'd do if we could have had one more conversation with him.

Beth has kindly allowed me to share hers with you.

The Beach

My dearest Elliot. We meet at the beach. It was always your favourite place. You used to scamper over the sand and jump the waves as a chubby, naked toddler. Later, when you were a little older, you'd spend hours digging the most intricate tunnel networks while your father and I sat in the half-tent and watched sun-kissed families walk by with their matted hair, picnic hampers, and excitable dogs.

It's the hottest day of the year, but the sun is low now, and soon it will be night. Your father and I are the only ones with the energy to venture out of Aberdyfi. We meet you on the long, empty, unbroken stretch of golden sand where you played as a child, but you're a young man now. So bright and full of promise. I want to lose myself in your embrace. I long for time to stop and for us to hold each other forever. But we part, and by the glorious sunset that makes everything so perfect, I tell you not to do it.

Please, Elliot. Don't do this. Let me go.

I look at your father and see the stored years of anguish. I was gone. He'd grieved for me and one day he might have moved on. But you, he never expected to lose you, and I can't be a substitute for his son. The hole in his heart is vast, and I just don't fit.

'Live your life,' I say. 'Let me go. Stay with him.'

But then I think about our other children and how they

wouldn't exist but for the choice you made. I think about their every smile and am pained by the idea of a world without them.

As I search for the right advice to give you, the waves roll in, stroking the sand as they have for aeons, and I ponder the choice you faced. The sun falls further, consumed by the distant sea, and darkness begins to creep in.

I died. I was nowhere, with no one, feeling nothing. If there is an afterlife, I wasn't gone long enough to get there. You gave me a second chance and created a new beginning for me, your father, and your brother and sisters. It makes me so sad you'll never meet them, nor they you. You'd have loved each other so much.

I thought I knew what I'd say to you, but I don't any more. I don't even have the frame of reference to think the way you do. You've made a choice that would have broken me, and you've done it with calm resolve. I think of all the time we spent with Ben, and never once did you give away your secret. I can't begin to understand what goes through your mind each day. How you've suffered.

How did you find the strength?

What you've done, the places you must have been, who you are – these are all beyond me. I won't presume to tell you what to do, because I can hardly understand how you've done it.

Instead, I take your hand.

'Thank you,' I say. 'Thank you for everything you gave us. I love you, Elliot.'

'I love you too, Mum,' you reply, and you hug me and your father. 'I love you both.'

My dream, the happiest of endings, is that the three of us never have to make any difficult choices.

We simply hold each other, and stay in that moment forever.

Chapter 62

For many years, I thought Beth blamed me for the loss of our son, and she believed I hated her for the sacrifice he made. Neither of us thought we could measure up to the other's grief, but over time we learned that wasn't what we needed. The loss would never be healed, but that shared grief bound us, and although we could never be substitutes for Elliot, we could make life better for each other. So we did. We focused on the good we could do for one another, rather than the ways in which we failed to fill the void left by our son. We worked hard, and slowly we learned there was a life beyond the pain.

We live on the edge of Tasman Bay on South Island in New Zealand, and it's as close to paradise as I could have ever hoped to get. We watch the sun go down over the hills each evening, and think of our son out there somewhere.

Even as a physicist with decades of scientific training, I used to think of Elliot stuck in a never-ending loop, a cycle of suffering. It wasn't until I found the letters that I knew about his life with Harri. Now I understand more about the true nature of time, I feel a greater sense of peace with the sacrifice he made. I embrace the block theory of the universe because if time doesn't pass, if all moments exist simultaneously, my son and his love are out there right now, somewhere in the gathered multitude of moments, watching the sun go down from their own house. Each evening, Beth and I like to raise a glass to the horizon and think of our child doing the same, still alive, still happy, living with Harri in the Elsewhere House.

She's calling me again, and I can see the sky turning pink, so I really must go. Before I do, I hope you'll indulge me and allow me to go back to the beginning. I want to show the courage that still makes me so proud.

Think of Elliot when your life is hard.

I find it helps.

Perhaps you will too.

Chapter 63

It was a balmy August day and Ben Elmys shifted uncomfortably. He didn't want to be in this chair, in this office, but it was a necessary part of the journey.

Elaine Hardcastle, the ceaselessly cheerful care home manager, sat behind her desk and studied the paperwork that would make him legal guardian of the child.

Elliot Asha.

Himself.

Ben shifted again. Sometimes his mind balked at the disjointed reality he'd created, but he'd had to do it and the child would have to do it again. He was the link between moments in time that ultimately saved his mother's life and brought her back to his father so they could be together, and he would do it endlessly, because that's what it took.

Elaine looked up. She was slightly overweight and her plump cheeks were creased with smile lines. She showed her teeth now.

'Everything seems in order,' she said. 'Shall we?'

She crossed the carpeted office, but her heels started clacking the moment she stepped into the corridor. Ben followed, trying to keep his eyes off a ladder in her tights that ran up her left leg and disappeared beneath her pencil skirt. She seemed too bright and cheerful for such a blemish.

She took Ben to a reception area where the walls were the colours of sweet wrappers. Smiling faces and cuddly toys crowded posters that covered the gaudy walls, but despite all the cheer, the room seemed permeated with sadness. There was a corner unit of fabric-tile chairs of the kind found in job centres and doctors' surgeries, and in front of them lay a graveyard of toys, battered and broken, fallen warriors maimed in battle by tiny hands.

'If you wait here,' Elaine said with a smile, before stepping through another door.

Ben heard her clack away. He tried to prepare. This was another crucial moment, and he scoured his memory. This one was old. From childhood. How did it go? Did it matter if he remembered? Wasn't he fated to get it right?

Was he an actor in a play, trapped by lines written by his future self? Or did he have agency? Are our paths set? Or our futures undecided? Ben never could make up his mind.

He tried to recall the words and paced the space until Elaine returned with another woman, this one much younger and less smiley. And they brought Elliot Asha with them.

Ben smiled uncertainly at his younger self, but Elliot was distraught.

'I don't want to go with him,' he said the moment he saw Ben. 'I want Mum and Dad.'

'I know,' Elaine responded, 'but Mr Elmys—'

Elliot cut her off. 'I want Mum and Dad.'

Grief glistened in the ten-year-old's eyes. He pulled away from Elaine and ran into the corner where he slumped down with the broken toys.

'Elliot, your mummy and daddy wouldn't want you to be sad. They'd want you to live a good life. They'd want you to smile and laugh and be happy,' Elaine said as she approached him. 'They wouldn't have left you with Mr Elmys if they didn't think he was a good man.'

She reached for his arm, but he lashed out with a petulant cry. He turned and started trying to hit her. She held him at bay, and the younger woman rushed over to help restrain him.

'Gently, Steph,' Elaine cautioned, and the two women spoke soothing words and tried to calm the distraught boy.

Ben watched, anguished at the pain, tormented by his own memories of the moment. He knew exactly what the boy was going through and that the two women couldn't say anything to ease his suffering.

'I'm sorry,' Elaine said. 'If we can't calm him down, we'll have to do this another day.'

Ben stepped forward. 'Would you mind if I tried? He knows me, don't you, Elliot? Maybe if I could speak to him alone?'

Elaine looked at Steph, who was stroking the shuddering boy's hair. She shrugged.

'OK,' Elaine relented, and she and Steph stepped away to the opposite side of the room.

Ben crouched down and tried to catch Elliot's eye, but the boy was staring at the floor.

'I know how much you miss them, Elliot. I really do. I know how hard this is, little man. I know what you're going through, but I'll make a deal with you. It's the same deal someone once made with me.'

Elliot lifted his eyes from the floor. Ben remembered this. His interest had been piqued. The words had cut through the pain.

'Come with me, and I promise you will see your mum

and dad again,' Ben said. 'You can't ever tell anyone, because if people learn about this secret, they will do anything and everything they can to take it away from you. It's a kind of magic, but one that won't work if others take it from us. If you come with me, and keep this secret forever, I promise I will make sure you see them again.'

A glimmer of hope took hold in Elliot's eyes. The fairy-tale hope of magic and miracles and happy endings children cling to.

'You promise?' he asked earnestly.

'I'll show you how,' Ben replied. 'I promise.'

Elliot reached out his little hand, and Ben took it and helped the boy to his feet. Ben led a changed child over to Elaine and Steph, and he could sense their astonishment.

'How did you do that?' Elaine asked. 'What did you say?'

'We made a deal, didn't we, Elliot?' Ben said.

The boy nodded.

'What deal?' Elaine asked.

'I can't say,' Elliot replied. 'It's a secret.'

'A secret?' Elaine remarked with more than a hint of suspicion.

Ben nodded. 'I made him a promise.'

Sitting here
On the other side of night
I owe everything
Good and bad
To my son
The boy who kept his promise

David Asha

Acknowledgements

I'd like to thank my son Elliot, who inspired this book with a question he asked while we were walking in the Roaches. I'd also like to thank my wife, Amy, and our other children Maya and Thomas, who've been very patient with my attempts to wrangle time and shape this story over the years.

Thanks go to my editors Loan Le at Simon & Schuster and Vicki Mellor at Pan Macmillan, whose thoughts were invaluable in helping develop *The Other Side of Night*. I'd also like to express my gratitude to my agents Hannah Sheppard and Helen Edwards for their feedback and enthusiasm for the book. Thanks to Fraser Crichton for his attention to detail during the copy-edit, and to Kate Tolley and the rest of the team at Pan Macmillan for their hard work and dedication.

Thanks to Tony Kent, brilliant thriller writer and barrister, for his advice on legal procedure and the language of the courtroom. I'm also grateful to storyteller extraordinaire Anthony Horowitz for reminding me of the power of perspective, and to thriller master James Patterson for all the lessons in keeping the pages turning. I'd also like to thank the many authors, booksellers, librarians, reviewers, and readers who've supported me over the years. This book is quite different from my previous work. I hope you like it. If you did, please review and share the book, but don't give away any spoilers.

I've read a few books on time as part of my research for *The Other Side of Night*. If you're interested in exploring the subject further, I can recommend *Your Brain is a Time Machine: The Neuroscience and Physics of Time* by Dean Buonomano as a great place to start. *Interstellar* is an excellent film that relies on block theory and challenges the notion of paradox.

Finally, I'd like to thank a man whose name I don't know. We met in the woods outside the Hurst in Clunton and walked together for a while. You talked about the loss you'd recently suffered. Your wise words on grief inspired some of the reflections in this book. You honoured your daughter with them.

More praise for *The Other Side of Night*

'A real brain-bender of a book, I'm still trying to wrap my head around the extraordinary ending. Just mesmerizing'
– Victoria Selman

'Wow! It takes a special kind of writer to pull off a story like this. Adam Hamdy's brave, intriguing, thought-provoking book will leave readers breathless'   – Mari Hannah

'An elegantly written and compelling genre-bender of a story, which left me thinking about it long after I'd read the last page. It is destined for the big screen!'   – Marnie Riches

'Inventive, clever and completely original, Hamdy's latest effort is simply terrific. Don't miss it'   – J. T. Ellison

'A thrilling novel with multiple tricks up its sleeve. Part detective story and part philosophy, Adam Hamdy has written a clever and moving concoction'   – Peter Swanson

'In this inventive and intriguing novel, Hamdy mixes in just the right amount of mystery, uncertainty and relational tension and brings them all simmering to delicious effect. Stunningly good writing. Don't let this one slip you by'
– Steven James

'This genre-bending novel is absolutely brilliant! So cleverly constructed, with a central mystery at its core that will keep you turning the pages, it's also a poignant meditation on grief, love and loss. Fantastic. Deserves to be widely read and I predict it will be a massive hit. I loved it'   – Amer Anwar

Newport Community
Learning & Libraries

28-09-22

PILLGWENLLY